THE GAMES WE'VE PLAYED

ACES HIGH, JOKERS WILD BOOK 8

O. E. TEARMANN

THE GAMES WE'VE PLAYED

Amphibian Press
13820 NE Airport Way
Suite #K471902
Portland, OR
97251-1158
United States

ISBN: 978-1-949693-29-4

www.amphibianpress.online

www.oetearmann.com

Printed in the United States of America

Character Credit: The following characters have been used with permission by their creators.

Azzie and Eber have been included in this narrative courtesy of Michael G. Williams

Lily and Clark have been included in this narrative courtesy of Salma Ahmed

Amp, Sherry and Benny have been included in this narrative courtesy of Alex Silver

All songs quoted are properties solely of their authors and have been quoted under Fair Use standards. All songs quoted are given a full citation in the back of the book.

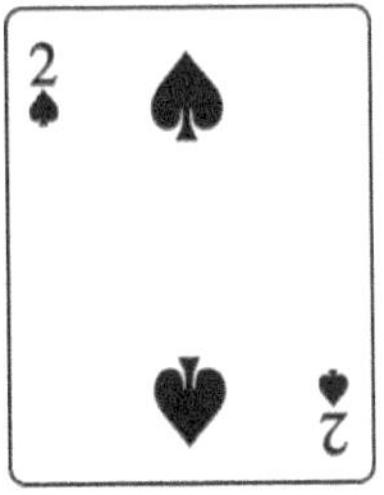

There's never an easy route to the things that matter.
~ Charles de Lint

Reader Advisement

Themes of police brutality, injustice and abuse are explored in this volume. Included are romantic and sexual scenes between people whose genders may not fit your expectations.
If this offends you, consider yourself warned.
If you want to be involved in the kinds of communities discussed in this story, there are resources for the real world in the back of this book and at www.oetearmann.com.
Buckle up for the ride.

AI Usage Statement

The Personnel Officer's Statement:

No artificial intelligence was used in the production of this text.

The Wildcards' Statement:

Tech bros who thought it was cute to make algorithms that scrape the Net and run it through a plagiarism blender, then try to pour the mess that comes out in front of people and call it art? Those tech bros can go screw themselves. And the engine they rode in on.

The Personnel Officer's Secondary Statement:

I apologize for the bluntness of my crew's previous statement. The sentiments were correct. The delivery was… not.

Table of Contents

Event File 01
File Tag: Unit Activation
Timestamp: 14:45-04-03-2162

In the silence, Liza's voice rang like a dropped girder.

"Deliquisha, turn on the news. Zoncom Station 6."

The teen nodded. The screen effervesced into life, mid-broadcast. "—last ditch bid to quell disaffected workers and protect the nation, water and power has been shut off in all major urban hubs. Please be assured, the infrastructure is not damaged. Amenities will be restored to all citizens who remain in accordance with their Citizen Contracts. In order to be reinstated as a citizen of good standing, please follow these steps—"

"Turn it off," Aidan's voice was quiet, but it was obeyed.

Kevin closed his eyes. One moment. Just one moment to sit in wonder with their baby in his arms. Tweak and Inyoni's daughter. *His* daughter. A tiny girl named Bao Li, a treasure made from three genomes, gazing at them with placid brown eyes and gently waving gamma ears. They were supposed to be celebrating her first week of life today. One moment to marvel at the existence of this beautiful child. That was all they got. And now the world exacted its price for even that fleeting breath of joy. Damn it all.

He drew a breath, opened his eyes, and did his best to smile for the newborn in his arms. "Once more into the breach, little treasure," he whispered, brushing his lips over the tiny brow. Then he raised his head, shoving his glasses back up his nose. "Billie? Will you take Bao Li? I'm afraid the rest of us will need to move."

"No shit!" Tweak exclaimed. Bouncing up, she took their daughter from his arms, turned—and wobbled, because this was Tweak and she had, of course, dismissed the fact that her body had just endured nine months of pregnancy and topped it off with a traumatic delivery— and handed the newborn off to her best friend. Billie took the baby with a worried smile. Tweak whipped round, stumbled, and let Inyoni steady her. Her eyes flicked to their commander.

"Boss?"

Kevin looked up at his husband. No. Mental correction. His *commander*. Today Aidan was the commander of the Wildcards unit, a leader in battle. Every line of his body stated the fact. Aidan wasn't a big man, but at times like this he stood like a lighthouse in the dark.

"Okay," Aidan began. His quiet words brought silence in their wake, the crew hushing themselves to listen to their leader. He drew a deep breath. "Okay." Slowly, Aidan met each of their eyes in turn. Kevin felt his heartstrings twang as the man he loved held his eyes for a breath. There was so much to be said, and no time to speak.

"The Corps have passed the point of no return," Aidan stated, his voice rising now to fill the room with the strength of his convictions. "Those seven corporations have run this place for almost a hundred years. They've just about buried this country in dead bodies so they could keep sitting on top of the pile. But they always managed to convince somebody they knew what was best, or that they were just doing business, or that they were on top of things. And somebody always listened, because it was convenient for them, or because they were scared. But the Corps can't pretend anymore. They just turned off water and power to an entire region. They just stopped pretending that they care about anybody's life.

Now, we stop pretending too. We stop hiding. And we will weather the storm."

"We will weather the storm," Kevin repeated, and he heard his family speak the words in one voice around him.

Aidan nodded. "So let's see what we can do. Liza, call the civilians here on the farm together for a briefing. We don't need everybody panicking because of the news from the feeds. Naomi, Sarah, go with her in case anybody gets out of hand. Damian, call Sector Medical, see if they want med staff. Kev, you and me are going to get on the screens. I'm calling Sector Command to see what the orders are. Janice, sit in with us; we'll need you to help us start thinking about how we get water into Denver fast. Really, really fast. Everybody else, sit tight until we get the word. Keep your heads in the game."

Aidan had never placed a call so fast. "Sir, Unit 1407 reporting for orders."

"Headly." Sector Commander Magnum dropped into his seat. *Man, he's breathing hard,* Aidan thought. *Has he actually been running? That can't be good.*

"Those personal water condensers that you've been distributing plans for. How many households have printed themselves a unit?" His superior panted out.

"Based on what we got recorded, 'bout a third of the Union folk," Janice explained, bringing up her records. "That's maybe a fifth of the population 'cross the front range who's got one."

"And your water pylons. What are their production numbers?" Magnum asked.

"We got two thousand, one hundred and seventy-eight water production pylons making up the wall 'round our compound, makin' thirty-seven thousand gallons of water a day," Janice came back rapid-fire, rattling the numbers off the top of her head.

"How much of that can you spare?"

Aidan brought up the table Janice had made for him. "We use seven thousand gallons a day for two acres of land, and about four thousand gallons a day for a hundred and fifty people. We're sending the extra back down to refill the Hogback aquifer."

Behind him, somebody cleared their throat. He ignored it. Whoever it was could wait.

Magnum nodded. "So you can spare twenty-five thousand gallons a day without hardship."

"Um, excuse me?" A voice peeped at the office door.

"Yessir," Janice agreed, glancing over her shoulder. "Hang on Jill, lemme finish this up."

Aidan watched as Magnum ran a hand over his face. "A fifth of the population equipped with water condensers in this Sector. A couple thousand gallons of water. It's not enough. Not nearly enough. But it's a start." The older man sat up. "I'm sending you water trucks, Danvers. You'll need to fill each truck as it comes in. We won't start draining the aquifer unless we're in true extremis. For now, we'll siphon off every drop beyond the immediate budget of the Four Aces Farm."

"Yes sir," Aidan agreed, his throat dry. "The news is accurate, sir?"

Magnum gave a little hack of laughter. "Headly, if it wasn't, would I be giving these orders?"

Aidan nodded. "Understood sir."

"Excuse me?" The voice behind him piped again. Aidan could feel the static of distraction starting to buzz behind his eyes. Head in the game. Stay focused. The distractions could wait.

"This is not a Regional issue; utilities have been shut off to all major cities across the nation," Magnum continued. "Anything that is labeled in the corporate systems as a civilian personal use item has its user license disabled, which means that everything from cars to can openers are failing their users right now. Power is off, and so is water. The corporations are instructing their employees to register on a database and submit their social feeds and communication devices for review in order to restore their credentials. The unions are telling their people to refuse to comply, and to go to their nearest Equal Standing Space for the support they need to get through the crisis. The task of the Force is to supply those spaces, each sector working out supply chains for their civilians. That brings us back to our area. Bases 1401 and 1404 are handling emergency power generation. Regional is supplying refrigerator trucks for citizens to store everything they have, now that their refrigerators are out of commission. What we need from 1407 is food and water. There are three water tankers headed your way as we speak. They should arrive in two hours."

"What are we doing to keep these water trucks under the radar?" Kevin asked at Aidan's side.

"The documentation is being sent to your tab now," Magnum replied. "We're in conversation with the unions about next steps. For now, we need to get food, water and cooling apparatus to the Equal Standing Spaces for distribution to the communities. Everything else is a secondary priority. McIllian, you're on supply networking. I want anyone who can beg, borrow or steal 3D printers to start producing water condensers. Get on it."

"Yes sir," Kevin agreed. "Janice, tell me what we need in order to—""

"HEY GUYS!"

Aidan swore he jumped a foot. God damn, Tweak's voice was broken glass in the ears when she pitched it that way.

On the screen, Magnum blinked. "Officer?"

Tweak stepped into the room, Jillian beside her.

"All that. W-water trucks. M-maybe we don't need that. J-Jillian's g-got an idea."

For a moment, Jillian stood like a block of wood, slotted eyes hidden behind her curtain of hair. Tweak elbowed her gently.

"C-c'mon. Talk."

The room was so quiet that you could hear it when Jillian gulped.

Beside him, Janice gave an exasperated sigh. "Girl, get in here an' tell us what you don tol' Tweak."

It was hard not to get impatient with someone hanging back when they were in a situation this dire, but Aidan bit his tongue as Jilian sidled into the room. *Give her time and she'll get there. Just be patient, give her time.*

"The factory I used to work at basically just ran on print schematics," the new member of their crew mumbled. "Mostly, it was printing plastic toys, cheap ones. Some electronics, CPS stuff. We—the personnel—we were just there to pick the defective units out and recycle them, check that the boxing machine got refilled, do the floors. That kind of stuff. The agar plastic and all the printer precursors are stockpiled; there's lots. So I was thinking, if we could get inside and change the print schematics, change what it's printing, make it print condensers and chill vests and stuff, then we could just hand stuff out." She swallowed, raising her head. Now he could see her slotted eyes darting between them. "Sorry for interrupting. It's just…I've still got my pass card from the factory. If we can reactivate that, and get people inside? Maybe that'd help?"

Aidan stared at the woman for a beat, his brain on standby. He shared a look with his husband and his friend. He could have sworn he saw the lightbulbs flick on behind their eyes.

"Now that," Magnum's thoughtful bass rumbled through the speakers, "that has possibilities."

Standing, Janice put an arm around her subordinate's shoulders. "Jill, c'mon in an' sit. Ain't nothin' to be ashamed of. Fact is, that's somethin' to be damn proud of!"

"Let's hear more about this factory," Magnum suggested. "And about this keycard."

"I can go get it?" Jillian suggested, smiling awkwardly under Janice's wing. Magnum gave the nod.

"Go ahead, Jillian," Aidan supplemented. "We'll wait."

Janice laughed softly as the woman's footsteps faded down the hall. "She's thinkin' like a Wildcard now!"

"She is that," Magnum agreed thoughtfully. "Yes. She is that."

"I'll grab some extra chairs," Kevin offered. "Tweak needs to sit down whether she admits it or not." Tweak rolled her eyes, but she didn't complain.

A couple minutes later Tweak and Kevin were checking over the little card Jillian had brought them. Tweak caught Kevin's eye. He nodded, grinning. She snorted a little laugh. "Thought so! This's j-just an R-RFID. These g-guys are d-dipshits!"

Janice crossed her arms, glancing between the two officers. "So I guess that means you can reactivate it?"

Tweak grinned like a wildcat with a kill. "Can I? Y-yeah! L-let me at it!" She started to push herself out of her chair, but Janice put a hand on each of her tiny shoulders as she tried to stand. "Ah, little mama, you stay in that chair. Don't go jumpin' around. Jus' take my tab an' talk us through this. How're we gonna do it?"

Tweak took the tab and brought up the note taking app, hanging its window in the air where everyone could read it. Her fingers moved almost too fast to see as she typed.

"All I have to do is override this with a basic proxmark cycle code to run through the possible codes on the locks."

She glanced up at them, huffed a sigh at their blank faces, and typed again.

"It's some really easy canned code. Takes me like, five minutes to get it set up. And then I write that master code to a card. It'll find the right code on the doors in about twenty tries. That's like, half a second of holding it in the door. Easy!"

"And if their security is as antiquated as this across the board, I doubt we'll have much trouble with the other safeguards either," Kevin speculated, glancing between the others. "Jillian, did you use the same key card to turn on your assigned machines as you did to access the building?"

"Yeah," Jillian agreed.

Tweak gave a little laugh of straight-up mischief, typing away.

"If I'm right, I can reverse engineer it to give it full access to all systems. We'll be able to make any changes we want when I'm done."

Kevin snapped his fingers. "Easy as that! Let me get some building schematics brought up. We'll still need a few water trucks this week, to get everyone through the interregnum, but if we can set this to printing today and distribute through the equal standing spaces…and after that the main issue is cold food storage for the general population, safety for the factory occupants and maintaining a defensible perimeter. Jillian, can I get the address of the factory?"

"Hold on, guys." Aidan turned back to his superior. "Commander Magnum. Permission to evaluate this method and create an actionable plan for a vote on the Common Ground?"

Through the screen, Magnum studied each of them in turn. Aidan held his breath.

"Permission granted," Magnum's voice weighed on the air like distant thunder. "McIllian, redirect your efforts. Work with Officer Carlan to get in touch with your civilian network and start talking about plans for water distribution and factory occupation. Follow that up with supply resourcing. Once we take these factories, the Corps will stop supplying them with printing precursors. We need to be ready for that." He parceled a look out between them. "We have a window of twelve hours, everyone. Get to work."

"Yes sir," they chorused.

With a nod, their superior signed off the call.

"Janice, go get Liza," Aidan stated as he stood. "Kev, help me move things around so we can have a hologram call with the union reps. Jillian, sit down with Tweak and Topher and start telling them everything you remember about the factory and its printers."

The next four hours were a blur of conversations, plans and decision trees between Aidan and the command chain, between Liza and the union reps. It paid off when the hologram of Noct Fredrickson gave a thumbs' up, a few of the members of the Fabrication Workers' Union they represented standing around them.

"The vote's official, and we've got plenty of volunteers," Fredrickson began. "You guys get down here and get us inside, we'll take care of occupying the factory. The infrastructure union is going to take care of barricading the roads and redirecting Go-enabled vehicles away from us, so if EagleCorp wants to come at us, they'll have to do it on foot. If that key card works the way your tech people think it does, we're going to take over this and three other factories with it. My people are getting prepped; what's your ETA?"

"We'll be down there in two hours," Aidan stated. "I'm sending my hydroelectrics people, my logistics officer and my print-rig specialist down to you in a water truck, along with my munitions officer to set up security. Two other bases are sending you support staff as well."

"Got it," Fredrickson agreed. "We'll be ready as soon as you get here with the key. See you."

"See you," Aidan agreed, shutting down the screen. He nodded at his team. "Okay, the last water truck's getting filled. Let's get prepped."

Half an hour later, he kissed his husband in front of an idling water truck. "See you soon," Kevin murmured.

"See you soon," Aidan repeated, resisting the first thing that wanted to come out: *fingers crossed.*

The heavy water tanker rumbled away into the dust. Aidan watched until it was out of sight.

In her seat, Janice gripped the panic-bar and hung on for dear life. "And after we're done with this, I have to get back and take Alice and Damian out to the Broomfield Equal Standing Space on a delivery run," Topher was explaining with that tone of someone talking for the sake of filling up the silence as he fought the steering wheel. "We have to take an evasive route; it's going to take us almost three hours. They want medics up there to treat a bunch of people, and we're closest. I'll drop them off with the food and water supplies"

"Makes sense," Janice agreed, hanging on tight as a gust of wind made the tanker swerve a little. She watched the Dust roll by out the window, grit devils spinning up across the scrubby land."Hey, Toph. Here's an idea. Why don't you take Truck C for that trip?"

"C's in repair. Speakers are still broken on that one," Topher pointed out distractedly.

"An' that's why you oughta take it," Janice suggested. "Damian an' Alice, stuck in the back of a quiet supply truck for a couple hours. See where I'm goin' with this?"

She could see it when the light came on behind the kid's eyes. Shoving his fedora back, he stole a second to grin at her. "Even they're going to want to talk about something after that long in a quiet truck."

"Got that right," Janice chuckled. "And maybe they'll finally get off their asses an' sort what's goin' on between 'em. Go ahead an' see what happens, yeah?"

"Yeah," Topher grinned. "You got it."

"Five dollars on the failure of that particular gambit," Kevin threw in. "Damian's not such an easy nut to crack."

"Ten bucks says we see them together after this," Janice came back. "Not before time neither." She glanced Naomi's way. "You want in on the betting pool?"

Naomi gave a little laugh. "Not on your life. When Damian wants to make somebody regret it for throwing him into a romance, I'm going to be over here watching the show."

"Same," Jillian agreed, yellow eyes on the badlands spooling out ahead.

"Heads up, everyone hold on," Topher interjected. "We've got high-speed gusts incoming."

The wind didn't let up until they headed down into the valley of Denver proper. The roads were clogged with cars right up to the I-25 spur, littered with accidents caused by people trying out the manual steering for the first time. They made better time on the roads into the city: those were empty as condemned houses.

Looking around the city, Janice could feel the crackle of a storm about to break in the air. She watched a dark jellyfish of a lethal-grade security drone float down the sidewalk. Out of the corner of her eye, she spotted another one down an alley. Her skin prickled with tension.

"Shit, Eagle's got kill-drones patrolling at street level now. Ain't never seen that before."

"I've told Tweak," Kevin murmured. "She's on it; we'll make sure those things leave our allies well alone." She nodded, glancing out the driver's window. "How're we cammo'ed?"

"We look like a supply truck for the factory; we passed the word to the union about it," Topher murmured distractedly. "Don't talk to me for a minute; this thing has a fat ass and these roads are tiny."

Janice simmered down; when another professional was working, you didn't interrupt.

The truck crept down the streets into the warehouse district. Janice's hands hurt with the tension that had balled them into fists. She had to tell herself to shake them out.

"How much further?" Naomi asked quietly.

"Couple more blocks," Topher replied. They'd both lowered their voices, Janice realized. On enemy territory, they were already talking as if the enemy might hear them.

Slowly, the truck eased its way into the parking lot of the factory.

"I'm going to roll down the windows, see if we hear anything the sensors are missing," Topher murmured. Pulling into the lot, he cut the engine. The quiet buzz of the motor died out.

"I don't see anybody," Janice poked her head out the window, glancing around the parking lot uneasily.

"That's because we're behind you."

Janice jumped, banging her head on the window casing. "The fuckin'...oh. Hey Fredrickson."

"Hey Danvers," the president of the Fabricators' Union replied, giving her a grin she could see now that they'd deactivated their slick poncho. The air around them rippled as the members of the Fabricators' Union pulled down hoods, deactivating slick tech. As they powered down the fiber optic gear that had been hiding them across the electromagnetic spectrum, a cavalcade of union members came into view. Now that she could see it, Janice realized that there was a whole damn crowd lining either side of the truck.

"We saw you coming in, so we walked in with you," Noct Fredrickson offered, tugging at the hood of their gear. "Useful things, these slick ponchos. Thanks for the printing schematics."

"I see you've put them to good use," Kevin laughed, climbing out behind Janice. "How many people have we got?"

"About a thousand, spread across the four factories," Fredrickson tossed out easily. "That's more than a full working compliment for every facility. And another thousand have signed up in reserve. We figured we'd come in shifts and hang out a few months, y'know? We got the roster set up for occupation, food, all that. And we brought the gear to fit solar panels on the roof, so we can power this baby off-grid in no time flat. You get us inside and keep the guns off us, we got it from there."

"Well alright then!" Taking the key card Tweak handed her, Janice held it out. "Mx. Fredrickson, welcome to the building."

With a grin, Noct Fredrickson sauntered up to the factory door and popped the card in. After a couple red blips, it turned green, and the door chonked open. Turning in the doorway, Noct grinned, holding up the keycard. "Who's ready to make something?"

The union sent up a cheer that just about rocked the pavement. "Definitely going to need to set up security after that noise," Naomi grumbled. "Okay! People! Inside, inside, no standing out here like targets in the street, thanks!"

"You heard the lady," Noct shouted in a production-floor foreman's bawl. "Team A, I want you on the roof laying the solar mats and fixing the wiring like yesterday! They're not turning off our power if we're making our own. Team B, accommodation! Team C, with me! Let's get this baby working!"

On the factory floor, the fabricators' union fanned out like it was just another day on the job. The staff already on the floor cheered, and a couple came jogging up to their union president. "Building overseer's locked in his office with a jammer outside the door, Mx. Fredrickson." Noct nodded. "Great work. Let's escort him out and take his key card. We can use that to get into the system just that little bit faster. Have somebody drive him to the other end of town and dump him where it'll take a while to report to the Corps, kay?"

The factory worker grinned. "You got it!"

"I'll give you a hand with that," Naomi offered. "After that, I need ten people to help me take over the place's security system and beef it up. Then I'll need a ride to the other factories."

"Got it," Noct agreed. Turning, they gave Janice and Topher a quick handshake. "You two, on the other hand, I'm not letting out of my sight now you're here. Come on, let's go see what the printing supplies look like, and we can put our heads together and see if we need to adapt the plans you sent."

When Janice saw the boxes of plastic and 3D-printing precursors packing a room bigger than her base, she just had to grin. "Well, looks like we're set here."

"Looks like more than it is," Noct corrected with a rueful smile. "If the factory's going flat out—and it will be—this will last us maybe two months."

Janice waved a hand. "By then our logistics folks will getcha more, don't worry 'bout that. Do we got what we need to put together batches of metal-organic framework for the water condensers?"

"Now that, we gotta talk about," Noct replied.

For the next couple hours, Janice didn't look up much. There was a hell of a lot of figuring to do. Luckily these factories were what the Corps called 'at will fabrication hubs', which meant the machines were multipurpose and all you had to do was put in a print schematic to get out a product. There were lots of these places primed to print out the next fad in whatever, and that made them easy to repurpose.

"Quick ask," Janice put in during a lull in the conversation, watching Topher and a couple fabricators run calculations.

"Yeah?" Noct acknowledged quietly, pulling on their vape-stick and exuding smoke that smelled like bubblegum.

"That lady over there, with the eyes," Janice nodded to where Jillian was helping set up some modular bunk beds for the fabricators' stay. "She used to work here, an' it weren't no good. I want her to be the one who hits the button that starts this factory up on our watch. She oughta have that. Work for you?"

Noct smiled. "Yeah. I like that."

"Okay, that'll work," one of the fabricators exclaimed, and they were all on the run again. The union guys got into the recoding job like anything. In no time, they'd reworked the plans for a personal print rig to scale it up to factory level.

"Okay, hit it, Jill!" Janice called. Grinning from ear to ear, Jillian hit the button in the foreman's office, and the line rumbled into life. Bots grabbed the coded chitin boxes full of the right agar-based precursors and shoved them onto the line. The next machine pulverized the boxes, mixing the agar packed inside with the chitin of the box until a flat pan of powder moved to the next station. It looked a little like a sandbox; in the sand, lasers started to play. As the plastic precursors were precision-melted into shape, another set of machines on another line was already making the buttons and internal materials of the water condenser unit. The smell of singed fingernails rose in clouds. At the end of the line, both systems terminated in a box as big as a house, enclosed in plasticine. It was a little hard to see what went on in there, but there was no trouble seeing what came out. Finished water condensers, ready to go. They tested the first four units for water quality with a teaspoon of their emitted water and the tests Janice had brought; every drop passed with flying colors.

"We're good!" Janice declared. "How many can we get out the door today?"

"The line'll make six thousand an hour," Noct explained with a quick grin. "Got a truck coming to pick them up and deliver them to fifteen of the local Equal Standing Spaces in ten. Your guy over there took care of it." They nodded at Kevin, who was talking to a group moving a pallet in through a loading door. "Factory B is on portable solar mats, Factory C is on chill vests and Factory D is working on portable air conditioners."

Janice grinned. "Well alright then! We're still sendin' out the plans for all those, yeah?"

Noct pulled a face. "Yeah, but ZonCom has locked down all the consumer print rigs. Keeps saying that people are going to print weapons. So anybody who doesn't have a jail-broke print rig at home is gonna need to get units from us some way."

Janice sighed. "Fuckers."

"For sure," Noct agreed. They glanced around the factory floor, a project leader checking everything was running smoothly. Then they lowered their eyes to the conversation at hand again. "Hey, can you stick around in case we get surprises? Run quality checks on this design of yours and all that?"

Janice nodded. "My junior's shapin' up good an' our pylons just about run themselves. I can send her back to base an' stick with you folks for a bit. Lemme clear it with my transport."

"Cool," Noct agreed with a quick smile. "Thanks much."

Jogging over to where Topher was watching the machines doing final assembly, Janice put a hand on his shoulder. "Toph, you go 'head an' move out. I'm gonna stick around these factories an' keep an eye on the water quality. You get ahold of everybody else an' get outta here." She glanced around the bustling floor. "Where is everybody else, anyhow?"

Topher shrugged. "I'm going to pick them up in a borrowed van; we're leaving the water trucks here. Naomi's at Factory C setting up their security. Kevin's got to go to Factory D and help them with their plans in a minute."

"When'd Naomi leave?" Janice asked, blinking.

Topher laughed. "In the couple hours you had your head down with Noct."

Janice had to laugh at herself. "Okay then. Don' mind me, I'll be in town for a bit. Jus' you get on, you gotta give Alice an' Damian a ride still."

Topher opened his mouth to say something more, but the blare of an alert cut him off. Janice's gut went tight as tension wire.

"Proximity alert!" a union guy built like a brick wall hollered. "Stations!"

Circling up, the union people headed to stations. Janice glanced around, taking in what they'd prepared. They'd turned those ball-tossing machines that Secure Standing folks got sometimes for their tennis and skeet shooting games into wall-mounted weapons that could shoot hard rubber balls at anyone coming too close, and now those stations were manned. Naomi had put up portable hands-off arcs on every entry point. Those little security gadgets would send a nasty shock through anyone who touched the door while they were active, so the doors were protected. Add everything together, and they had a decent start on a security system.

Would it hold though? That was the question.

Heart hammering, Janice jogged up the stairs to the foreman's office. "What we got?" Jillian turned a white face to her, her yellow goat's eyes wide. "A whole crowd of people."

"Peacekeepers?"

Jillian shook her head. "No, just people." Noct shouldered their way in, taking a look. Their eyes narrowed as they studied the camera feed. "Okay…okay, that looks like regular folks." Slowly, they nodded to themselves. "I'll go talk to them." Leaning over the railing of the catwalk, they shouted down. "Toby, Kat! With me! Max, get me the bullhorn willya?"

In the foreman's office, Janice watched the screen. Beside her, Jillian was subtly vibrating. "I'm gonna turn the sound up," Janice muttered tightly. Through the speakers, Noct's voice came clear. "Can we help you folks?"

The crowd rippled and murmured like a reservoir lake against a dam. Finally, a nervous little voice piped up.

"We…heard we could get water here? And…help?"

Janice had to smile. Over the speakers, Noct's voice warmed. "Folks, you came to the right place. I'm gonna call a lady who can get you set up with the water rig. Anybody who doesn't have a container, we'll lend ya one. Let's make a line."

Getting out of her seat, Janice trotted down the stairs and into the blazing sun. "Hey everyone! Step right up, water's in this big rig! Let's get y'all a drink!"

"How the fuck did they get water?" the CEO's voice blared through Kevin's speakers. "We turned off all the taps! We shut down the printers! They can't do this!"

The voice of the man they were currently eavesdropping through spoke now, dryly.

"Apparently they can, Walton. Because they just did."

Through the surveillance nanoids that had colonized Agustus Lynch's eyes, Kevin watched the room full of corporate heads, aides and sycophants. There hadn't been a whisper of this meeting. This event alone practically paid for the biologically based surveillance nanoids that Kevin had managed to feed four of the seven CEOs who were currently scrabbling for control of the country.

He noted that Bezo-Mars was absent, but Marcus Z of TechoCo was there in spite of the promises he'd made to the workers' unions and the UN. Trying to play both sides against the middle. Well, that was going to cost him. Kevin double-checked that the record feature was working as Lynch set about excoriating everyone within tongue lashing distance.

"I can't believe I let you coerce me into this travesty. One big push, that's all we need, wasn't that your phrasing, Hamilton? One big push and then the population will fall into line?"

The perspective changed as Lynch, Kevin assumed, stood up. A finger pointed down the table at the heavyset man who ran EagleCorp.

"Because of your idiotic idea, they're out there taking over factories that Bezo-Mars and Z paid for and burning through their stockpiled inventory without a dime in profit. I'm watching billions go up in smoke as the international markets take note of what's going on here and sell off stock in our corporations. We're losing billions more in revenue every damn day because of this ploy. Is this what you call falling into line, Hamilton?! Is it?!"

"You put that finger down if you want to keep it," Hamilton snarled. "And quit your whining, you signed up for this push just like the rest of us, and that was *after* you made promises to the other side, so I don't see where you get off talking to me."

Lynch's fist smacked the table. "I get off talking to you because you're destroying us, you—"

"We can leave it to the recording AI to alert us when the argument is over and strategy is being discussed," Quadrant Commander Ouray cut in, shutting down the surveillance screen they'd been sharing.

"Make that 'if,'" Regional Commander Hall observed, and Kevin shared a quiet chuckle with his superiors. He had been taking a certain savage delight in watching the CEOs verbally flay one another, but Commander Ouray was right. Watching the CEOs bicker in pure schadenfreude wasn't intrinsically useful.

"Based on the intelligence gathered via bio-surveillance, this is what we know," Commander Hall offered. "Lynch and Marcus Z were lured into one last attempt to suppress the population by Hamilton and the other hardliners. But they're weak links; if we keep up the pressure, they'll crack and flip right back to bargaining with the United Nations."

"The UN is helping with that," Quadrant Counciolor Hernandez added. "They're offering settlement deals for the upper management to get them out of this mess on a personal level, providing that no further human rights violations are committed. They're still going out of power and they're still giving up the bulk of their wealth in fines and redistribution, but if they deal it'll be more of a haircut than a beheading."

"Given a choice between the barber's chair and the guillotine, hopefully they'll choose the former," Kevin agreed.

"We can hope," Hall observed wryly. "Speaking of which, McIllian, when the full recording is complete we want your analysis of body language and tone for all the present CEOs and the corporate officers who have standing. Can you get that to me by Friday?"

"I'll do my best, ma'am," Kevin replied. "Our sector is fairly stretched in the logistics department at the moment, what with supplying the unions and their dependents. We've got water handled now, and we've been redirecting food trucks in coordination with the Grapevine, but I may be pulled away in the short term. I'll have the report to you by Tuesday at the latest."

"Understood," Councilor Hernandez agreed. "Hopefully that supply strain will ease up soon; the UN has been gathering shipments of food and supplies for some months now to support us, and they're sending us four neoliners of supplies stocked with staff to help us in this push and freight drones that will make the deliveries inland. If they aren't attacked en route, they should be here in a week."

That set Kevin back on his heels and no mistake. "The UN is sending us supplies and personnel directly, sir? Publicly?"

Hernandez nodded, broad face graced with a smile. "Things are changing overseas regarding us, Officer. Big things are happening. You'll hear about them pretty soon."

Kevin nodded, dumbstruck. The UN was publicly supplying them in their fight. He'd always worked with international contacts, but it had always been clandestine. For a man who'd lived in the shadows as long as he had, opening his eyes to this brightly lit moment was a bit overwhelming.

Commander Hall didn't give him much time to adjust.

"In the meantime, we have problems closer to home. McIllian-Headly. Your technical officer has been tracking bounties and surveillance?"

"Yes ma'am," Kevin agreed on automatic pilot. "We've noted a sharp increase in surveillance flyovers. Granted, we have the ability to deactivate the drones within firing range, but the increased attention is worrying."

"More than you may have realized," Hall observed. "I'll be giving this briefing to your base commander shortly. Long story short, the Corps have heard about the Wildcards and Four Aces Farm. They're not just looking for any Duster any longer, McIllian. They're looking for you. In particular."

"Ah." For the moment, it was all he could think of as a reply.

He supposed it was inevitable, really. After all they'd done, all they'd achieved, the idea that they could remain under the radar was infeasible to the point of lunacy.

Still. He'd thought they'd have more *time* than this. Damn it all.

"What steps does Command recommend?" he managed.

"We want you to sit down with your commander, technical officer and munitions officer and discuss an integrated defense plan that will increase your security," Hall explained. "The other bases in the area have orders to help you remain secure. These days, you people are the meal ticket. But I want you putting your heads together over there and working on the problem too. You're going to have to put it off for a week, but when you get back from the next assignment, that's your priority."

"Assignment, ma'am?" Kevin asked, numb with all the shocks to the system he'd gotten so far.

Hall smiled. "Your base commander will be briefed shortly. In the meantime, McIllian, start thinking." She glanced at the alert that had flicked up. "Alright, the voices have dropped below the sixty decibel level; let's see if the CEOs are saying anything useful at this point."

She flicked the video the nanites embedded in the bodies of the CEOs were streaming, and voices came through the speakers.

"—a moron, Hamilton, and if you had a single thought beyond how many guns you can shoot in a day—"

"And you make plenty of cash off those guns, so don't get on your high horse with me!"

Kevin had to smile. So much for the argument being over.

Eventually, he was alone in his office again. He checked the messages that had come in when he was occupied, responded as needed and got a few more shipments of food and printing precursor on their way to the appropriate destinations. That done, he sat back in his chair, head cushioned on his palms, and let his mind turn over everything that had been said today.

Start thinking, that was Hall's order. She didn't have to tell him. He couldn't have stopped the thoughts if he'd wanted to. He only wished they weren't going in circles around those words.

They're looking for you. In particular. They're looking for you.

"Headly-McIllian. I want you and your pertinent senior staff in California by the seventh."

Aidan hoped it didn't show on screen when he froze.

"Um…Commander Hall. Ma'am. With all due respect, I'm kind of holding the lid on a disaster here."

Commander Hall didn't turn a hair. "You and everyone else. What particular duties are you concerned with leaving for a period of a week?"

That'd be all of them, his brain replied. He cleared his throat.

"The civilian supply operation is going well, and I can leave that in the hands of the other base commanders in my sector. But, to speak freely ma'am, it feels like my people are keeping Eagle off us with duct tape and spit. We've blocked the Corps' drone surveillance and long-range projectile capabilities for now, but it's iffy. We're putting everything into the protection and evasion work that'll keep the civilians safe, and I don't want to turn my back on that." He drew a breath. "I also have a lot of new civilians at my base. Given our current infiltration problems, I'm concerned about leaving a gap in leadership and coordination. It's a hell of a vulnerability at a time like this."

Hall nodded. "A valid assessment. However, your base has what so many don't: a solid underlying infrastructure for day to day tasks. Your base services officer, your hydroelectrics officer and your munitions officer can keep your farm running and secure for a few days."

"I don't actually have a hydroelectrics officer, ma'am," Aidan amended cautiously. It was an easy mistake to make. Hell, he'd called Janice an officer often enough himself, because in his head she *ought* to be one. But she'd set him straight more than once about trying to move her up the ranks. She liked it where she was, and he wasn't arguing.

Hall smirked, the starburst scar on her cheek pulled to one side by the expression. "You do now. I put the paperwork through personally. Danvers will simply have to deal with the rank; she's ducked it for too long as it is."

Well that's going to be fun, Aidan thought with a kind of tired amusement. *Who needs fireworks when you get to watch Janice fight with the brass?*

He straightened in his chair. "Of course ma'am. And the civilian protection?"

"The Guardians' Union is sending a contingent of their people from Cascadia Quadrant to do civilian defense and aid in the Denver Metro," Hall offered with a wry smile. "These people worked for Eagle quite a while themselves. They know everything there is to know about what the security forces will be doing. This meeting is bigger than the problems of today, Headly."

"Ma'am?"

The older woman held his eyes steadily. "This order comes down from the National Council: all high-achievement personnel from every Quadrant are to attend. This is the meeting where the United Nations will ratify us as a legitimate military force and declare all corporate officers resisting the legitimacy of the democratically supported government to be criminals. Additionally, this is the meeting where we'll be planning the procedure for removal and arrest of said criminals. So, is that a meeting worth being at?"

♠

Three days later, Kevin clambered out of the compartment hidden under a load of soybeans and drew a deep breath of California air. Pulling his bag from the hidey-hole as his companions climbed out, he worked the kinks out of his back and stole a moment to add drops to his eyes. His contacts had really started to dry out on this last leg of the trip.

It had taken them a fairly cumbersome twenty-four hours to make it out here safely, but when the National Council told you to be somewhere on a given day, that, quite simply, was where you were.

He smiled at his team as he shouldered his pack. Aidan was rolling his shoulders to work out a kink in his neck, and Liza was wobbling on a leg that had apparently gone to sleep. Tweak was the only one who looked none the worse after their most recent leg of the journey; five hours in a space that just barely let them sit up, staying quiet beneath a load of field crops. She was picking at the long sleeves that hid her scaled arms, but that was, for her, fairly innocuous behavior.

"Here, Tweak," Liza murmured. Tweak glanced at the taller woman, who was holding out a sweatshirt.

"Hunh?" Tweak cocked her head.

"You're leaking," Liza offered. Kevin watched Tweak look down at herself and the two wet patches over her breasts. He felt a blush kindle in his cheeks as he glanced away again. It was ridiculous to blush at something as natural as a woman's breasts doing what nature intended, but that was indoctrinated shame reactions for you. He busied himself with luggage and let the ladies get on with business.

"Shit shit shit," Tweak rattled out. "Thanks L-liza." The oversized sweatshirt she'd pulled on when Kevin looked up made her look even smaller.

"From here out we're on legitimate transit, so we can get ourselves stretched out," Kevin reassured over the sound of their automated ride heading back to the highway. "We're here to blend in with the tourists taking a bus ride through the ecological tourism zone maintained by the Karuk tribe on an Argus Eco-Tourism license." He pulled the sheets of synth he'd packed out of their coolant-lined envelope, checking the names he'd written on the back of each sheet of synthetic skin as he passed them out. "Let's get these situated and be on our way, shall we?"

"You've got your holo-mask, right Tweak? Turn it on now," Liza added, turning to look down at the smaller woman with anxious eyes.

Tweak sighed. "Yes *mom*." Reaching up, she tapped the holo-emitter glued beneath her hair, just under her ear. With a flicker, her features were covered by the appearance of a younger Asian girl.

"You're going to have to stop using that line, now that you're *actually* a mom," Aidan teased.

Tweak barked a laugh. "As if."

Liza sighed.

Aloof from the banter for the moment, Kevin nodded to himself as he wrapped the printed sheets of skin cells implanted with their nicely coded genome around his hands. Yes, Tweak would definitely pass muster. Nobody would spot the Golden Dragon under the disguise. He did a visual double-check of everyone's appearance against their forged credential cards as he passed them out. Since these disguises were only covering them on a bus in the middle of a tourism zone, he hadn't been too elaborate in working them up. A good thing too; putting everything together for this out-of-the-blue jaunt had been the very devil of a scramble. He tapped his own holo-emitter, giving himself the appearance of brown hair, brown eyes and a rather distinguished set of graying sideburns. Aidan's disguise gave him the appearance of an Asian man the right age to be pseudo-Tweak's father, and Liza had changed her appearance with a holo-mask of a made-up face and auburn hair, a good match for Kevin's persona. A casual glance would put them down as a couple on a jaunt and a father showing his daughter the sights, and their falsified credentials would back that assumption up.

"Bus leaves in fifteen minutes, up at the top of that hill behind us," he remarked brightly. "Let's move everyone; we don't want to miss our ride."

"Mr. fricking sunshine," Tweak grumbled, but even her sourness couldn't bring him down today.

They hiked up and up through the open woodland, the smell of pine and water a bright leitmotif in the air. "We're looking for the sign that reads 'Happy Camp Tours,'" Kevin called over his shoulder. "Shouldn't be far!"

"Kev, can you slow down?" Liza asked. "Tweak's falling behind."

"Am. Not!" Tweak exclaimed in her sharpest tones of affront. Kevin glanced over his shoulder. Tweak was indeed a good fifty feet back, though she was gamely keeping up in spite of her shorter legs. That was what he got for taking in the scenery too enthusiastically, he chided himself. He really shouldn't have been so situationally unaware as to leave one of his team behind.

"Not far now," he offered cheerfully, dropping back to walk in the middle of the group. "Just up ahead."

They heard the chatter of the crowd well before they reached it. A nice mix of international and domestic visitors stood chatting in small groups, waiting on their bus.

"Okay folks," a chubby youngster with the face of a teen called, waving his arms, "let's line up for our seats!"

They'd timed it perfectly; there was no time for anyone to engage them in conversation and put any sort of chink in their disguise. Kevin trusted his own ability to keep up appearances, and Liza's, but Aidan wasn't the best at speaking like a corporate citizen. And Tweak was most definitely the worst. Kevin had hoped it would time out like this.

Obediently, the crowd lined up, flashing their travel permits in the case of the nervous international folks. It was strange to realize that people were still vacationing as the country convulsed itself with change, but that was people for you. The domestic travelers simply ran their hands over the bus door's genome reader; they'd been trained too long to be anything but blasé about the checking of their genome against their registration record and the travel permission from their corporations.

Kevin followed their lead courtesy of the synth on his hands, ensconcing himself in a window seat near the front. Liza slipped in beside him, with Aidan and Tweak taking the seat across from them. At the front of the bus, a tour guide with black hair tied up in a gleaming braid stood up and started off on his spiel.

"Good day everyone! My name is Bernie Hockaday. Who's ready to see some beautiful country?"

Polite clapping pattered around the bus. Out of the corner of his eye, Kevin spotted Tweak rolling her eyes. Her natural proclivities were actually an asset here, for once. She might be well into her twenties and a mother herself these days, but between her size and her attitude, people would easily believe she was a teen dragged along for the ride.

"I'm your tour guide for today and in this tour, I'm going to show you one of the cleanest and healthiest forests in the Western Incorporated States!" Bernie kept up his talk as the bus rumbled into motion. Kevin relaxed into it. From here—he mentally crossed his fingers before he so much as thought the phrase—things ought to run smoothly. 'Ought' being the operative word in that sentence, of course. But they'd just have to see.

"If you're looking for a chance to experience California wilderness, you've come to the right place!" Bernie burbled on. "You're about to embark on a trip down the Elk Creek road: originally built to service a gold mine, today it provides access to much more. There's so much to discover here! As we ride this road, you'll catch a glimpse into the interior of wild California. Today, you may see a soar—that's the collective noun—of bald eagles perched in our incense cedars, a bear and her cubs wandering through a meadow, or a pair of snow geese gliding across a lake."

Kevin watched the scenery out the window, mulling over the new term. A soar of eagles. Yes, it was a perfect descriptor; powerful, evocative, and beautifully encapsulating the magnificence of the birds. "These animals are protected by ArgusCorp, for your viewing pleasure!" That last sentence soured the moment for Kevin. Of course the bottom-line obsessed infrastructure giant that was ArgusCorp would monetize this wilderness every which way they could without actually destroying it. And that included ubiquitous sales plugs.

Outside, a lovely coniferous forest flowed past. It was a bit like being up in their own Rocky Mountains, riding through these green-clothed hills, but this forest was so much more lush. Spires of white fir, lodgepole pine and incense cedar soared cathedral-like overhead, sunlight gleaming between the branches. Kevin had read about the way the Karuk tribe cared for the forest they'd fought so hard to keep on terms that pleased the corps, and he could see that the reports hadn't been exaggerated. This place was gorgeous.

"— you'll see majestic mountains," their host was saying when Kevin tuned in again, echoing his own thoughts, "shaped by glaciers and tectonic plates, set within breathtaking landscapes. There is also a fascinating history of people who have made this land their home, both in the past and in the present. Shortly, we'll be stopping to let folks who've booked rooms in one of our local resorts off the bus. Please be cautious and take care, as there may be uneven surfaces, potholes, and washouts. Driving around the Klamath River can be an adventure! Have fun and take it slow. Drink in the beauty. And take notice of the rich interplay of the wildlife, people, and landscape around you—all held in trust for you by ArgusCorp!"

Kevin resisted the urge to roll his eyes. As a distraction, he glanced down the aisle, idly watching as a young boy ate a calorie bar. The wrapper dropped to the floor as the boy chewed his snack. In the seat behind him, an old lady with a tight-pursed mouth pulled out her tab and started to tap. Ugh. A goody. Kevin loathed the new Good Citizen, Good Samaritan app that TechoCo had come out with in the past year, and the people who used the damn thing. That bloody app encouraged citizens to report even the most trivial infraction. His crew had worked their rears off to take the Citizen Standing Score system down, and now the Corps were trying to use that nasty little application to recreate the whole thing. They'd started incentivizing neighbors to tattle on each other through it; the person reported on lost fractions of a Citizen Standing point — or more — and the person doing the report gained the same. Some sanctimonious or avaricious people were actually making a livelihood as goodies these days, reporting every little thing to the app for perks and higher Citizen Scores. As if their nation hadn't sunk low enough; now they had professional tattle-tales and prod-noses.

Oh well. They were going to fix that in the long term. In the short term, he needed to have a word with Tweak about disabling that bloody program. And for the moment, he could do something small. Worming his way past Liza, he leaned out of his seat and picked up the wrapper before the goody could take the requisite image as proof, holding the old woman's eyes. "No harm done, ma'am. Nothing to report."

The old goody sniffed. In the seat, the little boy's mother looked up from what she'd been reading, fear in her eyes. She glanced between her son, the floor, and Kevin, comprehension dawning. After a beat, she gave Kevin a relieved grin, holding out her hand. "Thanks for the catch." "No trouble," Kevin agreed, tucking the scrap of trash into her hand. With a quick nod and a smile, he took his seat once more. Now Bernie was going on about something to do with fish.

"—adult salmon begin this migration cycle by swimming upstream to build a nest, spawn, and deposit their eggs. These fish return to the stream where they were born, bringing the gift of life. In the Karuk language, they are known as áama, and they are sacred to the Karuk people. After spawning, the fish die, and their decomposing bodies become food for other animals and enrichment for soil within the watershed. Throughout the summer, biologists keep track of the numbers of returning salmon. Careful monitoring is essential, to guarantee that healthy salmon populations are maintained.

"If you'd like to fish along the Klamath River, pick up a copy of the current fishing regulations at the Slana Ranger Station. While you're there, a park docent can tell you where to obtain an Argus Approved Recreational Fishing license, which is required for anglers age six and above. You can also inquire about any other resources within the world-famous Klamath River basin!"

More sales spiels, Kevin thought wearily. *But I suppose sales did keep this place pristine. After all, if the Karuk people hadn't proven they could turn such a high tourism profit, this part of the country surely would have been ripped up for resources long ago. I suppose we have to count our blessings.*

He felt the slowing of the vehicle in his muscles before he consciously registered it, but the change pulled him out of his reverie. Bernie touched his tab, and a light flicked on in the bus HUD.

"Guests for the Klamath River Resort Inn, please grab your bags! Your stop is coming up."

"That's us," he murmured to Liza, nudging her gently. Liza nodded. The bus left them in front of a series of long, white ranch homes snoozing in the sun.

"We want the main hub," Kevin offered, throwing his pack over his shoulders. "Allons-y."

Reaching the door, he led his team inside. A woman's round face greeted them at the rather rustic concierge desk. "Well hi folks! You booked in ahead, or are you hoping for a night?"

"We're booked ahead, ma'am," Kevin replied with a nod. He relished the code words as they crossed his tongue, loving the sound of the Karuk language. "We're here for the Pik-ya-vish."

He'd thought the woman had been smiling before. Now her face blossomed in a beaming grin. Coming out from behind the desk, she clasped first Kevin's hands, then Liza's. "Welcome to Amikîiáram. It's good to have you here. Did you come far?"

"Colorado, ma'am," Aidan offered. The woman shook her head in wonder.

"Colorado. And there's people from even further away too. What a day." She patted Aidan's shoulder. "Come on in and we'll get you settled with the other guests. The meetings start tomorrow; right now, let's get you some rooms, some food and some sleep in real beds. Tomorrow, we fix things."

"Everyone's got their signal-blocking fobs on them and activated, right?"

"Yes *mom*," Kevin and Tweak's voices chorused as everyone got unpacked. Liza let it go. As long as they were following security, she didn't care. She was glad they had a little time to think before the big day. Once they were settled, she took them through the attendees they'd be seeing and how to address them, mostly so Tweak wouldn't make a mess of that. Kevin drilled them on the vocabulary he thought they should know that afternoon: Amikîiáram, the Karuk name for their part of California, and Turtle Island, what the Indigenous folks called North America. Aidan still wasn't giving them meeting details; he kept saying he hadn't been cleared with a patient smile. By lights out, Liza was pretty anxious. By breakfast, she was completely wound up.

"Wondered when you guys would get in," a familiar voice greeted them as they pulled out chairs at a table they'd chosen. Liza turned to give the Walkers of Coomb Olwen a smile. The siblings who represented the small and unaffiliated communities of the nation gave her identical grins in reply. Today both of them had pulled their hair back into frizzy ponytails as an attempt, she guessed, to deal with the humid heat of the river valley. "Good to see you too!" Kevin enthused. "I thought we'd get a chance to catch up. Oh, here, I have something for you…" Digging in his jacket pocket, he pulled out an actual analog book. Liza would never know how he managed to carry those around. "Appreciate the loan, this was a lovely read," Kevin smiled as he held the book out to the members of the community who protected so much of America's genetic diversity in their mountain seed vault.

"Glad you enjoyed," Brendan acknowledged, taking the book and tucking it in his satchel.

"Oh, hey, there's somebody you should meet." Standing on tip-toe, Brandi waved both her arms. "Autumn! Autumn, over here! Come sit with us!"

At another table, a plump Karuk woman looked up, disengaged herself from a conversation and came over. "Hey Brandi," she greeted easily, "You're going to scare these Duster types yelling like that, they're jumpy as cats already."

Liza had to smile a little when the woman met her eyes; there was something in her face that said 'I've been there too, so let's laugh about it together.'

"Guilty as charged," she admitted, "but I'm blaming my superior officer. He's brought me here with no details on what this meeting concerns."

"Yeah, it's pretty hush-hush," Autumn agreed, flipping two heavy black braids over her shoulder as she took a seat. "This whole space is signal-blocked, and we're still asking people to wear personal signal-scramblers, just in case." She was probably somewhere in her twenties, but she spoke with the assurance of someone who knew exactly what she was doing.

"Seems Brandi wanted me to meet you folks. Ayukîi. I'm Autumn Maddox, acting intercultural liaison for the Karuk Tribal Council."

"Aidan Headly-McIllian," Aidan replied with a friendly nod, "Base Commander, Unit 1407. And these are my officers—"

"The Wildcards!" Autumn cut in, brown eyes dancing as she glanced from face to face. "I knew I'd seen a few of you somewhere! The Queen of Clubs and the Golden Dragon, of course!" She grinned across the table at Liza, then at Tweak.

Liza straightened in her chair, pride swelling her chest. "Pleasure to meet you."

"Pleasure's all mine," Autumn replied with a laugh. "I knew you people were on the list, but everything's been under so many wraps that I'm only starting to put names to faces. No wonder I had to be so careful setting all this up." Leaning over, she kissed Brendan's brow. "Thanks for calling me over, Path-Finder."

"You organized this?" Liza asked, perking up. "It must have been an incredible undertaking."

The round-faced woman shrugged. "I coordinated most of it for the Tribe and worked to make sure that all reservations for the meeting hall and the rooms we're letting to all of you appear legitimate to ArgusCorp. They think we're good dogs, and we need them to keep thinking that if we want to keep providing Tribal land as a safe place for gatherings." A sly smile made Autumn's brown eyes dance. "Good thing they don't know my ceremonial name."

"May we ask what that is?" Kevin asked with a polite smile. "If it's alright to tell outsiders, of course. I don't mean to impose."

Glancing up at him through her lashes, Autumn gave him an impish grin. "Here in Amikîiáram, I'm Coyote Who Is Grinning."

They were still chuckling when a bell was rung at the front of the hall.

An elderly woman stood at the little podium at the front of the room. She was dressed in what must be traditional Karuk clothes, because Liza had never seen anything like them. A round cap covered in geometric patterns topped her head. A bright purple shirt covered in a shoulder-length cape of what looked like long beads was set off by a gorgeous leather skirt decorated with mother-of-pearl beading. It was quite a look, and it brought the eyes of everyone in the room right to the woman. She smiled.

"Ayukîi, everyone, and welcome to the Pik-Ya-Vish. I am Sarah Walking Backwards Thom, Chairperson of the Karuk Tribal Council." She held her arms open to the assembly. "We are glad to see this gathering happen on our land, because this is the right place for such a gathering to happen. The Karuk have called ourselves The People Who Fix Things since time began. Today, on this land that we call the center of the world, we are gathered to fix poor Turtle Island. We've been keeping the purpose of this gathering awful quiet, haven't we? Well, now I can let you in on the secret." She grinned at the gathering. Liza heard a little chuckle run through the room.

"Pik-Ya-Vish translates as 'to fix all of it'", the chairperson continued like a grandma telling secrets to beloved children. "And today, we begin to do that. We need three things. First we need justice. Then we need healing. Finally, we need a way forward. Today we begin with justice. Please welcome to the stage Ms. Punthea Chea, Special Envoy for the International Court Of Justice."

She traded places with a short, powerful-looking woman with a helmet of graying black hair. Eyebrows riding high on a lined brow, Ms. Chea looked around the room as if she knew exactly how much trouble each person in it had caused in the course of their lives. Liza met her eyes for a moment, and they were black as obsidian: sharp, and full of knowing.

Punthea Chea. Liza had read everything she could get about the woman. A Cambodian with an incredible legal career under her belt, Ms. Chea was the one who went after oligarchs, designers of destructive business practices and leaders who cheated their people around the world. Liza was embarrassed to admit it, even to herself, but in spite of being a ways into her thirties, Ms. Punthea Chea was what she wanted to be when she grew up.

"Good afternoon, colleagues and attendees," the international lawyer stated. "Today, I am tasked with reading out the following indictment." She pulled a holo screen up. "The accused carry out the functions of president, officer, deputy officer and management staff in the following entities and their subsidiaries: National Banking Corporation Of America, Argus Infrastructure Corporation, TechoCo, Cavanaugh Corporation, American AgCo, and ZonCom. The crimes committed are, in summation: illegal imprisonment, confinement in inhumane conditions, abuse, depravation, establishment of caste-based systems of administration, illegal medical experimentation, use of explosives against citizens, deliberate acts of extermination against citizens, use of internationally banned biological weapons, and other breaches of human rights committed against civilians as well as political dissidents and those defined in law as prisoners of war. The accused are charged with crimes against humanity and war crimes against prisoners of war under article three, article four, article nine, article twenty-four and article twenty-six of the Geneva Convention."

Liza held her breath as Punthea Chea read the words.

"Furthermore, the accused are charged with crimes against life. The crimes committed relate to the wilful pollution of watersheds, the causing of carbon releasing events exceeding two hundred tons and the negligence in mitigation of such events, three hundred counts of non-human species depredation, and seven hundred counts of depletion of natural resources across a landmass exceeding ten acres. The accused are charged with crimes against life under articles one, five, sixteen, nineteen, twenty two, twenty four and thirty of the International Abundance Accords."

The only sound in the room was the squeak of the lawyer's shoes until she spoke again.

"The prosecution will prove the allegations of the indictment with the testimony of a large number of witnesses, including victims who were mistreated in this corporate administrative system, as well as the submission of several thousand pieces of evidence.

"The indictment has been delivered to the International Court Of Justice for confirmation. The indictment has been ratified. The accused are required to present themselves for trial. Those who will not comply will be forcibly brought before the International Court of Justice by the sworn officers of the court."

Liza could hear her heart beating in her ears.

Chea looked around the room. "Commanders of the Democratic State Force. As the enforcement arm of the Democratic National Council of America, you are responsible for the apprehension and humane delivery of war criminals and human rights criminals to the International Court. Please stand."

Liza watched as Aidan stood along with the eleven Quadrant Commanders of the country and who knew how many of their sub-commanders, numb with the unbelievable thing that was happening.

"Place your hands over your hearts," Chea continued, flicking a holographic window showing text into the air. "Repeat after me. By the dignity inherent in life, I swear that I shall enact and instruct my subordinates in the delivery of those accused of crimes to a fair and public hearing by an independent and impartial tribunal. I do swear to act and give orders for action that accord strictly with fair and impartial justice, in the recognition of the dignity of all living things. In discharging my duties as an officer of the International Court, I will carry out no act nor give any order that is not rooted in impartial justice. This I so swear, by the life in my body."

The room swelled with the words, carried on so many tongues.

Slowly, the holographic screen holding the words faded away on the air. Ms. Chea bowed to the room. "You are now sworn officers of the International Court of Justice. Carry this responsibility as befits its gravity."

Nobody spoke. It seemed like nobody *breathed.*

On the stage, Ms. Chea nodded decisively. "Now that you're sworn in, we'll make plans. Hurry and eat your breakfast, everyone. We have a lot to do."

Liza was numb through breakfast. She was numb for the rest of the day, as the general guidelines for making arrests and meting out responsibilities for capture of the corporate heads who refused the summons to the Hague went on around her. She just couldn't believe what was happening. Blankly, she followed the directions and sat down with the team working on plans for her region. She interacted as best she could through lunch, and through dinner, conversations she could barely take in going on around her.

In the quiet of the little four-bed dormitory where the Wildcards had been housed, eased by the dark, she managed to speak the words that had been caught in her brain for hours.

"Is this real? Is this really happening?"

There was a rustle of sheets as someone sat up. Kevin's voice was as soft as hers. "Another man who fought for freedom said something once. First they ignore you. Then they laugh at you. Then they fight you. Then you win."

"So we're winning now?" Liza asked, almost afraid to speak.

"Maybe we're fighting. And maybe we're winning." Kevin murmured. "I believe in our victory. If we're going to have it, we have to believe in it. *Believe,* Liza."

Tears itched behind her eyes. She swallowed hard.

"Okay."

"Members of the Inter-Quadrant Technical Solutions Committee," the desk jockey with the overseas accent glanced from them to his tab again. "Er…I understand you call yourselves the…code monkeys?"

"Yep," Tweak agreed. The desk jockey glanced at her. "And you are?" "Lung Tung Mei. C-c-cordinator." She nodded at the rest of her team. It was so great hanging out in person. "D-d-Deniki Koyah, First N-nation. Rhin Po, T-tidewater. Nathan Ed-ed-ed.." she swallowed, grabbed her tab, and turned on the text to sound as she typed. It was annoying to hear her voice coming out of the tab, but it did the job. "Nathan Edenshaw, Midlands. Lulu McGyver, Appalachia. Daniel Brown, Freshwater. Fatima Abdulfattah, Gulf. Fidencia Rodrigez, El Norte. Darnisha Collins, New Netherlands. LaQuan Matthews, New France. Ethan Smith, Cascadia. I stand for the West."

Everybody nodded or waved a hand as they were introduced. The UN guy blinked a few times and cleared his throat. "Ah. Well then. Thank you for the introduction. So, the work we'd like your aid in is this: assisting in tracking down hidden financial accounts belonging to the indicted. Your command has given approval; here's the signed document." He flicked a screen into the air. "We've locked down the international assets of all persons involved in the indictment, but we are absolutely sure we're missing things from the outside. So, if you can assist us internally, our chances of success are much improved."

Nathan whooped. "Oh hell yes, let me at it!"

"Mm, hold up," Darnisha put in. "Sir, we can't go ahead on this unilaterally."

"Excuse me?" Their contact asked. He sounded floored.

"We have a problem with people's goods and assets being arbitrarily seized already," Darnisha explained. "We start doing the same thing, we're just the new head guys in the same shit system. So, we're going to need to put this up for a national vote."

"That is going to telegraph your moves," the UN advisor pointed out.

Rhin shrugged. "So? They knew we were coming. Maybe we even want them to know. If they try to run, they out themselves. If they try to bury their money in an international hole, you guys snag them." Xe shrugged. "Their problem. Not ours."

"Totally," Ethan agreed.

Tweak laughed, typing out the words the speakers said for her. "Yeah! Love it."

"If that is your decision," the aid replied carefully.

Tweak bobbed her head, giving talking a try now that she didn't have to say so much. "Is. Let's send it up the l-line. To the brass. See if we can put it on the C-c-common G-ground for a v-vote."

"On it!" Fidencia declared, fingers already racing across her tab. "Setting the final tally for the day after tomorrow if the brass approves."

"Sounds good," Tweak agreed. She gave the UN guy a grin. "Our people say we do it, we d-do it."

A little taken aback, the guy from overseas nodded. "Er…I see. Thank you very much." He didn't seem to know what to do with his hands. This wasn't going the way he thought it was going to, Tweak guessed. He was probably used to a lot more diplomatic back and forth. Yeah well, that was his problem.

He took up a few more minutes stalling, but eventually he got out of the room. Now they could *relax*.

She glanced around the table. "Kay g-guys, what's up with you?"

"With us?!" Darnisha leaned in, grinning. "Girl, what's going down with you? I mean, I get it, we got shit to do, but we *gotta* take a break for baby pics!"

"Yeah, how old is Bao Li now? How is she doing?" Rhin asked, planting xir elbows on the table with dancing eyes. "You brought pics, right?"

Tweak rolled her eyes, but she pulled up her pic folder. "Okay, yeah. Here. She's two w-weeks old now." She fanned the pictures out in an arc of cute.

The chorus of 'awwwww!' just about rattled the table. "She's perfect!" Rhin squeed. "Aw precious!" Lulu cooed. "And those ears! She's like a little plushie!"

Tweak realized she was smiling. "Yeah. Okay. Wanna go home and s-s-see her, so let's work! How we d-doing with the s-s-supplies for the c-c-c..." she rubbed her throat and grabbed her tab.

"For the communities?"

she continued in type. Man, the stutter was being an *asshole* today.

"Pretty good," Lulu answered. "The Corps automating everything is coming back to bite them in the ass now. For water, here's the deets: eighty percent of non-corporate households have access to personal water condensers now, and that number's being pushed up fast. That jail-breaking trick is working like a charm on factories all over. We only had five failures nationally, and that wasn't on the code. Eagle got to a couple factories before they got their defenses set up all the way and nailed them."

"Gotta work on that," Deniki suggested. "I'll go through the record of those, see what we can do to stomp on Eagle the next time."

Tweak had to smile at that. Stomping on problems was what Deniki did; that's why his name meant Moose in his language.

Lulu nodded. "Definitely. Anyway, Food trucks are all getting redirected to community centers now, so we're good there. Only..." Lulu glanced down. "Only a lot of coordinates are getting leaked. Mostly out of your Region."

Tweak winced.

"Sleepwalker?"

she typed. "Sleepwalker," Deniki agreed. "And those coordinates…well here." He pulled up a window. Tweak blinked at it. She felt her heart begin to pound.

"Shit. Send my tab a copy of those."

"Will do," her buddy agreed. She was pretty sure he looked worried.

Tweak nodded, letting herself close her eyes for a second, Okay. Panic later. Work now.

"Okay. Thanks." She swallowed hard. "So. Tell me how things l-look in your q-q-quadrants. How's everybody d-doing j-j-jamming Eagle? I know they're working with Techo to try to block our jailbreaks. I been out a couple w-weeks. Catch me up."

It was a subdued group that gathered at breakfast a day later. Looking around, Liza saw a lot of abstracted expressions and far-away eyes. So apparently she wasn't the only one who couldn't believe they'd gotten international sanction to put the cuffs on the Corps.

Today, Chairperson Walking Backwards waited until most people had finished their food before she got up on the podium. Sunlight through the windows caught on her gray hair, giving her a silver halo under her neat little hat. She stood with her hands clasped, looking out at them until the rattle of flatware fell silent.

"Good morning, everyone. Yesterday we began in justice. And that is not an easy thing." Spreading her arms, she smiled. "But now the ground is clear. Now we can speak of healing. Madam Envoy? Will you take the stage?" At the United Nations table, a stately Indian woman in a business suit that set off the gleam of her dark hair stood. She bowed to the Chairperson of the Karuk Tribe, hands before her brow, as the First Nation elder offered her the podium.

"Thank you Chairperson Walking Backwards. I'm honored by your welcome," the lady acknowledged gracefully. Taking her place, she smiled at the gathering. "Honored colleagues. I am privileged to speak to you today in this time of crisis. I am Ravitri Kumar, currently the Special Envoy for the United Nations Economic And Social Council. Your Democratic National Council has submitted an application to the Secretary-General of the United Nations, accompanied by a letter formally stating that it accepts the obligations under the United Nations Charter. We have thoroughly considered this application, approved it, and put it before the General Assembly of the United Nations. Your case was escalated due to the denial of basic infrastructure access by your governing corporations. Today, we come before you to announce the Assembly's findings and our decisions." Looking over the room, she smiled warmly. "The United Nations has not held a meeting in the former United States since 2100. In 2115, the seven entities that make up the United Corporations of America were deemed a threat to international economic stability. Since then, we have imposed numerous sanctions and levied fines to punish the corporations for their human and environmental rights abuse. But there was only so much we could do from the outside. Until now. This past eighteen months, the international community watched in wonder as a democratic movement swept across the former United States. To date, we've recorded actions in the tens of thousands, occurring in every part of this country, held by the people in support of a new democratic government and an end to Corporate hegemony. "

The room shivered with silence. Liza could hear her own breathing pick up. In a whisper, Kevin was praying.

Envoy Kumar leaned into the podium, eyes sweeping the room. "The United Nations General Assembly has ruled that, in light of the shocking human rights violations committed by the United Corporations culminating in their refusal to supply something as basic as water to their population, they are declared illegitimate as a governing body. The Democratic National Council is deemed the legitimate governing body of the country. It will be required to prove itself capable of holding a free and fair election and ratifying a constitution approved by at least sixty percent of the population within a year of this meeting. As of this date, the Democratic National Council is recognized as the legitimate governing body of this country by the United Nations."

The room exploded in cheers. Liza clasped her hands to her chest. Recognition from the United Nations. That made the National Council and everyone under their leadership legitimate in the eyes of the world. So much would come with that recognition. Resources. Supplies. A seat at the international table. Real power to push back against the Corps. Victory. That's what it was. Victory.

Tweak was looking around like she couldn't figure out what the big deal was, but Aidan and Kevin were hugging, and Brendan had wrapped one arm around Brandi and the other around Autumn, kissing both their brows as they laughed. Up at her podium, Envoy Kumar stood quietly smiling, letting the excitement work itself out.

"For the next week, we'll be working with this assembly to agree on a roadmap for your path to a ratified constitution and government. We understand the threats that the corporations in this country are currently bringing to bear, and that, of course, is your immediate concern. Working with your Quadrant Councilors, we will arrange humanitarian supply drops. We have seen the works of this democratic movement, and we are more than confident that it can succeed in neutralizing the powers of the Corporations and bringing democracy back to a country which once prized it so highly." She clapped her hands. "Now. Plans for working groups have been sent to your tabs. Let's start work! We have a lot to do before the end of this conference!"

Tweak felt like she did nothing but *talk* for the next few days. It was great to climb into their transport home and be *quiet* for five minutes in a row. She needed a break before the conversations at home.

Transport handed them off from a consumer-goods shipping truck to a long-haul grain truck to a ride with an auto broker hauling junked cars to the scrap yard. Tweak thought about telling Aidan her info a couple times along the way. But then she's just have to repeat it to Naomi. Nah. One conversation was better. Plus, more secure.

The last leg, they rode in the back of a Fringer's pickup that had no shocks left at all. Tweak hated every second. She was still sore and crampy, even this long after Bao Li was born, and the ride was making it worse. And she was *still fucking leaking* from breasts that fucking ached, even after she'd pumped breast milk the way Alice had shown her every day of the trip. More than that, she was just plain *tired.* All she wanted to do was curl up and *sleep,* and that fucking *sucked.* She didn't want to be tired, but her body had never cared what she wanted before. Looked like it wasn't going to start now that she'd had a baby either.

When the truck stopped in front of their compound and she saw sunset light filtering through the water pylons, Tweak almost started to cry with relief. She swiped a hand across her face, growling under her breath. Stupid after-baby hormones, jerking her around. Like she needed any more body stuff.

"Hey boss," she called as Aidan climbed out of the truck. He turned to her, and she realized she wasn't the only one who was tired.

Okay, she'd make it short for them both.

"We're not done. Yet. Get Omi."

Aidan blinked at her for a second. Then he nodded. "Okay Tweak. My office in five."

"I'll get our gear put away," Kevin offered.

"You two look wrecked," Naomi observed as she took a seat a few minutes later. Aidan gave her a janky little grin. "Yeah, we are. After this I'm passing out. So what's up Tweak?"

"This." Tweak pulled up the map her coding buddies had made, hanging the holographic window in the air. "C-code m-monkeys collated all the c-c-coordinates the fucking S-sleepwalker's been handing out. Put it on a map. Lookit."

Brother and sister leaned in. Naomi gave a little grunt. "That's a spiral. Zeroing in within ten miles of our base, looks like."

"Looks like it," Tweak agreed quietly.

Aidan sighed. "Crap." Leaning back in his chair, he ran a hand over his hair. "Oh crap. They're trying to use this asshole to pinpoint us now that the drones don't work. And we can't move anymore. Fuck."

"Nasty question, but I gotta ask," Naomi stated. "How come he hasn't already pinpointed us?"

Tweak shrugged. "He's using a n-net en-nabled bug. It's uploading whenever it can ping a d-d-drone or a s-satellite. But it can't be big, and it c-can't be s-strong. So it's g-giving out all the time, and our slick tarps s-s-suppress the signal. Good for us, but the c-coordinates he's feeding out are doing a s-scary good job of t-triangul-l-l…triangulating." She massaged her throat with one hand, staring at the screen.

"What are the chances that we could find a bug if we had everyone on base strip down and do a non-invasive medical check for bugs and micro-tags?" Naomi asked.

Tweak shrugged. "Eh. Heads or tails. Has to be s-skin l-level and has to be on to get d-detected. And if it's inside an imp-plant, somebody's eyes or l-leg or something, you'll never know. C-casing and electric s-signal would m-m-mask it. D-doesn't hurt to try, I guess."

"Anything we can do to passively improve our security?" Aidan asked. Naomi looked at Tweak, and she worked to hold the other woman's eye.

"Seed the Dust around here with signal disruptors?" Naomi suggested.

Tweak nodded. "Sure. Two m-mile r-radius. B-better if we c-c-catch the g-guy."

Aidan coughed out a little laugh. "Yeah. Wouldn't that be nice." Standing, he stared at the map. Then he turned his head and looked her in the eye. "Thanks for telling us. Truth is, both you and me need a couple hours of sleep before we can make good plans, and that goes for everybody who was on the trip. Especially you, Tweak."

"I'm. Fine." Tweak retorted, standing and crossing her arms so fast her scales rasped on each other. Aidan gave her a tired smile. "Yeah, but you're a brand new mom still recovering. That *is* fine. And I want you taking care of it, and yourself. You get me?"

Tweak sighed. "Fine. Yeah, I get you. Not wrong," she tacked on, pissed that it was true. And she'd gone right into fight mode with Aidan too. That pissed her off on top of it. Which probably meant he was right, and she was on overload from the trip. That pissed her off most of all.

"You guys go get some rest," Naomi suggested. "I'm on this."

"Thanks Omi. Love you," Aidan offered, giving his sister a quick squeeze.

She chuckled. "Yeah yeah, go get some sleep before those circles under your eyes get to be permanent." She glanced at Tweak. "That goes for you too."

She rolled her eyes. "Yeah. Yeah."

She didn't love to be *told* to go rest, but she was really, really glad to do it. Opening the door of her room felt like the real coming home.

In the armchair some of the crew had squeezed into a corner while Tweak was finishing up pregnancy, Inyoni looked up, ears perked. The bottle in his hand wobbled as Bao Li sucked on it.

"Hey," Tweak murmured, sliding the door shut. "How's she?"

"She's good," Inyoni offered with a smile. "Almost asleep. You?"

"Same," Tweak sighed out a laugh. "Hard same."

Inyoni nodded to their bed. "Go lay down, I'll bring Bao Li over and we can chill."

"Kay," Tweak agreed. Kicking her boots off, she walked over to the bed and flopped onto it.

Inyoni's long, slim body spooled out beside her. The bundle of Bao Li was laid gently against her shoulder.

"She good? She eat okay? When I was g-gone?" Tweak asked. When had her eyes closed?

"She was great," Inyoni agreed. "Milk you left was plenty."

"Good, 'cause it sucked g-getting that r-r-ready," Tweak grumbled.

Inyoni breathed a laugh. "Yeah, getting demoted from dragon to cow must really suck."

"Shut up," Tweak laughed.

For a moment, they lay quiet, just Bao Li's little baby noises murmuring between them.

"You done good? Those meetings go okay?" Inyoni asked.

Tweak nodded. "Went g-great. Am-mazing stuff. Tired. R-real t-t-tired."

"Then how 'bout we chill out here," Inyoni murmured. "You get some sleep. Bao Li'n me'll stay here with you a while." His lips brushed hers. She smiled.

"Like that. Yeah."

"So where are we?"

Aidan blew out a breath, clasping his hands behind his head as he leaned back in his chair. "Okay, so, the public vote went through; the population voted to freeze the assets of all officers in the Corps, and Tweak's on that."

"A nice tit-for-tat gesture," Kevin agreed with a sharp little laugh. "They can get a taste of what it's like when the taps are turned off."

Aidan worked up a smile for him. "Yeah. So, little picture, Naomi grabbed a couple of the newer folks and they're out seeding the Dust around the base…um, farm, with signal disruptors. Alice and Damian are back, they're working on getting everyone organized for the medical-level infiltration check. They're explaining it as a full physical for all members of Four Aces Farm and a preventative measure to make sure we have everything anyone can use when the supply chain disruptions happen. Some people don't like it, but it sounds like it's mostly going okay." He stared at the ceiling, feet absently rolling his chair from side to side. "Big picture, we're going to see drafts of articles for a new Constitution to get voted on in a couple weeks. Any base that has spare hands is supposed to help collate the posted suggestions on that into data that makes some kind of sense and send it up the chain of command. The

UN observers and task force officers are going to arrive in a month; then we can start putting together the arrest details for the CEOs and corporate officers who aren't turning themselves in. The big cities are getting food and medication drops now, so that's good. Until the UN is ready to work with us on active arrest details, there's a lot of work going into tracking the upper-level officers of all the corporations, 'cause now that they know they're war criminals they're running, and there's a lot going into heading them off before they book it. One of our big assignments is to help out with capturing them. The brass says we have…kind of an edge on catching the big fish, they think."

"What kind of an edge is that?" Kevin asked, his amusement grating on Aidan's raw nerves. "And what's got you worked up, by the way?" His husband tacked on.

Aidan swallowed. Man, this sucked. "They…somebody in the Dusters figured out a way to get bio-surveillance nanoids into the bodies of a couple of the CEOs. So we're getting the info directly from their eyes and ears."

"Well done," Kevin quipped. "Did they tell you who's getting the medal for that?"

Aidan closed his eyes. "It's not a joke, Kev. It isn't funny."

There was a moment of silence. Then Kevin's chair rolled on the floor, and Kevin's hand rested on his thigh.

"Something wrong, love?"

Aidan winced. "Sorry. I just…sorry."

"Sorry for what?" Kevin's lips brushed his brow. "Don't play the silent martyr with me. You know better."

Aidan breathed a laugh. "Yeah, okay. I just…" He drew a long breath. "I thought we were better than that. Nano-surveillance? That's corporate shit. I hate that our people are stooping as low as them. I hate that one of us even suggested that shit."

"It is for a good cause, love," Kevin suggested quietly. "These are the CEOs, remember. They've more than earned the punishment, and we need the information."

"Yeah. The Corps told me the same thing when they had me in a cell," Aidan muttered. "They told me that I'd…that I deserved what they were doing to me. And that the information they needed made it okay."

Kevin's chair squeaked, and his arms enfolded Aidan from behind.

"They were going to inject me with stuff like that," Aidan whispered against his husband's shirt. "I can't believe my own people are doing the same shit as them. This is…it gets to me, okay?" He swallowed. "It gets to me. Sorry."

Kevin was quiet for a long time, holding him. Aidan sat tense, trying to get his breathing under control.

Kevin laid his head against Aidan's, soft and warm and without a word of judgment. Aidan felt himself ease back, his breathing smoothing out. This was what he needed. When Kev didn't make him think or explain, when he just sat and offered his comfort on the bad days, that was everything to Aidan.

"War is hell," Kevin murmured against his throat.

Aidan sighed the words out, repeating them in acknowledgement. "War is hell." He shook his head, sitting up a little. "Sorry. I just…yeah."

"Do stop apologizing one of these days, will you?" Kevin kissed his brow. "Now, what do we know about our role in the apprehension scheme?"

"We know that two of the big guys are sticking here in Denver," Aidan offered, feeling his system starting to ramp up all over again. "And they're the priority for us." When Kevin heard this, Aidan wasn't sure what he'd do. "Bezo-Mars turned himself in to the UN, so did Lynch. They told the ZonCom and Natbank officers to turn themselves in; we'll see if they do. Evers booked it out to Tidewater with a bunch of the AgCo brass. Marcus Z headed for that island he owns in the Seattle Archipelago and told the top guys at TechoCo to take cover. Hamilton and the Eagles sticking with him are here in Denver; they're turning Eagle headquarters down on sixteenth street into a fortress, basically. They're not even pretending to be a civil peacekeeping force anymore."

"Color me surprised," Kevin grumbled. "I saw that coming months ago. Alright, we can plan for that. And who else is going to ground in our Sector?"

Aidan glanced up at him. "Um…Harrington. He's got a bunker in the Rockies, and he's settling into it."

Kevin sat up very straight. "Ah. Of course. The summer retreat." Aidan blinked at him. "Hunh?"

"The summer retreat," Kevin repeated quietly. "Mr. H. used to invite us up to his mountain retreat in the summers, up on Mount Elbert. I remember him talking about how well it could be secured. It was a point of pride for him."

The soft quiet in the room had gone cold now, brittle as sheet ice. Aidan watched his husband stare into the middle distance.

"What are you thinking?"

Kevin's eyes, when they fell on him, were cool and flat. "You know the answer to that, Aidan."

Aidan resisted the urge to hunch down in his chair. He squared his shoulders. "You want to be on that team. To go after him."

"Unquestionably. I have first-hand knowledge of the property. I can make myself valuable to the endeavor."

"And you want to be the one who goes for him."

Solemnly, Kevin dipped his head. "And that, of course."

Aidan ran a hand over his hair, clasping the back of his neck. "Kev…" He drew a breath. "You almost shot the guy once. Full disclosure, I'm having trouble feeling right about sending you on this."

Kevin nodded. "Fair enough. I did try to shoot him, once. Caught unawares and faced with my…" Kevin froze.

Aidan glanced at him. "Kev?"

Bewildered, Kevin gave a weak laugh. "You know, I can't pinpoint the proper signifier. I've hated him so long, and yet I never bothered to put it into words. Enemy is too weak a term, opponent doubly so. If I say arch-nemisis I sound like I'm quoting a trashy movie script. Anyway, he's not my nemesis in the proper usage of that word; I very much intend to be his." For a moment, he hesitated. Then he snapped his fingers. "Ah. of course. Bête noire. Faced with my bête noire, I acted purely on instinct." He flashed Aidan a razor-thin smile. "We've talked about this since. You know where I stand now."

"Yeah, but will you keep standing there when you see him again?" Aidan asked.

Kevin nodded once, decisive. "I'm absolutely sure I will. I believe my resolve has been tested, and it's held. I can do this, Aidan. Trust me."

Aidan swallowed. Trust Kevin, who'd gone insane the last time he'd seen Harrington anything like face to face. Right. Easy to say. Harder to do. For now, Aidan smiled. "It'll be a while before that happens. We've got to wait on the go from the UN. Give it time."

Kevin's smile grew gentle again. Leaning in, he kissed Aidan's brow. "I'll do that, love."

On the desk, Aidan's tab fizzed to life. A hologram of Liza shot up.

"Commander, you're needed in the med bay. We have a situation."

Aidan pulled a face that only Kevin could see. Kevin gave his hand a squeeze.

"Yeah, Liza?" he asked, turning to his desk. He sat up a little straighter at the look on her face. "What's up?"

"Behavioral health incident, sir. Edged weapons involvement. Contained," the personnel officer replied tightly. "It's a situation you'd be best at defusing."

"It's not Tweak, is it?" Aidan asked, praying it wasn't.

Liza shook her head. "One of the new arrivals, sir. Please come down to the med bay."

Aidan nodded. "On my way."

As Liza's image flicked out, Aidan pocketed his tab and smiled faintly at his husband. "Back me up?"

Kevin stood smoothly, offering him a hand. "Always."

♠

The silver blade sliced the air in front of the bundle of nerves in the corner. Tucked into the very back of the last curtained cubicle in the medical bay, the young man was stick-thin and shaking, the scalpel in his hand shivering through the air in crazy zigzags. The eyes were full of pure terror when they snapped to Aidan.

"Who the hell are you?!" He was trying so hard to sound tough, and that made it worse; he sounded like a child faking a grownup voice.

"Hey. I'm Aidan," he offered. "I help run things around here." Stepping between Liza and Naomi, he squatted on the guy's eye level. "So…what's going on?"

"I'm not taking my clothes off!" the boy spat, trying to grind his shoulder blades into the wall behind him. "I'm not taking my clothes off, I'm not!" The last word was almost a shout.

Aidan sat back, crossing his legs into a more comfortable seat. "So, did they tell you why they need you to take off your clothes?"

The panicked boy licked his lips. "Medical shit."

Aidan nodded. "Yeah, medical checks. We're doing them for everybody, so we can make sure you're okay and you get the care you need."

The boy shook his head so hard the rest of his body shuddered. "I'm not taking my clothes off."

Aidan nodded slowly. "Okay. For starters, let's cool down in here…Naomi, Alice, can you give us some space?"

Naomi nodded, turning towards the people peeking out of their medical cubicles or frozen in the act of picking up their prescriptions. "Okay people, clear the air, come on, out this way."

A beat later, she stood with her arms crossed, leaning with deceptive ease against the door that most of the onlookers had left through.

Aidan kept his attention on the boy. Shit. There were no good choices here, were there? If this whole thing was a performance to hide an infiltration and he didn't get the boy checked for a bug, he could get his people killed. But if this wasn't an act, if this was a traumatized kid going through one more humiliation…

Shit.

"I know this is all a lot. And it's easy to get freaked out," he began quietly, "We're trying to help everybody here. That's why we're running checks."

The boy snarled a bad imitation of a laugh. "Heard that before."

"Yeah, and they lied," Aidan agreed. "But I'm sitting here in front of you. And I'm not lying. I need to know things so I can take care of everybody here. That's my job." He waved a hand — really, *really* slowly — around and behind him. "These are the people who help me do that. Damian chooses the meds and supplements every one of us needs. Kevin gets ahold of them for us. In the kitchen, Billie gets the food balanced out to get all the vitamins and minerals we need into something you want to eat." He smiled lopsidedly. "So yeah. That's what we do. We help each other. If you want, you can be part of that. That starts with us helping you get healthy."

"Why?" the boy demanded. "What's in it for you?"

"There's you being okay," Aidan offered. "Because one of these days, there's going to be you finding what you're good at here, and that's going to help everybody else. Maybe you'll be good with some plant, and we'll all eat better. Or you'll be good with printers, and I'll finally have boxers that don't slide off when I turn around fast." It was a stupid line, and it sounded stupid coming out of his mouth. But Aidan needed to break the tension here one way or another.

The boy gulped, shaking his head. "I'm not taking off my clothes. I can't. I can't."

"Maybe you've got something going on under your clothes that you're scared about, and I get that," Aidan offered quietly, "But I bet you five bucks it isn't anything that our medical staff haven't seen before, and I know for a fact it's nothing you need to worry about. Seriously. One of my best crew members is trans, and so'm I. Four of my crew are Gamma.

A couple of us have to deal with stuff about our bodies, and our mental health, and stuff other people did to us without our say. Damian and Alice have some psych training; they can help with that."

Leaning in, he held out his hand. "Whatever you're scared of. Whatever's going on. We'll work it out. Okay?"

The boy hesitated. The scalpel shivered in his hand.

Aidan gave him a smile. "I didn't get your name."

The boy was breathing a little slower now. The scalpel had stopped going all over the place, at least.

"Matt," the little guy managed. "I'm Matt."

"Okay," Aidan acknowledged. "Matt. How about we do this. How about I stay in here, and Damian gives you a health check, and we get you set up?"

"I'm keeping the knife," Matt snapped.

"Okay, but let's put a cover on the blade," Aidan suggested. "Otherwise you're going to end up giving blood the old fashioned way."

Finally, the kid actually relaxed. Well, kind of.

"I…yeah. I guess."

Event File 07
File Tag: Civil Works
Timestamp: 10:00-04-19-2162/13:30-04-19-2162

"Come on, come on, let's get these trucks unpacked before the next flyover!"

"I *told* you," Inyoni tried for the millionth time, "We got the flyovers handled."

The Fringe guy gave him *that look*. "Yeah, you keep telling us that, Donkey."

Inyoni let it go and grabbed another water condenser off the back of the truck. That was what he had to do, keep leaving his holo off and being polite and letting it go, much as it sucked. He just had to give it time. Nobody bought what you were selling right off the bat. They didn't trust him here at Sky House, because he hadn't given them a reason. He just had to keep showing up. Doing good. Giving them a reason. Some time they'd trust him out in the Fringe camps. Some time he'd feel like they trusted him on the base too. They told him they did. Maybe some time, he'd buy it.

Fuck, he wished Yvonne or Kevin had come with him on this. They told him he was ready to make Fringe runs on his own, do deliveries and represent at the routine meetings. But if that was true, how come he felt so far over his head out here?

"Okay, we're good," he called down, shoving the last water condenser off the truck's tailgate to the hands waiting to catch it. "How're we on time?"

"Ten minutes before the get-together," one of the guys helping him unload replied, glancing up at the sun. "Bes' get this truck covered an' get inside."

Inyoni nodded, trying for I-got-this chill. He was pretty sure he wasn't pulling it off. Pulling on his signal-blocking necklace, he tapped it on as they headed in. Everybody was supposed to do that during meetings now, just in case. While he was at it, he double checked the sensor bracelets on his wrists. The two swallows inlaid in the silver were a nice bright blue, so as weird as he felt, his body was in decent shape. Okay. He could do this.

Walking inside Sky House was still one of those things that set off all his alarms. It was too tight in here; too closed in, too few exit doors. Not that long ago, he wouldn't even walk into a place like this; way too many red flags for him. But this wasn't the grid. And he wasn't a bum no more. He had to keep remembering that. He was a Duster, not a bum. He was a Wildcard. He was here because they wanted him.

He still felt like the walls of the hollow rock tower were too close, and the people too. Fuck, he never should have said he'd stop turning his holo on around these guys as a gesture-of-trust thing. The rest of Logistics said it was a good idea, and yeah they were probably right, but all these *looks* were weirding him out. He fiddled with the signal blocker around his neck as he waited in the crowd with the rest of the Fringers and UN people helping them out.

"Alright, y'all, settle," the old guy who ran stuff around Sky House was saying up front, getting up on the crate the Fringers used for a stage. "We got a lot to talk 'bout today, so let's get to it. Remember your manners y'all, and don't jaw the sun down."

That got him a laugh. Old Pat smiled real quiet, and cleared his throat. Inyoni started his tab recording like Kevin had asked as Pat started to talk. "First things first, everybody take home water condensers to help out, an' plans if'n you wanna print more. Thank the Wildcards for them." He tipped his hat to Inyoni. Great, now everybody was looking his way. He felt his ears go flat, but he smiled and waved all the same. "And speakin' of the Wildcards an' such," Pat continued, "they sent ahead some drafts of the new Constitution they're workin' on. Now y'all know every one of us gets votes on all these things through that Common Ground app; les' go over this together. Vote on this draft's due in a month, so I wan' us to start havin' this conversation an' thinkin' it over. We can call other folks real safe an' talk it over with other people who can't travel so far as this if we want on another day, but les' start with who we got and see what we got right now. Now jus' lettin' y'all know, there's some folks recordin' right now; I want y'all to simmer down and let it be; they're sendin' those vids to the UN an' such an' makin' sure the Corps don't get 'em. Everybody got a look at them recording consent forms; if y'said no, then your image will get blurred."

"How come the overseas folk are steppin' in for us now?" Someone called in the crowd. "Never gave two shits about us afore."

There was a mutter of pissy agreement from the rest of the listeners.

"Legally, we weren't allowed to get involved until the population of the country proved that they considered their current government illegitimate and wanted a change," the UN lady with the messy long braid stepped up to say. "We have rules about how and when we get involved in the UN that keep us from being nothing but a big bully on the international playground. But once you proved that the corporations of America didn't speak for you, then we had the legal right to get involved and help you get a government you really want."

That chilled out the piss and moan club. Inyoni even heard a couple little whoops and cheers. He still had trouble believing all this was for real sometimes. Tweak had shown him how the whole thing worked, how the Common Ground was wired up to secure an equal vote for everybody in realtime on whatever issues their individualized hashtags had access to. Some stuff was just regional or town votes, and those didn't let people from across the country vote on what time the food deliveries would happen in Denver. All the hashtags were signed up for this vote though, and everybody using the Common Ground was voting on stuff about the new constitution. Kevin called it direct democracy, Tweak called it something big and long about hash tracking and validating signatures. Right now Inyoni just called it pretty cool. Kind of a lot, but pretty cool.

"So, first article of this here," Pat began. "I got a voice like an old gate; Diego, c'mon an' read this."

Pat's grandson stepped up on the crate, taking the tab from his grandpa's hands. "All public power in the country proceeds from the people and the communities they choose to form. This democracy is founded on the free formation of opinion and on universal and equal suffrage. In recognition of this, the country will henceforth take on the name of the United Communities of North America. The power of the United Communities is realized through a direct self government. This system will be served and maintained through a public works infrastructure and an assembly of public servants at quadrant, region, municipality and community levels. Public power shall be exercised with respect for the equal worth of all and the liberty and dignity of the individual. The personal, economic and cultural welfare of the individual shall be fundamental aims of public activity. In particular, the public institutions shall secure the right to employment, housing and education, and shall promote social care and social security, as well as favorable conditions for health.

"The public institutions shall promote sustainable development leading to a thriving environment for present and future generations."

The old man nodded. "Now, that's an awful lot of words. So let's—"

Inyoni felt his system shock up as something over his head went off like a garbage can rolling down the stairs. That fucking noise hijacked all his senses, pushing his heart into overdrive. The Fringers all grabbed for weapons and ducked into alcoves. Inyoni shoved his hands over his ears, flattening them and shutting out at least a little of the fucking noise.

"Get down! Intruders!" a Fringe lady shouted at him as she ran past.

"Thanks!" Inyoni shouted back. Looking around, he ducked behind a stone pillar with a couple other folks. The fucking alarm was going to crack his skull. His heart was hammering in his ears, and that just made everything louder. He scrabbled in a pocket for the earplugs Topher had printed him and jammed them in. Okay, now he could think with some of the noise gone. But what the fuck was going on? Who had...

Oh. Shit. Black-suited bodies came in like a swarm of soldier ants. At first Inyoni thought they were EagleCorp, but there was no white eagle insignia, and here and there were dark green and grey body-armor sets mixed in with the black. Nope, not straight-up EagleCorp. Contractors. Okay, security contractors, so less bad. But they were still armed, and they were yelling a bunch of stuff, and they were still going to capture or kill people, and he had to do something. The plan. He had to go with the plan. Okay, okay, first step of the plan.

Somebody shoved a long-bodied spray canister into his hands. He raised it and aimed.

From every corner of the room, spray canisters foamed quick-set concrete at the invader's boots and their legs. In the roof, a collection of nanoids came awake and buzzed down to burrow into every gun barrel, filling them up with contact cement. Foam trapped the contractors' arms to their sides.

The contractor's yells changed. It had been all kinds of stuff about 'get on the ground' and 'Eaglecorp authority to blah blah blah'. Now it was yells of 'what the hell?!', cussing and grunts of shock. Cocooned in foam and quick-set concrete, the people who'd come to do the capturing today had just been turned into prisoners.

A cheer rose from all around Sky House. Rising from their hiding places, the people of the Dust circled around their catch. "Perimeter's clear!" somebody shouted down the rock chimney over their heads. "Nobody but these guys!"

"Thanks Ted!" Pat hollered up. Turning, the head guy glanced at a buzz-cut dude on his left, and the woman with the messy braid on his right. "So, what's the call on this?"

"We'll take them into custody under UN acts against civilian statutes," the woman said with a professional smile. "Luckily it's an individual bounty-hunting team this time; if they followed standard contractor procedure they reported as little as they possibly could in order to prevent another team stealing their…ah…payday out from under them, so we should still be secure at this location. If the representative of the Democratic State Force…ah, good, officer, please call your chain of command and report that we'd like assistance in moving prisoners to holding."

It took Inyoni a second to realize she was talking to him. He thought about telling her he wasn't an officer, then realized that he hadn't put on his rank pin and it didn't really matter. She just needed a Duster. He jerked his head up and down. "I…yeah. Sure." Then he remembered what he was supposed to do and raised his hand to his forehead in a salute kind of thing. "Yes, ma'am. I'll turn off my signal-blocker and call my commander."

When his heart stopped banging in his ears, he would. When his system wasn't completely froze up with the freak out and realized he actually wasn't about to get nabbed and end up dead. Yeah. He'd call as soon as he didn't feel like he'd got a bunch of chemical pinballs rattling around in his head and his guts and he could hold a tab without dropping it. To show that he did actually care what they were saying, he reached up and tapped off the signal-blocking fob around his neck. Fuck. That had really just happened. Fuck. He glanced at the glued-down contractors, pulse still going crazy. One minute everything had been fine, and then there was screaming and attacks. Sure, it turned out okay, but fuck it all, this was too much. Where had these assholes come from? How'd they found Sky House? He thought he was safe in here. He thought they were okay here, and here they were, getting slapped upside the head by another attack out of nowhere.

He realized he was still getting stared at. He tried the salute again.

"Your tab's buzzing, Officer," the UN guy offered. Inyoni slapped his pocket and fumbled the thing out. He dropped it twice before he got it into his hands and the right way up.

"Uh, be a minute, sorry."

He stepped into an alcove, bringing up the call window. On the screen, his lady and Aidan were smushed together to get in the frame at the same time, big eyes looking back at him. Tweak made a funny little sound, grinning. Aidan let out a sigh and smiled at him.

"Hey, you gave us a scare. We got a report that Sky House got attacked. We've been trying to message you."

"Sorry," Inyoni answered, "we were dealing with bounty hunters. Had my signal blocker on. Everything's okay, we got them, but..." he didn't know how to put everything he was thinking into words yet, so he let it go.

"Anyone wounded?" Aidan asked. Inyoni shook his head. "We're shook, but everyone's good. They didn't get shots off. The UN people want help arresting them."

"I'll let Command know," Aidan said, glancing at Tweak. "You guys take a minute, I'll get the calls put in." Then he was out of the frame.

"You g-g-good?" Tweak asked when they were alone. Inyoni shook his head. "I'm freaked. I'm real freaked. We gotta talk when I get back, Dragon."

"Y-yeah. We do," she agreed. "Come home. B-be safe. K-k-kay?" Her eyes were so big, and so scared. Damn, he hated scaring her.

"Kay. Love you," he added. "Yeah," she agreed. "Same. Bye."

It took a while to get everything done he said he'd help to do at Sky House, and then he took an evasive route back to base. This time he kept his signal blocker on the whole way home, just in case. It meant nobody could call him, but if somebody was tracking him...well yeah.

If someone was tracking him. That was all he could think about. It was the only thing that made sense; seemed like everywhere he went, an attack happened while he was there or right after. So either he had the shittiest luck ever, or…

Yeah. Or.

He had to have Tweak check everything for bugs again. He had to check what he was doing with Kevin and go over his training; maybe he was missing a trick somewhere. He had to fix it. He couldn't be the reason somebody died.

Tweak was waiting in the garage when he got in, arms squeezed around herself. He hung his gear up and booked it across the garage, picking her up in a hug. He heard the gear slide back off the hook, but he didn't give a shit. In his arms, his girl shivered. Her scales were standing up, so he made sure he didn't cut himself on their edges where his arms pressed on hers. "Hi." Tweak whispered.

"Hi," he breathed against her hair.

"S-s-scared," she managed.

He ran a hand over her head. "Same. Room?"

"Y-yeah."

"Bao Li with somebody?"

Tweak swallowed hard. "Y-yeah."

"Kay. C'mon." Holding his girl in his arms, he carried her down to their room and shoved the door open with a foot. Walking inside, he sat in the corner of the room where they'd put an easy chair. He rocked her until the shakes let up, hers and his both. Slowly, her scales sank down until they were smooth gold snakeskin against his fingers again.

Inyoni drew a breath. "Tweak? I think I'm fucking up."

She raised her head, meeting his eyes. "Why?" He swallowed hard. "Everywhere I go, the Corps hit us. If it's me… I mean if I'm messing up and I keep getting people taken out wherever I go…" She rested a stick-thin finger over his mouth. "Hey. Bird. No." Man. He loved this girl like nothing else, no question. But times like this the way she talked made things tough. "No what?" He asked, thrown. She rested her head in the hollow of his throat. "No. It's n-not you. It's war. Corps. Going n-nuts. Hit anything."

He glanced up at her. "You sure?"

For now, she held his eyes, nodding. "Sure. I see you. In the t-trackers I r-run. You m-move like all the g-good l-logistics g-g-guys do. Sides. Kev t-t-trained you. He's a b-bag of dicks on g-grid. You did anything w-wrong on p-p-procedure, he'd tell you. He did that. With me. So I know it. So yeah. Chill. Got it?"

Inyoni swallowed hard. "Okay," he managed, "got it." She smiled, reaching up to stroke his ear. "Good. Don't forget." Man he loved it when she did that. On the outside, it made him want to melt. On the inside, having the bit of him he hated get treated like something good made him feel amazing. He managed a smile. "Y'know I'm a jackass. You'll remind me when I forget again, yeah?"

She kissed him. "Sure."

"They're really looking for us now. They're not playing."

Reading Tweak's typed words, Kevin smiled thinly. "Tell me something I don't know."

Tweak gave him one of those barbed sidelong looks of hers, let out a snort and typed again.

"The signal that got Sky House was the Sleepwalker again. When're you going to have time to help me track this guy?"

"When there are thirty hours in a day, probably," Kevin replied dryly, glancing from the console to the door. "Aidan should be here in a moment, he knows we have a call with Command today."

"He's probably just dealing with civvies again. Liza too,"

Tweak offered. Kevin nodded, quietly impressed. The fact that Tweak had come along so far as to offer reassurance to others really was something.

"It does seem to happen a lot these days," he acknowledged. "Dealing with civilians. I wonder if…there you are." He smiled warmly as his husband and his comrade came in.

"Got caught by somebody in the hall," Aidan offered, dropping into his seat. The hunch of his shoulders made Kevin long to reach out and soothe him, but there was no time for that now.

"Are we late?" Liza asked.

"No, Tweak and I are early," Kevin reassured as he flicked the screens to life. "Logo's still up; Hall hasn't started the call yet."

The logo made a liar of him by flickering out of existence, showing Commander Hall's face. She gave a small nod to the gathering.

"Officers."

"Ma'am," most of them chorused.

"I've scheduled this call to give the Wildcards unit their preliminary assignment in our next push." Hall began with the minimum of preamble. "You will have two sets of responsibilities: civil and military."

"Yes ma'am," Aidan agreed on their behalf. Hall brought up two new screens to hang on either side of the call.

"On the military agenda, we have the following intelligence. Among the corporate heads, Bezo-Mars of ZonCom has already voluntarily traveled to the Hague, as has Lynch of Natbank. They've advised all their officers to comply with us and our UN allies. Anyone who isn't complying is doing so against their explicit mandate.

"Marcus Z of TechoCo has run to his island in Seattle, and is trying to apply for asylum with the Tsardom of Rus for himself and his inner circle. In the meantime, he's advised the upper echelons of TechoCo officers to lie as low as they can. We have some of them in our Quadrant, and we'd like to assign operatives versed in covert works to lure them out. Several of your members are candidates on our list, and we'll be reaching out with assignments as needed."

No prizes for guessing who that'll be, Kevin murmured to himself. *Myself, Yvonne and Sarah, of course.*

"Other corporate officers will require a more robust military approach," Hall continued. "Hamilton has—surprise—given orders for every EagleCorp officer to fight to his last breath. We'll see which of them stand and which ones run, but they've closed the gates of the communities where the families of corporate heads live, and made themselves a foxhole out of their head office on Sixteenth Street in Denver. That will take an attack plan to clear out, and I'd like members of the Wildcards to sit in on that session.

"Walton has told ArgusCo people to stay at their posts and try to maintain the urban infrastructure as long as possible. He's barricaded himself into his skyscraper in downtown Chicago with the families of the most trusted ArgusCo officers; we're treating it as a hostage situation.

"And then there's Harrington; he's left the board of directors and his officers at Cavanaugh swinging in the wind, and bolted for his retreat on Mount Elbert. Many of his officers have already surrendered in exchange for plea deals."

Kevin hadn't realized that he'd reacted until Aidan caught his eye. He did his best to sit back and relax. Carefully, he modulated his breathing before he opened his mouth. "Permission to speak, ma'am?"

Hall turned her head, pinning him to his chair. "Officer?"

"I visited the Mount Elbert complex numerous times as a child and a young man. I'd like to offer my expertise on the capture of Harrington."

Hall pursed her lips, considering. "Let's pursue that in a separate conversation, McIllian. Schedule it, Headly, and I'll approve the meeting."

"Yes ma'am," Aidan agreed automatically. Hall spared him a grim little smile.

"And now for the civilian side of things. Obviously, Four Aces Farm will continue your work as a liaison venue for all factions of our movement, and a provider of food and medicine to the metro area. I want civil service to be Officer Carlan's main focus."

"Thank you, ma'am," Liza acknowledged.

"You'll also continue your work in founding satellite farms and passing seed stock to those who want to create their own small grow operations," Hall went on. "Command has discussed an additional, passive assignment during this time. A stock of seed will be delivered from our allies in the mountains; we are requesting that you plant it in a test bed, report on its viability, then begin to seed your surroundings with the mix should it meet our standards of germination and hardiness."

Kevin glanced at Liza, then at Aidan. His husband gave him a subtle 'don't look at me' shrug before returning his attention to the screen.

"What kind of seed is this, ma'am?"

If Kevin was right, Hall's eyes actually twinkled as she smiled. "This seed, Headly, is a collection of native prairie grasses and perennials that have been modified for survival in the conditions that currently exist across the West. If this works, we're going to help the Dust become a prairie again."

She glanced between the dumbstruck faces. "You wanted a revolution, officers. This is what a real revolution looks like. Reclaiming what is good, from the grass roots up. Literally."

Kevin could barely believe it. They were going to turn the Dust back into the thriving prairie land it had once been. They were going to bring back the grasses and the native flora. Carpeted in grasses and herbs once more, the Dust could cool itself and grow verdant, becoming the welcoming place for animals that it had once been rather than the hardscrabble ecosystem it was now. He glanced at his husband, and shared a grin with him for a heartbeat.

Commander Hall cleared her throat.

"In order for that to happen, there will be quite a lot of work for all of us. I'm delivering assignment packets to your system, including a rough timeline. Headly, please brief your crew and assign your subordinates accordingly. Call ahead for final approval of each action."

"Yes ma'am, thank you ma'am!" Aidan saluted with a will.

Hall actually smiled at him. "Thank you, Commander Headly. Dismissed."

Her image flicked out, replaced by the Force logo.

Once their superior officer was out of sight, Kevin got out of his chair, knelt beside Aidan's and hugged him tight. Aidan's arms wrapped around him, and for this one breath of time, he basked in the wonder of it. They were taking out the Corporate heads. They were taking back the Dust: not for themselves, but on behalf of the ecosystem, the land itself. They were taking *everything* back now.

He kissed his beloved, giddy with wonder. "We have to tell the crew!"

It took an hour to get everyone together in the oldest rec room, the one they'd always used.

"Okay, so here's the plans for the next actions," Aidan pointed out, hanging the map in the air and enlarging it for the whole crew to see. "Liza, you made sure nobody's hanging around the door?"

"It's locked sir, with a sign stating that this is Force business. The only civilians in here are Bunny and Jen," Liza agreed. Little Bunny waved a fist on cue, grabbing her father's ear. Aidan nodded while Tweak helped Inyoni extricate himself from their daughter's grip. "Okay, then here we go. I got our orders for the next few weeks." He pointed at the objective list. "Yvonne, Sarah, they want our best prank-pullers in on planning stuff that will out Corporate officers and put them in a spot to get arrested without getting anyone shot."

Yvonne bounced to her feet, giving the best salute of her life. "Yes *sir!*"

With a little grin for Yvonne, Aidan moved on. "Janice is staying down in town to keep helping the civvies with their water and power setups, we had a call yesterday. Milo, they're adding one more set of seed experiments for your division; seed's arriving later this week. Prep a bed with dirt that's in Dust conditions, I'll brief you on it later."

Joggling little Jen on his knee, Milo nodded. Kevin waited for Aidan to talk about the work he'd be doing to hunt down Harrington and his ilk, doing his best not to fidget.

"Jillian, you're running the hydroelectrics room," Aidan continued, "ask Topher and Dozer for help if any of the machines give you any trouble."

Jillian swallowed hard, but she nodded. "Yes sir. Thanks, sir."

Kevin strained forward, watching his husband. Was he going to leave it at that? He had to say something. Kevin had to be a part of the takedown, he *had to.*

Aidan nodded Jillian's way. "Liza is on working with the civil aides, deciding how the UN can help the unions get the new civil systems implemented. Kevin's going to be assigned for liaising with the justice side of the UN force, helping them scope out local places to keep prisoners, get all the intel they need and be their local point guy whenever they need him. Other than that, he's going to be doing work on the constitution with Liza and—"

Kevin's self-control broke. He raised his voice. "Ah, Aidan? That other assignment I may need to be on?"

Aidan looked at him, and he could have kicked himself. There was so much in his beloved man's eyes; a kind of pain, and a sort of fear, and an eternity of patience.

"Hang onto that Kev," Aidan suggested. "We'll talk about it later on."

Kevin subsided sheepishly, feeling like a bloody troglodyte.

"Your first assignment is to work with Liza as part of the team collating all the suggestions made for the Constitution in the West, and advise Councilor Hernandez on what we've got," Aidan went on. Kevin nodded automatically. Of course. A solid Constitution was essential to their long-term success. A glorious revolution was pointless if you didn't have a plan for picking up the trash and feeding the community the day after you won. That was what the community needed.

But that's not what I need, Kevin almost groaned inside his head. *I need to make Harrington pay! I've waited so long!*

Another thought smacked him like a sock full of sand. *Perhaps that's why Aidan isn't putting me on it. And perhaps he's right.*

Kevin gave himself a mental shake. Alright, enough of that. He was a professional. An officer. He wasn't a wounded child any longer. He would do what was needed, not what was satisfying. And he'd do it to the very best of his ability. He owed it to his Aidan, and to everyone else.

He pulled himself back into the moment, listening as Aidan walked the team through their assignments and their work. He took notes. He stayed focused. All the time, part of him paced and raged in the back of his head. But he was practiced at locking that part of himself into its cage, and he hid it well. He'd flattered himself that he had, anyway. He got away with it until he was up to his elbows in a mountain of collated civilian suggestions on the new Constitution, and caught Liza staring at him.

"Sorry, mind wandering," he offered. "You were saying?"

"I was saying, are you sure you don't want to do the final presentation on this for Hernandez?"

"Are you getting overworked? I can take something off your plate so you can focus here," Kevin suggested.

Liza shrugged. "The workload isn't the problem, but you love to talk and you haven't given a single big presentation yet. It seemed like it was your turn."

Kevin smiled, shaking his head. "We've been over this, Liza. You're a much better representative of our people than I am. And you've worked so hard to get us here."

"So have you, Kev," Liza offered gently.

Kevin sighed. "Liza. Let me put this bluntly. Men like me have been on podiums for generations, and look where it's gotten us. It's not my turn any longer. It's yours. It *needs* to be yours. And I have other work to do."

Liza eyed him for entirely too long. "You're planning something, Kevin. And it's something dangerous."

He blinked, taken aback. "Now what makes you say that?"

"You've got that look in your eye," she replied judiciously. "That blank one that says you're planning something, and you know I'm not going to like it, and so you're just going to hide it. I hate that look, Kevin."

He pulled on a smile for her benefit. "Don't worry about me, my girl. I'm only doing what I need to do."

"That's what scares me," Liza observed dryly. "I've seen what you think you need to do before." He kept his smile in place, deflecting her stare.

Finally, Liza sighed. "Don't shoot anyone, alright? And don't get shot."

"I'll do my best," Kevin acknowledged. But he did not give his word. He wouldn't want to be accused of breaking it.

"Hey Tom? Can I borrow you a minute?"

Tom looked up from the screen he was studying with Deliquisha. Yvonne still had to look twice at him some days. Not so long ago, he'd been all big eyes and elbows. Now he was old enough to enlist. That still threw her.

"Sure," Tom agreed with a quick nod. "Del? Pick this up tomorrow?"

"You got it. Your rank test is when again?" Deliquisha asked.

Tom shrugged. "When the brass has time. I'm ready, though. See you."

Tucking his tab in his pocket, he trotted over to Yvonne. "What's up?"

"Got something to go over, c'mon," Yvonne slung an arm around his shoulders, leading him down the hall to her room. "Grab a seat, Sarah's on her way."

Tommy gave her an eyebrows-up look. "Uh, why am I getting double-mom'd today?"

Yvonne rolled her eyes. Luckily, the door opened before she had to explain.

"Hey baby. Hey Tom." Sarah dropped onto the bed, giving their son a quick squeeze. The eighteen-year-old eyed her. "Okay…what's going on…?"

Sarah glanced up at Yvonne. Sitting on the bed, she smiled at their son, putting a hand on his knee.

"Tom, we want to talk to you because…well, because we kinda made a promise when you were little. We said one of us would always stay on base, so you'd never lose everybody again. Now, I know we kinda bent that promise sometimes, but this time…"

"You're eighteen now, Tommy," Sarah picked up. "You're all grown up. So we wanted to see how you would feel if me and Yvonne ran these next few missions together."

"These last few missions, maybe," Yvonne suggested with an encouraging grin. "It's looking more and more like we're going to win. So if this is our last chance to stick it to the Corps…how would you feel about Sarah and me going out as a team?"

Tom's eyes widened, and Yvonne's heart cinched at the way it made him look. He was so young still. The only thing in the whole world that could make her skip out on this series of missions was that look on her kid's face.

"Can I say something?" Tom asked.

Yvonne nodded. "Go for it."

Tom sat up straight, solemn-eyed and still. "If I go with you, you won't have to worry about who stays home. So why don't we do that?"

Yvonne stole a look at Sarah, who looked as freaked as she was by what Tom had just said. She wrenched her eyes back to their son. "Oh, Tommy, that…that just isn't going to work."

"Why?" Tom asked. "If it's the rank thing, I'm ready for my test as soon as the brass administers it."

"It's not the kind of mission we can take you along on, Tommy," Sarah explained gently. "We're going to have to be undercover a lot of the time; we can't have anybody but experienced folks on this. And we may end up doing some pretty gross stuff."

Tommy looked at her with questioning eyes. "What kind of gross?"

Sarah sighed. "Honeytrap stuff, probably."

Tommy cocked his head. "Is that sex stuff?"

Sarah shrugged. "Kinda."

"Okay, then I don't want to know."

"Got it."

Watching her wife and her son, Yvonne could have cried. Everything was so safe and happy right here, with the three of them. She wished it could always be that way. But Tom was almost a man. They were almost winning a war. And they had jobs to do.

"There's a lot you can help with on base," Yvonne reassured.

Tom glanced at her, his shoulders slumping. "I mean…I know that. But…"

"But?" Sarah coached gently, putting an arm around Tom's shoulders.

He leaned into her. "I just…I feel like…." All at once, he sat up, and his eyes were full of pain. "They killed Mom. I should be out there doing *something* for her. Something to make that…I don't know. Something! I just…I've gotta do something for her, don't I?"

"Oh Tommy." Reaching out, Yvonne pulled her adopted son into a hug. Sarah snuggled in on his other side.

"You know what Andrea would really want to see you do?" Sarah offered quietly. Tom looked up at her. Sarah smoothed his nutmeg hair back from his eyes. "Live a good life. That's what you do for her."

Yvonne nodded, so glad Sarah was handling this bit. Shit, she had hoped *so much* that Tommy wasn't going to end up like Topher with pain at the bottom of his eyes all the time, or like Kevin; hurting and hating deep down and pretending he wasn't. How had she missed how bad Tom was still hurting?

"It doesn't feel like enough," Tom muttered, eyes flicking down.

Yvonne gave him a squeeze. "It's what she always wanted, baby. It's what she fought for: giving you a decent life. So if you want to do something for her, really for her? Do that. Don't pick up a gun; pick up a shovel and go work in the garden. Forget the bastards who tried to wreck us. Grow up and live good. That's the real win over corporate assholes: not letting them make you into bastards like they are. You hear me?"

Tom swallowed tightly.

Yvonne joggled him a little. "Hear me?"

"Yeah," Tom eked out. Glancing between them, he managed a weak smile. "Okay. You guys want to go out together because you're pulling big pranks, and you want to have fun doing it one last time before there's nobody bad enough to really screw with?"

"You got it," Sarah agreed with a grin.

Tommy returned her smile. "Who're you aiming for?"

"We're starting small and obvious, and working our way up," Yvonne explained. "Remember the Folder?"

"Yeah?" Tommy nodded.

Yvonne leaned in. "We didn't let you see the videos when you were little; you ever watch them later?"

"Yeah," Tommy agreed, making a face.

"Well, we just got the word. Every Corporate officer we can name in those vids? We're taking them first. They're going to stand trial, and the evidence is right there on camera."

Tom glanced between them, and a slow smile spread across his face. "Oh man. Tell me about it later? If it's not sex stuff?"

"You got it," Yvonne agreed. "You'll get all the deets you want."

"When do you leave?" The man that their little boy had become asked.

Yvonne had to swallow before she said anything. "Later this week, once we accept the missions."

"How long will you be gone?"

She hated the answer she had to give. "We can't tell you, Tommy honey."

Tom nodded. He gave them both quick forehead kisses. "We better do laundry tomorrow so you can pack. You forgot last week. When you get back I'll have a rank badge to show off."

Yvonne pulled him into a tight hug. "Can't wait to see it."

"So who's our first target?" Sarah asked two days later, sitting on her duffel bag to make everything fit.

"The foreman of that AgCo Pets plant," Yvonne replied, flicking up the first set of paperwork on a screen that she guided to hang on the wall.

"The one the neighborhood burned down after they realized what was really going into the dog food?" Sarah asked as she shimmied out of her BDU pants and pulled on Grid-quality jeggings to check the fit.

"You got it," Yvonne agreed, studying the paperwork. "Yeah, I remember this guy…get this, all AgCo did was assign him to a new meat processing plant. He's doing hotdogs now."

"Oh great," Sarah observed with a grimace. "Somewhere *else* where you don't know what's in the meat. Where is he?"

"They moved him to Five Points. UN has him down for acting as a willful accomplice in genocide, extrajudicial killing, and criminal obstruction of an ongoing act of human rights abuse. That'll put him away for a while."

Sarah paused with one arm in her new shirt and gestured at the screen. It scrolled upwards, showing everything that was known about their mark. "Looks like he has a day off on Monday, so he'll be home and we can get at him then." Glancing at Yvonne, she grinned. "Baby, you know what? His home has next to no security. I mean it's in an AgCo neighborhood, but if we get Eagle uniforms and we code ourselves some credentials…"

She glanced over at Sarah. "You're thinking Housekeeping Act?" Sarah's grin matched hers. "You took the words out of my mouth. How long to get everything together?"

Yvonne ticked off the points. "Day to get the OK from command and let the UN people know, day for recon and planning with Kevin and Tweak, day to print us some gear and the synth, day for prep and double check. So we're out by Friday for a Housekeeping Act, that work?" Standing, Sarah grinned up at her. "Perfect." She looked Yvonne up and down. "Only, baby? Dump this shirt. It looks like crap, and it's out of date on-grid."

"Picky, picky," Yvonne chuckled, sneaking a kiss.

Four days later, they climbed through the maintenance hatch in the central train hub for the Denver Metro that the gang had green-lighted forever ago, the one that let them out into a locker room that a station maintenance crew only used twice a day.

"This shirt better?" Yvonne asked, doing a twirl for her wife after they'd changed.

"Totally up to date grid-girl," Sarah agreed. "So, plan: we get on the train in Grid clothes—got your 'buds?"

"Right-hand pocket," Yvonne agreed, patting the cloth. "We got the Eagle stuff in the backpacks. We get off the train at Alameda, we jump into an EagleCorp prowl car that Kevin got us the credentials for and change clothes on the way."

"Stripping in a car, it's like when we were twenty," Sarah quipped with a wink. Yvonne grinned, grabbing her hand for a quick squeeze.

"Let's go, baby."

The prowl car was right where Kevin had said it would be, waiting in a parking spot marked "Officers Only" in a parking garage. Yvonne input the pin code on the car's door, pressed her thumb against the reader below it, and popped the lock.

As the car drove itself to the address they'd put in, Sarah and Yvonne banged elbows and knees, squirming into the quasi-EagleCorp uniforms that'd been printed for them. This was one of the oldest tricks in the book. Everybody opened the door for housekeeping services, cops and that kind of thing, the same as everybody let waiters come close to them at tables in a restaurant. Nobody really looked at cops, or housekeepers, or waiters; they looked at *uniforms*. And in this case, all a scared little son of a bitch would see was two uniforms.

By the time they arrived, they were picture-perfect Peacekeeping Officers. Sarah rapped on the door.

"Peacekeepers, Mr. Harris. Please open the door."

Apparently this asswipe thought 'security' meant 'four locks on the front door.' Yvonne listened as each one clacked open. Moron. If she'd wanted, she could have used a thermo-electric pulse wand and popped them all at once.

The long, stringy guy from the Folder vids opened the door on two chains. Yeah, and if he thought that'd protect him he was a dumbass as well as a bastard.

"What?" The factory foreman snarled.

"Citizen protection detail, sir. We're here to take you to a place of safety," Yvonne stated in her best flat professional voice. "Threats have been made against your wellbeing."

The man's sunken eyes widened. *Welcome to being scared for your life, asshole,* Yvonne thought as she watched him. *You liked it when it was you standing over some poor schlub you got to shoot and throw in the dog food machine with no consequences. Not so much fun in the other direction, is it?*

"I got work tomorrow—" Harris started, but Sarah cut in. "We are escorting you at the request of your superiors, sir. Please follow us to the car."

The guy's watery eyes darted between them. "Lemme check this with the boss."

"Of course sir," Yvonne agreed. Good thing Tweak had figured out an AI to imitate the people this guy called and hacked his phone to place it ahead of time. The fact that she'd actually called up her UN liaison and checked it to make sure it cleared as a white hat hack still floored Yvonne.

The mark took his time with the call, eyeing them the whole time. It took a while, but eventually he hung up and walked out his door without a word. Locking his door took a hell of a minute; that done, Harris stormed over to the prowl car and dropped himself into it. You could just about see the steam coming out of his ears he was so mad. But he didn't bother to talk to them; after all, they were just the escort.

The drive felt like it took forever, but it was only an hour and something really. Up in an abandoned lot furred with plants breaking through concrete, they pulled in beside an idling bus that sat waiting.

"I thought we were going to a safe house?" Harris griped.

"The bus will take you where you need to be, sir. Please follow us," Yvonne replied in her professional soldier's tones. Grumbling, the murdering dickhead climbed out and walked to the bus. As he climbed the stairs, Yvonne neatly handcuffed him from behind. "Issac Harris, by the power invested in me by the International Criminal Court, I arrest you for the crimes of acting as a willful accomplice in genocide, extrajudicial killing, and criminal obstruction of an ongoing act of human rights abuse."

"What the fuck?!" Harris snarled as the UN officers waiting in the bus stepped down the stairs to grab him.

"You have the right to remain silent," Yvonne went on, repeating the memorized words as two big UN guys picked the skinny asshole up and carried him onto the bus. "You have the right to humane treatment under the UN accords regardless of your choice to speak. Anything you say can be used against you in court. You have the right to have a lawyer during questioning. If you decide to answer questions now without a lawyer present, you have the right to stop answering at any time."

"Fucking bitch!" Harris yowled as he was clamped into a bus seat. The driver gave Yvonne a quick salute. "Nicely done. He's on the road to the Hague. Take care, ladies."

"Thanks much!" Yvonne agreed, bouncing back down the stairs and off the bus. She grabbed Sarah and gave her a quick kiss.

"One down, a bunch to go. Who's next?"

"Is everybody here?" Liza ran her eyes over the packed warehouse. White heads, grey heads, bald heads. The occasional blue-rinsed or shockingly dyed 'do on an old lady who no longer gave a damn. And the green arm bands, of course. Hundreds and hundreds of green arm bands, wrapped around sleeves and jacketed arms and hard, wrinkled biceps.

Just in case, she turned the sound on her mic up a bit. "Are we waiting on anyone?" When you had more than a thousand names on your list, it paid to double check.

"I've checked off everyone who said they were attending," the Tomorrow Organization's founder offered, holding up her tab with a quick little smile, looking out at the crowd. "Everyone, welcome to the Great Walk For Tomorrow."

A wavery cheer and a smatter of clapping ran around the room. Signs made from recycled boxes waved over grey heads. The blonde woman at the podium beside Liza smiled. "As you know, Officer Carlan and her team will be helping us stay safe. If you need directions or any sort of aid, look for the people dressed in blue; they're the Caretakers' and Resource Distribution Workers' Union, and they'll help you out. If you see signs of danger, look for the people dressed in orange and wearing hardhats; those people are members of the Guardians' Union, and they'll help handle violence. We'll march down Broadway as far as Downtown, where the grandchildren's gathering and another set of Dusters will join us to march to Old Courthouse Pavilion in front of the Byron White Courthouse."

"What's she want with a mouse?" A wispy little gentleman with more wrinkles than last week's laundry asked the round woman beside him. She beamed as she leaned in and bawled in his ear.

"Courthouse, my lamb! We're marching to the courthouse!"

Liza kicked herself mentally, and turned closed captions and sign language filters on to run beneath her images as she spoke. She liked that they were using the landmark's original name instead of calling it Argus Pavilion. One of the best places to deny the Corps was in people's heads, and Amelia Boscombe knew all about that. She'd been running Tomorrow, a civilian alliance group, for nearly fifteen years now. Liza had heard about her now and again, mainly in casual mentions thrown out by Kevin, Jim and Yvonne. It was nice to finally put a face to the name. Amelia and her Tomorrow people had done so much good, well before the Dusters had managed to break the stranglehold represented by the surveillance and punishment system of drones and Citizen Standing Scores. These days the Dusters were the bones of the movement, and the Unions were the muscles. But it was mutual aid and reclamation organizations like the Diggers, Coomb Olwen and Tomorrow that acted as connective tissue in the movement and kept things accessible to people just trying to make it through. Liza was happy to be standing up on the stage with a woman like Amelia, wearing the green armband of her organization for the day. And this march idea of hers was genius. Grandparents and grandkids peacefully marching together for a better future; what could be more symbolic and less violent than that?

She glanced over her shoulder, where Inyoni was manning a tab and keeping an eye on communications from Kevin and his team. Inyoni gave her a thumbs' up, and she nodded. Everything was ready down at Kevin's end too. They'd broken things into two teams today; Deliquisha was with Kevin to help out with the grandchildren who'd be in the march, and Inyoni and Liza were taking care of the grandparents. Naomi had already set things up on the security side in concert with the Guardians who'd assigned themselves to this action. Yes. They'd covered all their bases. They were good.

"Let's go over our chants one last time," Amelia called out. "And then we'll all get moving to our staging areas for the march. First call: Who deserves a future?"

"The kids deserve a future!" hundreds of cracked and reedy voices replied together, sounding powerful in chorus. At her side, Inyoni put his hands over the sides of his head for a moment. His holo flickered. She raised a brow at him, and tapped her ear. He nodded, pulling out his earplugs. She really should have reminded him before this.

"Good, chant two," Amelia encouraged.

"It's been too long! We'll right this wrong! For! Our! Kids!"

The syncopated rhythm beat in time with Liza's heart.

"And last call, say it with me!" Amelia shouted out. The crowd roared the words back at her.

"Rip the contract up today, we won't sign our kids away!"

"Great," Amelia grinned. "Okay, next set, we do these with the grandkids, call-and-response style. Lily, start us off."

Stepping up onto the stage, two girls took places beside Amelia: a thin blonde girl with Ameilia's features and the straightest shoulder-length hair Liza had ever seen, and a curvy girl with a flannel jacket, her wild curls cut in an asymmetric fade. The bigger girl gave Liza the best grin as Amelia's daughter, Lily, took the microphone.

"Okay, next set! These we chant when we join the grandkids! What we want is human rights!"

"No more corporate-mandate lives!" The crowd cheered back.

"Next chant! It's our future, let us choose it!" Lily called, standing for all the young people.

"It's their future, give it to them!" the elders rejoined.

"Show me what the future looks like!" Amelia called, repeating it until the aged crowd chanted it with her. "This is what the future looks like!" Lily and her companion chanted back. The girls on stage grinned back at Amelia and Liza; she grinned back and gave her a thumbs' up.

"Wonderful!" Amelia called. "Now, let's get ready. Officer Carlan?"

"Let's have everyone move to our staging areas," Liza stated calmly. "Remember, everyone received a number on your tabs. Group One, you're at Sherman and Eleventh, in the pay-to-park lot. Group Two, you're at the ZonCom Auraria Campus. Group Three, you're at City Park Pavilion. The kids are all inside the Basilica of the Immaculate Conception at Fifteenth and Colfax, they'll come out and join us for the last leg of the march, a twenty minute walk straight down to the Pavilion. We've taken care of the Go systems, so vehicular traffic won't be a problem for us. We'll stay there for an hour, and then we'll disperse. If trouble comes up, the Dusters have camoflauged buses waiting at Champa and Eighteenth, at Champa and Nineteenth, and at Holy Ghost Church. Our assignment, in accordance with the vote you participated in, is to focus on protection of the participating children and assisting in any necessary evacuation. My colleagues are currently drilling your grandchildren on all these safety and evacuation measures one last time, and we know everyone in the Tomorrow organization has been training for this." She gave the watching crowd a smile. "Ladies, gentlemen and friends, let's go make a better future."

Cheering, the crowd headed out the exits. As they left, a couple people stepped up to say a few words to Amelia. Her first duty done, the organizer turned to shake Liza's hand. "That was great, you really got everyone's confidence bolstered."

"Glad I could be of help," Liza agreed, smiling from her to the teenagers standing behind her. Amelia glanced back. "Girls! This is Officer Carlan, the Queen of Clubs. Officer, this is my daughter Lily, and her girlfriend Clark."

"Pleasure to meet you," Liza offered, shaking hands with both girls. "Will you be joining the grandkids?"

"Yep," Clark agreed. "Probably too old for it, but hey. I never followed the rules. Not great when you're born EagleCorp, but…eh. Fuck 'em." She grinned at her girlfriend, slinging an arm around her waist. Lily tittered. "Miss Rebel." She kissed Clark's cheek, then stepped away to give her mom a hug. "We better go. Seeya Mom!"

"Be safe," Amelia called after them. "Chicken for dinner tonight!"

Lily laughed, waving a hand over her shoulder as she and her girlfriend hopped off the stage and headed to the door. Amelia waved, her eyes just a bit too bright.

Gently, Liza laid a hand on her shoulder. "She'll be okay."

Amelia swallowed. "Yeah. They both will." She gave a tiny laugh. "All of this started because I couldn't find chicken for her when she was little. The '45 food shortages, you remember. I kept promising her chicken tomorrow, and one day she looks at me, all tiny seven year old with big blue eyes, and said "don't worry mom, tomorrow will come." She drew a breath. "I swore I'd make tomorrow come, after that. A better tomorrow. Any way I could."

"And you're doing it," Liza agreed quietly. She could see why Kevin liked this one. There was fire in her, and strength.

Amelia straightened, shaking off the moment. "We better get moving."

"Of course," Liza agreed. "Inyoni, did Kevin say anything?"

"Just that they're ready," Inyoni offered, half-apologetic as always. They really needed to work on the boy's self esteem.

"Great," Liza gave him a tight smile. "Amelia, heard anything?"

"Eagle's Nest hasn't had too much going on," the organizer replied, slinging a backpack over her shoulder and passing Inyoni a bullhorn. "Even at the low-Standing part of the compound where I live, things have been relatively quiet. No chatter about the march. I think we're good. Let's move. We're in Group Three."

In the streets, you never would have known anything unusual was happening. The heat was just on the upper edge of pleasant, and citizens of all Standings were out enjoying these early days before the summer really bore down and they needed chill vests outdoors. Everything looked fine. But Liza could feel the sizzle of suppressed excitement in the air. How many casually walking people here were headed to their positions for the march? She checked her tab. Fifteen minutes to get into position. She picked up her pace. Civic Center Park was really more of a green pocket than a park, surrounded by CSS cafes and fences that protected the stretch of heritage Kentucky bluegrass. ArgusCo kept watering it in this part of town to show just how affluent Downtown was. Liza rolled her eyes at it. What a waste. Put some pretty agastache, rabbitbrush and catmint in there and you could hydrate six families on the water you'd save. The area would still look good, and it wouldn't be taking water out of people's mouths. But that was a problem for another day. Today, there were aged people walking on the heirloom bluegrass in spite of the posted signs, smiling at one another mischievously as they broke a small rule and prepared to go up against a much bigger one. Liza took the bullhorn Inyoni had been carrying for her. "Time, everybody! Let's walk!" With a cheer, everyone streamed onto the sidewalk. Liza nodded to the man with the drum, who started a slow beat.

"Who deserves a future?" Liza called through the horn. The response swelled up from dozens of throats.

"The kids deserve a future!"

Once they got started, Liza handed the bullhorn off and melted further back into the crowd, watching for trouble. Command had organized three responses: one for a lack of reaction from the security forces of EagleCorp. Possible, given that they were staying barricaded in their headquarters and might refuse to engage with what they'd call a disturbance of the peace on the grounds that they had bigger problems right now. They hadn't even gone after factories the unions had taken, so they might stay hunkered down for this march. Option two, the Corps attacked some group of marchers the moment they saw something happen; par for the course, given how they usually reacted to threats. Option three, Eagle attacked at the park. They'd planned for that too. Liza and Kevin had walked everyone through each step; holding an action this close to Eagle's headquarters on Sixteenth Street was a gamble, but the Cap Hill area was the beating heart of Denver, and the old Justice Center was the most iconic thing they could possibly use to symbolize their goals. And if everything really went to hell, they could bolt to the evacuation buses they'd arranged to have ready behind the Courthouse. They could also head back to the Basilica, an institution that had been helping get people in danger out of Denver for more than thirty years now.

People were stopping on Colfax, staring at them as they marched. As they walked down Colfax, the Basilica reared up on their right, gray spires like fingers stretching up to touch the sky. Liza tapped her tab, sending the prepared signal. As they came level, the gigantic wooden doors opened and the kids came pouring out. Ranging in age from eight to eighteen and flanked by blue-clad Caretakers, the youngsters found elders to hold hands with. A last round of the elder's chants went through the crowd.

"Rip up the Corporate Contract today, we won't sign our kids away!"

The kids set up a cheer of pure delight, and started on one of their chants.

"It's our future, let us choose it!"

"It's their future, give it to them!" the elders roared out, backing them up.

The crowd strode down Colfax like an autumn thunderhead across the plains. Liza watched from her place within the crowd. So far so good. She checked her tab, but so far her contacts hadn't spotted trouble. Maybe they were going to get Option One after all. Wouldn't that be great.

"Show me what the future looks like!" the elders called. "This is what the future looks like!" the children replied. Up ahead, Liza spotted Lily and Clark walking hand-in-hand.

They wound down through the streets around the gated High Standing park at the center of Downtown and passed the mess of dropped silver blocks that made up the ZonCom Denver Art Museum. Up ahead, the white marble of the Old Courthouse gleamed in the sun. The chants unfurled like banners of sound.

"It's our future, let us choose it!"

"It's their future, give it to them!"

"Not a bad shindig, if I do say so myself!"

Liza turned as Kevin came up beside her, grinning as he clapped her on the back. He'd gone with a black wig and beard for today's disguise, and it made him look like some kind of vampire with that pale skin.

"How were the kids?" She asked, raising her voice to be heard.

"Good as gold, the grandparents?" Kevin called back.

Liza gave him two thumbs up. "Word perfect and ready to go!"

Kevin grinned at her. "Sounds like Eagle's staying put! We're in good shape!"

"Great! Where's Del?" "Up ahead, leading a chant!" Kevin laughed back, pointing. Liza spotted the flower-tied hair wrap of pristine white that Deliquisha had gone with today. It really made her stand out, that and the bullhorn. Liza should have known she'd head up front.

Liza raised her voice with the chant, and heard the man who was a brother to her raise his voice beside her.

"Who deserves a future?"

"The kids deserve a future!"

They walked into the pavilion with drums beating and voices high, looking up at the white stones that had once represented fair and impartial justice. Today, they were going to bring that meaning back.

Later, Liza could have kicked herself for getting lost in that moment. It took her way too long to notice the alarm going off on her tab. It was Kevin who caught on first. She glanced at him as he pulled his tab, bringing up a holographic window. It blared into life.

ALERT! EVACUATE THE SQUARE! HELICOPTERS INCOMING!

When she looked up at him, Kevin's face was white as the building in front of them.

Whatever he started to say was lost in the roar of blades as black helicopters swooped in over the Old Courthouse, smoking canisters falling from their bellies like the hail storms in hell.

Inyoni's head felt like it was going to explode when the tear gas fell and the screaming started. Earplugs were nowhere near enough for this shit.

Whipping his head around, he scanned desperately for his people. Where the fuck was Kevin? Where was Liza? And Del, shit she was just a kid, she shouldn't be in this mess, and—

WHAM!

The explosion knocked Inyoni to his knees, head in his hands. Shit. SHIT.

Another explosion went off, and another.

Fuck. This was all going to shit. It was all going to complete shit.

No way he could stay here in this clusterfuck; he was dead if he did. They had a plan for this, didn't they?

Bus. Get to the bus, and take everyone you can with you.

"Bus!" Inyoni shouted, grabbing the nearest kids and their attached old folks. Pushing them in front of him, he headed out a side street, towards the…

For a beat, he didn't get what he was looking at. Then he did, and then it was worse.

The bus was a burning heap in the street. It was pretty much toast already, just a fiery blur punctuated by the charcoal lines of the chassis.

Around it, a couple bodies in orange clothes were already starting to smolder.

Inyoni had to repeat it to get it into his head.

They blew up the bus.

They blew up the fucking bus.

And there was another fire further down the road. Another bus burning. More corpses in orange.

Inyoni gulped.

"Get outta here," he told the scared people he'd guided this far. "I gotta go back and tell people the buses are a nope."

The grandad clenched his jaw, gave a nod, and shepherded the kids away.

Inyoni returned the nod without really thinking about it, turning back towards the mess in the pavilion.

As he ran, something pinged off his ears. For a second he thought it was raining, but then he felt something crunch underfoot. Nanoids. Tons and tons of nanoid robots, little metallic bodies crunching underfoot.

Nanoids that were supposed to be looking for and clogging up guns.

Inyoni's gut dropped. *Oh holy shit.*

EagleCorp assholes were coming down ladders from the choppers whup-whupping overhead, and they weren't fucking around. They started off shooting the Guardians the second their feet hit pavement And the weapon-blocking nanoids had gone down. *Fuck!*

A bunch of Peacekeepers herded a crowd of old folks and the last couple Guardians up against the steps of the Old Courthouse.

"Be it known that these citizens have committed willful espionage, breach of citizen contract and civil conspiracy! The punishment for this behavior is termination!"

The guns went off. The old folks fell across the stairs. Already, another group was being pushed over that way.

Inyoni's head was spinning with the overload, but he knew one thing he could do. He grabbed the hand of a running girl. She turned and scratched at him, so he dropped to his knees. "Hey hey, be cool! I got somewhere to go! Come with me!" Gasping, the girl nodded. Pretty soon, he had a whole pack of kids at his back; every time they passed another one, a kid would grab them and explain. Back where they started. That's where they'd go; it was safe up there.

They got into the sidestreets on the Art Building side of the pavilion, dodging between all the big civic show off buildings with lots of shrubs and plantings. The kids were panting and crying, wheezing a lot; their eyes probably hurt. Inyoni was having to blink a lot, his sight was fuzzy and his throat felt kind of tight, which meant him and everyone here had gotten tear-gassed. If he could feel the pain, he'd probably be moaning right along with the kids.

Kids. Kids and old people. They'd attacked kids and old people.

Don't think about it now. Not yet. Later. Get through now.

It took a long time, seemed like, to get back to the big-ass church where they'd started. Inyoni knocked on the back door.

"In out of the storm," he managed. His voice sounded weird, sort of scratchy. He dredged out that word Kevin had told him to use. "Sanctuary."

The guy in black with the white collar darted a look around, and threw the door open.

"Inside, into the basement. Hurry!"

In the basement, the priest moved some boxes to one side and opened a second basement that hadn't even looked like it was there.

"In here. It's EM shielded. There's cloths, medical gear and milk in the fridge in there."

"Great," Inyoni agreed. "Guys, in. Everybody, c'mon. In." The kids filed inside, too quiet. Big-eyed. Shit, they were going to be so messed up from this.

The priest patted his shoulder. "Get inside and I'll close the door. You're safe in the arms of God now."

Inyoni just blinked at him. Stepped inside. The door shut. Inyoni knew he should be taking care of the kids. But the world was tilting, and nothing felt real. He sat in a corner, and put his head down on his arms.

Slowly, little peeps of talk started coming up again. Sounded mostly like the older kids, the teenagers, whispering.

"I got milk, lemme see your eyes."

"Your arm's broke. I'll tie it up."

"Am I bleeding? There's blood on my shirt…"

"Nah, see, isn't even your blood. You're good."

"There's a bunch of medical stuff over here."

"Hey man, you okay?"

The last bit was said twice, and Inyoni realized it was being said to him. He raised his head. A teenage girl with seriously gamma curls in a side-shave was looking at him, hands on her knees.

"You got the shakes pretty bad," she observed. "You need a fix, or is it the scare?"

"Scare," Inyoni replied quietly. "I'm clean." Just in case, he checked his bracelets. The birds on them were blue; he wasn't bleeding anywhere. Good enough.

"Your eyes need milk?" the blonde beside her asked, hefting a white gallon. He shook his head. "Save it for the babies."

"Yeah man," the curvy one agreed. She reached out, putting a hand on his shoulder. "Back there. Thanks."

"Yeah. Yeah, course." He swallowed hard, looking up at the blonde. The organizer's daughter. It came back to him now. Lily.

"Your mom okay?"

The girl's mouth went tight. "She hasn't called yet. We're waiting."

He nodded. "Yeah. Me too."

He glanced down at his tab, but there was nothing on it.

He didn't know when it was when the door to their hiding place opened, setting the littler kids off into screams. The priest poked his head in, smiling. Behind him there were more kids, and a bunch of grandparents, and—oh thank fuck. Inyoni's guts came unknotted as Del came in, and Kevin, and Liza. Standing, he was going to head right over to them. But his knees gave out, and he fell down again. Kevin caught him before he hit the ground, pulling him into a quick hug.

"Glad to see you." He clapped Inyoni on the back, stepped back and gave him the once over. "All in one piece?"

"On the outside." Inyoni agreed blankly. Kevin met his eyes, and nodded.

"Best that can be expected for now. We can—"

"YOU!" Inyoni turned around with his hands up around his gut just in case, that voice had so much piss in it. An old lady came elbowing through the crowd, aimed like a gun at Kevin. "You were there to take care of them! You picked my Nadia up! You promised she'd be safe!"

"Is your child missing, ma'am?" Kevin asked, glancing around. "If you can tell me what she looks like I can—"

"She's DEAD!" The shriek just about split Inyoni's head. "She was shot on the stairs with her grandfather! She was twelve, you lying bastard! TWELVE! You people promised that we were going to make changes! You said things were going to get better if we marched! You promised that you'd protect us! And my Charlie and my Nadia are lying out there DEAD because we listened to you! You Duster trash!" Rearing up, she spat in Kevin's face.

For a moment, the whole world froze. Nobody moved.

The old lady turned and stamped over to a corner, dropping into it and starting to sob.

Slowly, Kevin pulled that little cloth he kept on him out of the pocket of the jacket he was wearing and wiped his face. "The Sisters are bringing us food and blankets," he stated, staring straight ahead. "We'll spend the night here. Tomorrow, we'll get everyone back to their families, best that we can."

Turning, he walked away.

The next couple days were, no joke, just plain shit. It took a week to figure out which kids still had families to go back to, which ones would need to evacuate with them, and which ones needed medical help. Inyoni threw up the first couple times he woke up after nightmares, and he sure wasn't the only one. Pretty soon the room smelled like a lemon factory from all the stuff they used to clean up after each other. That organizer lady showed up, gave her teenagers a big hug each and headed out with them and a couple more kids. Every noise the walls or ceiling made sounded like the weight of an EagleCorp boot to Inyoni, he was so on edge.

It was three more days in different cellars and hiding places before they could get on transport and get back out to the Dust. Then they had to camp in the Dust for a night to make sure they didn't take trouble home with them.

The whole time, the Wildcards team was mostly quiet. Kevin and Liza's faces, Inyoni couldn't read too good. He was so overloaded from the last week and some that he'd take the quiet, even if it didn't feel like a good quiet. Del looked like she was okay, but man was she pissed.

Tweak was waiting for him in the garage when they came in. He swept her up into a hug, holding on for dear life. He'd almost never seen his family again. He almost hadn't made it back here. Tweak clung like a baby sloth, hugging him so tight he felt her scales pressing into his skin.

After a minute, she kissed his cheek. "Bird. Down."

He put her down. She walked over to Kevin and Liza.

"We heard. Inside. Office. B-boss."

"Lead the way," Kevin stated.

Aidan looked up when they walked in, eye-checking every one of them. "Everybody take a seat."

Inyoni felt like a puppet on somebody else's strings.

"The Sleepwalker turned in the plans for the march. He had perfect intel this time." Aidan explained. He brought up the windows. He showed them the details.

At Inyoni's side, Kevin stood. "Aidan. This is the chair you said you needed to recycle, yes?"

Aidan blinked. "Um…Yeah?"

"Thanks." Picking up the chair he'd been sitting in, Kevin took it out into the hall and, face blank, kicked and stomped the thing into little pieces. Standing in the wreckage, breathing a little fast, he closed his eyes for a second. Then he shook his head, picked the pieces up, stacked them neatly by the door, and rested his shoulder blades against the wall where the chair had been. Inyoni couldn't help but lean away from him. Then Kevin talked, and it was like nothing had happened at all.

"Could you place a call to Commander Magnum, love? We'll need to report in."

They did the things. Made the reports. Gave the statements. Finally, Aidan gave him a little smile. "Inyoni, you're on leave for a couple days. Go get some down time. Go with him, Tweak?"

He nodded. Turning, he walked down the hall with Tweak's hand in his.

In their room, Bao Li was asleep in her crib. Letting go of his hand, Tweak walked over and scooped her up.

"Bird, sit."

Inyoni did what he was told.

Tweak laid their baby in his arms. Bao Li didn't even really wake up; just yawned and rolled over closer to him. He bent his head over her.

Tweak's hand stroked his ear softly, from the top of his head down to his shoulder.

"Bird. Talk?"

He shook his head.

"I…ain't got nothing real to say.""

"Just. Talk." Tweak offered. He swallowed hard.

"Tweak…I…Tweak. They just…lined people up and…blew them away. Old people. Kids too. People who couldn't do nothing to them. They just…blew them away."

"Yeah. They did." Tweak agreed. Inyoni swallowed.

"The noise Tweak…and the smell…it smelled like…everything smelled like blood and tear gas. I feel like I still smell it." He shook his head. "Thought I knew all about 'dangerous'. I knew *I* might end up face down. But a bunch of grandmas just…bang. I saw it and I just…" He bowed his head over his daughter, and tried to catch his breath. His wife rubbed his back.

"Why, Tweak?" Inyoni asked. But Tweak didn't try to answer him.

Inyoni gulped back something that felt like it was clawing up his throat.

"Tweak…what if I'm the reason why? What if I fucked something up and they got us because—"

"No," Tweak stated flatly. "Talked. About. This. Before. Yeah? It's n-not you. It's war. Corps. Going n-nuts. Hit anything. Hit everything."

"Yeah but if it's always the places I am that get hit…" Inyoni started. Tweak shook her head. "Not. You." She stroked his ear, then his hair. "War. Bad shit happens. If it h-happens where you are a lot? That's 'cause it's a w-war."

"But what if…I don't know, what if I did something?" He met her eyes, his heart going double time. "I gotta know, Tweak. I can't be the reason people keep dying!"

In his arms, Bao Li jerked at the pitch of his voice. She made that little 'I'm gonna cry now' sound she did sometimes, and he rocked her, using two fingers to stroke her ears and hoping that felt the way somebody's hands on his ears always felt to him. "Sorry Bao Li. Sorry. Sorry. Papa's sorry. Sssh, ssh, it's cool. Sssh…"

Slowly, their baby closed her eyes again, and Inyoni's heart slowed down. Okay, no raising the voice around the kid with hearing just like his. He needed to chill the fuck out. He didn't get to lose it with his little girl in his arms.

For a while, Tweak just petted him. When she spoke, it was soft and matter-of-fact.

"You want me to r-run a bunch of d-diagnostics, bug checks, make sure? I'm on it. Prove it's n-n-not you. When I do, you d-d-don't say it's you n-no more. B-bad for y-you. So, I prove it. You quit it. Got it?"

He swallowed hard. "Okay. Got it." She smiled, reaching up to stroke his ear. "Good. Don't forget." He managed a smile. "After those bug checks. Start on them ASAP, kay?" She kissed him. "Yeah."

Event File 12
File Tag: Cryptoservice
Timestamp: 05:30-05-09-2162

"We need to talk."

It was the first thing Kevin said to his husband in the morning. Well, he actually said it to the ceiling, in the dark. He knew Aidan was listening.

"Yeah?" Aidan's voice murmured softly.

"I know we have meetings with the civilians coming up, and I'm more than happy to sit in and offer strategy for the rest of the week," Kevin said quietly, beginning the speech he'd been planning while he waited for his man to wake. "For one thing, I want to figure out exactly how Eaglecorp neutralized our weapon-disabling nanoid swarms and help come up with a work-around for that. But after that, I want to be taken off the civilian side of our work completely. I need to focus on the arrest detail for this Sector."

"What's your reasoning?" Aidan asked with all the calm Kevin was struggling to maintain himself. He closed his eyes, forcing himself to breathe steadily.

The crack of a slap. The woman's eyes, brimming with tears. The blood, flowing across white marble. The fire in his chest. He needed to articulate all of it now. He chose his words with care.

"I need to hunt these…these *beasts* down, Aidan. The ones who are giving orders for monstrous acts. This rage for these atrocities is burning me up inside. I *need* to use this anger in a way that makes it valuable. If I can't eviscerate the Sleepwalker — and the truth is, I can't catch the bastard in order to do so, much as I hate to admit it — if I can't do that, then *please.* Make this rage an asset. Let me hunt prey that I'm uniquely qualified to capture."

For a long time, Aidan was quiet. Finally, he sighed.

"We'll call Command today. See what they think."

"Thanks," Kevin breathed in the dark. Aidan didn't answer him. In a rustle of sheets, he got out of bed. Kevin let him have his quiet.

He didn't go to breakfast. He didn't need food on a day like this, and he knew he couldn't stomach it. Instead, he worked. He used the time until the call Aidan had scheduled to analyze the videos of the routed march, along with every other action in the Sector that had failed of late. He considered. And he planned.

At lunch, Aidan knocked on his door.

"Hall sent us word."

"Yes?" Kevin asked, sitting back in his work chair. Aidan stood awkward in the doorway.

"She's coming here with Magnum and a contingent representing the Diggers organization from Nebraska, and the UN people are convoying in with them. Some union reps are arriving tomorrow. We've got a couple days of planning ahead; Hall and Magnum say they can spare you half an hour when they get in. Hall said if you can prove your case in half an hour, you can be on the arrest detail."

Kevin nodded. His man looked so awkward in the door that he couldn't help but stand and try to soothe that lost-boy look. Stroking Aidan's hair, he kissed the sun-tanned cheek. "I know you don't like this. I know it worries you." Gently, he leaned against the door and pulled his husband into a hug. Aidan sighed against his throat. "Fact is, Kev? I *hate* this. I think it's a stupid idea. I'm worried that you'll get hurt, or…" he shook his blond head, lost for words.

"Or I'll turn into somebody we don't want me to be?" Kevin finished for him.

Aidan met his eyes. "Yeah," he sighed. "That."

Kevin dipped his head for a soft kiss. "I know. I know you hate this. And that's why I'm saying thank you. Thank you for letting me do what I need, and not what you want."

Aidan looked away. "Just don't get…wrecked, okay? And don't get killed."

"I'll try," Kevin murmured gently.

Aidan's eyes snapped back to his, and now their blue depths held the glint of steel.

"Trying isn't good enough, Kevin. Not for this."

This time it was Kevin who glanced away. "Let's see what Hall says. Will you sit in on the meeting?"

"I will," Aidan agreed. "After the meeting, I want to hear an answer from you, about whether you'll be careful. A real one."

"Duly noted, sir," Kevin replied quietly. With gentle hands, he set his husband back from him. "We've got work to do."

It was late that afternoon, and Kevin was deep into the logs of the failed nanoid swarms that had so badly let the protesters down when Aidan came to fetch him.

"They're in the guest office down the admin wing, and they're waiting," he stated stiffly. "Come on."

Kevin stood, feeling like a heel as he followed Aidan. Damn, he'd really done it this time. If they had a moment, he'd talk to Aidan, comfort him, ease his worries. But they didn't have the luxury of time, so he'd have to let the situation lie for now. It seemed like there was never enough *time* these days.

Well. He'd stated his opinions. Aidan had a right to his views, just as Kevin did. It wasn't up to them to decide who was right; that was a responsibility reserved for their superiors. The emotional side, he'd sort out later. He promised himself he'd find a way. Aidan didn't need to hurt and worry over his decisions. He deserved better than that.

Commander Hall's face, when Kevin closed the door behind him, was thoughtful. Magnum's was rather impatient.

"Officer," Hall began, "I understand that you've requested an assignment to our arrest detail."

"Yes ma'am," Kevin agreed. "I feel my skills would be pertinent in the sphere."

Hall tipped her head, ever so slightly. "To date, your skills have been very pertinent in civilian protection. What's your grounds for the change, officer?"

Well, here goes nothing, Kevin thought.

"Commanders, if I may speak rather candidly: I am the son of a corporate owner. I've been in and out of the houses of most of the high-ranking officers in Cavanaugh, as well as the homes and leisure areas of other CEOs and high-level targets. I used to sleep over at Tim Gould's house; he's now the CFO of NatBank. He still lives in his childhood home. I played laser tag and tennis on the property of Gloria Tweed-Bright, who is now an executive and Walton's right hand in ArgusCo. Harrington had us up to the Mount Elbert retreat for weekend events. I was young, but I remember these buildings. I know the properties, and I know the people involved. I want to offer that knowledge."

"You were very young when you acquired this information," Magnum observed patiently.

"And I'm very genetically modified," Kevin replied. "I don't forget details." And oh, how he *wished* he could. How long would he see blood flowing across white marble? That broken woman's face, right before she'd spat on him for his catastrophic failure. He'd see her face when he closed his eyes for years to come.

Focus on the here and now. Job to do.

Hall eyed him appraisingly. Glancing down, she tapped a stylus on her desk.

"I'm concerned about the vendetta element of this, McIllian."

Kevin's chest tightened.

"But given Commander Magnum's input, as well as your past infiltration record and your previous assignments, we'll agree that you have proven yourself to be less motivated by the personal revenge element than I had expected."

Kevin could feel his pulse pounding in his wrists. Hall looked up, and gave him a nod. "Consider yourself on the arrest detail. A briefing packet will be sent to your tab within the week. Next operation is next week. The arrest detail will reach out tomorrow." Kevin breathed again. In. He was *in.* Now he could really do some good.

"Thank you, ma'am," Kevin agreed, saluting Hall, then Magnum. "Thank you, sir."

He glanced at Aidan, but his husband was staring straight ahead.

The rest of the day slipped away like sand between his fingers. It was late when Kevin stepped into their room and found Aidan sitting on the bed, tapping in a desultory manner at his tab. He slid the door shut quietly, and smiled. "Done for the day?"

"Yeah mostly," Aidan agreed. "But I need to check in about some stuff."

"And what would the stuff be?" Kevin asked, taking his seat beside his husband. Aidan wasn't looking at him; never a good sign.

Reaching over, he cupped Aidan's cheek. Aidan closed his eyes. "What did Hall mean about infiltration, Kevin? What've you been doing?"

"What Hall's assigned me to do," Kevin replied quietly. "I haven't done anything I wasn't explicitly assigned to do. I swear it, my beloved."

"Were they the right things to do?" Aidan asked. Kevin leaned in and kissed him softly.

"In this time, in this situation? They were."

"Are you going to tell me about them?"

"Someday I will, Aidan my love. But I'm under orders. I can't divulge clandestine assignments. I know what I've promised. No secrets, not between us. But…this is different. This is my duty."

Aidan held his eyes. "Yeah. This is different. This is something you're volunteering for, Kev. It's not like doing the stuff we do as a unit. This is…this is something else." Aiden turned his head, closing his eyes as Kevin spoke.

"And it's my duty," Kevin replied gently. "We are each given what we need in this community we've built, love. And we each serve with the skills we have. These are my skills. I know how to make things happen inconspicuously. I know how to keep secrets. I know how to hide who and what I am beneath a veneer of what's appropriate to a given situation. I know how to hunt monsters. If we want a world where my skills aren't necessary, then I have to finish using them before I can lay them down."

Finally, Aidan opened his eyes: blue lakes of aching anxiety. The look in his man's eyes made Kevin nearly frantic to soothe the pain away. He restrained himself with an effort. Now was a time to be candid, not to cover this wound.

"Remember what I said earlier?" Aidan asked. His voice was uneven. "I want to hear an answer from you."

"About whether I'll be careful," Kevin acknowledged. "I remember."

Aidan nodded. "So. Say it."

Kevin kissed his brow. "I will be careful. I won't become a monster as I hunt the beasts. And I *will* come home."

Aidan studied him far too long. Kevin tried to smile for him.

"You swear?" Aidan asked. The note in his voice made Kevin's heart turn over in his chest. He rolled close, wrapping his arms around his husband.

"I *swear* I'll come home. I've got you to come home to, my best beloved, not to mention my entire family. Good God above, Aidan, I have *a daughter* to come home to now. I would never abandon a child of mine to be dragged through childhood by Tweak and Inyoni. Think of the tragedy."

But even this little bit of humor didn't make Aidan smile. He was still staring at Kevin with those great, pained eyes.

"Make me believe it," Aidan whispered. Kevin smoothed his wheaten hair back from his face. "I swear to God and the Mother of God, *I will come home.*" But those words weren't enough. That look was still in Aidan's eyes. He needed the right words to do what his beloved man asked. Closing his eyes, he laid his lips against Aidan's brow and considered. Words. Words about leaving, and coming back. Ah yes. Khalil Gibran. Of course.

"The wind bids me leave you," he whispered against Aidan's brow. " Less hasty am I than the wind, yet I must go." He kissed his way along the line of Aidan's jaw, lingering over the soft skin under his ear.

"We wanderers ever seek the lonelier way,

and no sunrise finds us where sunset left us.

Even while the earth sleeps we travel."

"I'm serious, Kev," Aidan admonished, one hand gently pushing at his shoulder. Kevin raised his head to kiss him, long and slow.

"So am I. You wanted me to promise. I'm making my promise, and sealing it in the most profound manner I know. My body and my voice; this is how I make you believe."

He lowered his head, kissing Aidan's throat as he deconstructed and remixed Gibran's 'the Farewell'.

"We are the seeds of the tenacious plant,

and it is in our ripeness and our fullness of heart

 that we are given to the wind and are scattered."

Reaching down, he unzipped Aidan's pants.

"Brief are my days with you, and briefer still the words I have spoken."

He stroked Aidan through his boxers, and Aidan wriggled.

"Sexing me up isn't getting you out of this," Aidan grumbled, but his voice had a note of play in it that made Kevin grin against his chest. He had been so hoping to hear that laughing note in his man's voice again.

"But should my voice fade in your ears, and my love vanish in your memory, then I will come again," he murmured against Aidan's skin, sliding his hand inside Aidan's boxers to palm the hardening length of him.

"And with a richer heart and lips more yielding to the spirit will I speak."

He shoved Aidan's pants down to his knees as he spoke, giving himself the room he needed to do the job properly. Lowering his head, he kissed the exposed skin below Aidan's navel. He took the length of Aidan in his mouth a moment, and his husband whimpered.

"Yes, I shall return with the tide,

"And though death may hide me,

and the greater silence enfold me," Kevin murmured as he slid back up the bed to trace Aidan's body. He kissed his man and continued speaking softly as his hand slid along the dampened length of him, "yet again will I seek your understanding.

And not in vain will I seek."

Aidan was breathing hard now, eyes wide and glassy. Kevin smiled down at him, and sped his hand.

"And if this day is not a fulfillment of your needs and my love,

then let it be a promise till another day.

Man's needs change,

but not his love,

nor his desire that his love should satisfy his needs."

He watched Aidan's face as he pushed the man towards his climax. Kevin teased him just a little longer as he finished the poem, keeping his touch just a hairsbreadth below the threshold of sensation that would tip his man over the edge.

"Know therefore, that from the greater silence I shall return."

Bending his head, he trapped Aidan's lips with his, and added pressure and speed to the strokes of his hand.

Aidan whimpered and bucked beneath him, then gave that little squeak that always squeezed Kevin's heart as he came. Kevin drew the orgasm out of his man using every skill he possessed, making it last as long as he was able. When Aidan was completely limp, he laid his head on his beloved man's shoulder, smiling.

"Oh man." Euphoric with orgasm, Aidan kissed the top of his head."Still doesn't get you out of it, though. You do a handshake when you make a promise. That wasn't a handshake."

"Hands were involved," Kevin equivocated, raising his head and kissing the tip of Aidan's nose. Aidan gave him a wide grin now, tipping his head. "How about we get more hands involved?"

"Oh?" Kevin asked, the word inviting. For answer, Aidan rolled on top of him and undid his fly.

"Your turn."

"Oh. My. God." Yvonne couldn't help it: she jumped on the hotel bed, and gave Sarah the biggest hug. "Oh my god oh my god oh my GOD! Sarah! Sarah honey! We just got assigned. To take down. Marcus Z the Fifth. Oh. My. GOD!"

"Oh my god seriously?!" Sarah asked, eyes gone wide.

"Seriously!" Yvonne agreed, pulling her in for a kiss. "They're shipping us out to Seattle tomorrow! Oh my god! Oh. My. God!"

For a couple minutes, all they did was squee and hug and go a little nuts. Then they opened the files.

"What've we got on him?" Sarah asked.

Yvonne flicked the windows into the air. "Here's the intel."

Leaning comfortably together, they read over the dossier of habits, hobbies and routines.

"Oof. Look at all that security. This's gonna take some work…"

"You're telling me."

"Big classical music fan, hunh?"

"Looks like he's a really big fan of world acts…" Tapping her lip with one finger, Yvonne thought it through. Then she grabbed the tab and started to type. The image on the wall fritzed and blitzed as she joggled the tab doing the projection around.

"Let's see if our international contacts can get ahold of her..."

"Who're you thinking?" Sarah asked, watching over her shoulder. Yvonne looked up at her, and grinned.

"I'm thinking Nicole Ma."

Sarah sat back. "Nicole Ma, huh! Even I know that name."

"Yeah, because everybody knows that name, because she's amazing," Yvonne agreed, hitting send on the message she'd just created. "Musician from a family of musicians, been a famous family since her great grandad. She plays great-grandad's cello, plays a violin, absolutely huge in world fusion music. If she's okay with it, then this'll be perfect!"

"It'll take time to set up," Sarah cautioned. Yvonne shrugged. "Well yeah. But we don't know anything until we know if she'll buy in. So let's start there."

Sarah hadn't been wrong either. It took a week just to get an answer from Nicole Ma's publicity agent. But when they got it, the reply was a request for a vid call.

They brought up the call at the agreed time. A cute little co-housing unit with a view of the Eiffel Tower out the window showed in the screen. Front and center, a stately woman waved at them. Nicole Ma was part Kenyan, part European and part Chinese by blood, and she had landed the best bits of all the genomes; she was drop dead gorgeous. When she spoke, her sweet French accent lilted out of the speakers.

"My agent got word to me about this action to capture human rights criminals using my performance as the bait? Is this right?"

"Yes Ms. Ma," Yvonne agreed, "We're hoping to lure out Marcus Zuckerberg the Fifth and his inner circle. If you were to perform in Seattle, and the show were to be publicized, we think he'd show up and an arrest could happen without bloodshed."

Ms. Ma's eyes opened wide. "Him? Really! That would certainly be something!"

"Him and his inner circle. We can work out the logistics on our end," Sarah offered, "but first we just need to know: would you be willing to help us out?"

Ms. Ma bit her lip for a moment. Then she drew a breath. "Could I have an hour to talk to my husband and think about it?

"You can have all day," Yvonne reassured, "we're in the preliminary planning stages, and there's no rush."

"Thank you," the musician replied with a sweet smile. "Whatever we decide, please know how much I admire the work your force is doing. I'll give you a call by the end of the day."

The rest of the day was probably the longest wait of Yvonne's entire life. They called in to command and passed on the word on what they were doing, and then they tried to kill time with games, a book, and some talk. It didn't really work. When the tab buzzed, they both went for it so fast that they cracked heads.

"Mrs. Ma?"

"Hello ladies!" This time, the performance artist was holding her violin on screen, cradling it like a baby. "And please, call me Nicole. Arsene and the kids and I talked. This is the kind of thing that my work's always been about; helping people with my music. This is the kind of thing Papa Yo Yo would have done, and he'd be proud of it. So I'll bring his cello back to the former United States, and I'll do this show, and you'll catch this worm."

Sarah and Yvonne shared a grin before Yvonne looked at the screen. "Nicole, you got a deal. It's going to take time for us to lay the plans, but we'll be in touch as soon as we can."

When the call ended, for a moment Yvonne just stared at her wife.

"Nicole Ma. Is in. On a prank we're planning. *Nicole Ma.*"

Sarah pulled her in for a long, hard kiss. Leaning back, she grinned.

"Let's call command before she changes her mind!"

They had to wait on that too; damn near everything took waiting these days. But finally, Regional Commander Hall's face was on the screen.

"Are these notes accurate, specialists? You've reached out and recruited…Nicole Ma? As in…*the* Nicole Ma?"

Yvonne had to bite back a laugh. Wow, she never thought she'd see Commander Hall thrown.

"Yes ma'am!"

Hall blinked. "Well...alright. Then I have people to call."

And that started one of the longest weeks of Yvonne's life. Every day was eaten up in hours and *hours* of talking. There was no time to get food, and no time to eat full meals; Sarah and Yvonne lived on calorie bars and caffeine. Shipping them out to Seattle got delayed; instead, they got introduced to Base 4246 over the screens, and got to know the members of the team responsible for Seattle; their handle was the Seahawks, and they were definitely sharp enough for it. They also had some really great out of the box thinkers who came up with some super approaches to getting the word on this fake world tour out and getting Marcus Z to come out of hiding and see it.

"We're basically lunch if we try to get into his compound, unless we bring serious firepower," Cally of the Seahawks explained as they went over the image for what felt like the fiftieth time. "But Benaroya Hall, this is where all our big acts show up, now this we can prep with all kinds of things that'll tilt the playing field in our favor and help us land this fish. For a full on operation like this, we gotta check every detail, but I think we can get in there if we work with the Actors' Guild." Cally had used the phrase "full on operation" so many times in the last week that Yvonne swore she'd scream if she heard it one more time.

Sarah and Yvonne jumped right from that call to *another* conference call with Nicole Ma's touring team. The amount of logistics that went into a world tour was truly terrifying.

"We'll line up Viking Entertainment Logistics to put together realistic paperwork for stops in eight American cities," a tight-faced woman on the other side of the vid stated in that weird, water-over-rocks accent that Yvonne had learned was from a country called Wales. "They're well versed in the lack of room for delays, damage or errors in scheduling during a tour like this. How's Ms. Ma's publicity coming along, Yvette?"

"We're doing roughs of the promotional material as we speak," a French lady with a perfect bun almost shot back. "We aren't accustomed to rushing."

Yvonne started to apologize, when the lady that Yvonne had started to think of as the Welsh Attack Dog cut across her. "Too bad. Now—" she pinned Yvonne with a hell of a look. "What are the *exact* plans for Mrs. Ma's protection?"

Yvonne had given less scary presentations to National Councilors. Mrs. Glamfyres—which was what the Welsh Attack Dog was actually called— took what felt like every word she said apart. When Yvonne was absolutely done and Mrs. Glamfyres still wasn't happy, they called up and looped in the UN team who'd be acting in concert with them. At least *they* were able to satisfy the lady. It was good to be sure about safety, but *man.*

As Mrs. Glamfyres grilled a United Nations guy, Yvonne crunched a calorie bar; she swore she couldn't remember the taste of real meals anymore.

Finally, the call was done, and Yvonne flopped backwards on the bed.

"Ow…my brain…"

"I swear pranks used to be easier than this!" Sarah groaned beside her.

"Baby, this isn't a prank," Yvonne replied with a weary laugh. "This is a Full On Operation."

Sarah groaned, swatting at her. "Doooon't!" she whined. "You know how sick I am of those words?"

Yvonne chuckled, grabbing Sarah's arm and pulling her in for a hug. For a bit, they just snuggled.

"So, we got a couple weeks to kill while they get the publicity out there," Sarah suggested.

"Mm-hm," Yvonne agreed.

Sarah kissed her forehead. "Better pick a local target; no sense wasting time."

"No sense getting bored either," Yvonne agreed. "So, who's next?"

"Commander Headly-McIllian. Good to meet you." The woman with spiky hair held back by a tie-die scarf shook his hand.

"A pleasure, Organizer Caurollo." Aidan agreed, shaking hands with the rest of the Diggers. "And welcome to Four Aces Farm. Everyone else is waiting down the hall; we'll have time out in the gardens during our mid-morning break."

"Forget about breaktimes," Regina Caurollo replied with a grin. "We're here to work with you on this national march. We want to get at it!" Her Diggers whooped around her. Aidan grinned. "Sounds good! Please follow me and Officer Carlan, and we'll get you introduced."

At the door of the big canteen, Tweak and Naomi stepped up, just like they'd talked about. "Hey guys," he offered, sticking his arms out.

"Any non-biological implants?" Naomi asked in her disinterested 'just doing the job' tone.

"Sexual health implant in the arm," Aidan replied in matching tones. "Bone and cartilage reconstruction nanoids in the feet. That's it."

The two wands beeped.

"Clear," Tweak stated. Naomi nodded. "Clear. Thank you, Commander."

Now that he'd given the example to everyone following him on the procedure, he stepped inside and surveyed the room. They'd had to use the newest and biggest of the canteens to fit everybody for the meeting; the Duster brass, the Diggers, and all the Union presidents and reps who'd made it for the meeting. A bunch of holographic representations of folks who couldn't make it in person were milling around to one side, tethered to their projectors. Aidan had to smile at one lady's hologram: a cat kept appearing and disappearing as it stepped in and out of the imaging area. The lady's hologram was blitzing as she tried to shoo the cat off.

All around, people looked up, noted his entrance and grabbed seats. He nodded.

"Good afternoon, everyone. I'm Commander Aidan Headly-McIllian. This is a joint civilian-military meeting; as custodian of Four Aces Farm, I'll be acting as moderator. We're all here to discuss our next big action: the National March Of Memory."

Turning, he flicked up a wide screen Tweak had programmed for him ahead of time. On it, the faces of dead Dusters and civilians formed a grid. Everyone who'd died in the Courthouse Massacre were shown front and center.

"Everyone's already voted to approve the general premise of this action: we're marching to bring the human cost of current Corporate life home to people still enmeshed in the system. We also want to provide all our allies and participants a chance to mourn their losses together in public, as a first step towards accountability and healing. Recently, my area has suffered a terrible loss." He flicked the tab, and the pictures of the gunned-down marchers filled the screen. "Seventy five people were executed on the grounds and the steps of the Denver Courthouse. Twenty of them were members of the Democratic State Force and of the Guardians' Union, killed trying to protect people. Forty-three of them were senior citizens, averaging around seventy years in age. Twelve children were also murdered."

A ripple of murmurs ran through the crowd. Aidan let the images stand behind him as he spoke. He drew a long, slow breath.

"Okay. For a second, I'm going to talk to you like a normal guy, not an officer. We've all lost people. We're all hurting. And we all need to talk about that: both because the assholes up top need to hear it, and because we need to talk about it." He closed his eyes for a beat, letting the emotion run through the room. Then he straightened. "And we need to do this to make sure that nobody else ends up on the list of the remembered. So let's start planning, and figure out how to do this in a way that's safe for participants and impactful for everyone watching." He nodded at his superior. "Commander Magnum, the commander for this Sector, will explain our protective measures for the new march."

"Thank you, Commander Headly," Magnum strode to the podium. "Ladies, gentlemen and comrades, I will be frank with you: we made mistakes recently, and those mistakes cost lives. Currently, we're laboring under the weight of an infiltration issue. We are actively hunting the infiltrator. Until they are apprehended, this is our most potent weapon: layered security. No single tool can be treated as our shield."

He gestured at the walls of the room. "Let me assure you that this area is protected; technical officers and munitions officers have set up every possible defense against surveillance and infiltration. This is a space where we can share thoughts on our best choices for civilian defense."

Aidan flicked the screen up. "This is the general idea: in every Sector of the country, marchers will print pictures of people who they've lost due to corporate neglect or aggression as big as they can, and walk through a set route of streets with them. Each march will end at a local icon that has plenty of room to move and lots of escape avenues, that way nobody gets kettled on site."

"We'll set the criteria for site selection at the national level via the Common Ground; local site selection is the responsibility of organizers at the Sector level." Magnum continued. Aidan brought up a new window for him as he talked. "We've got a series of chants and songs available that would suit this march; voting for which ones we'll use is starting on the Common Ground today, and it's running until next week." Flicking that screen away, he brought up a new one. "These are the civilian defense mechanisms that have been successful to date. Today, we will discuss how we should recombine them. Recently, we've become dependent on gun-blocking nanoid swarms as a movement. Commander Headly, please explain."

"We're not sure if it was the infiltrator that cued the Corps in about the nanoid swarms, or whether we just used them too many times, but we saw what happened when the Corps caught on at the Courthouse Massacre." Aidan began, scanning the crowd for reactions. "We discovered after the event that EagleCorp launched a signal disruptor designed to shut down nanoids at the frequency that construction-grade nanite tech works on. And that meant their guns didn't get blocked up this time. So, yeah, we can't depend on nanite tech anymore. We'll use it in concert with other techniques; if anything, nanoid swarms can be our decoy move. If we can make it look like we're still leaning hard on them, the Corps won't go looking for what else we're doing to protect our people." He brought up the next option. "Slick tech is available, but since the whole point is for us to be seen by cameras and people around the world doing this march, that's only useful in specific circumstances. We can also print protective clothing for participants that'll mitigate the dangers, but that runs into problems with distribution, and the fact that you just know there'll be at least one guy who forgets his vest or his goggles."

He waited a beat for the laugh to ripple around the room.

"One thing we need help from our civilian allies on is medical assistance: we didn't have nearly enough medics on site at the Courthouse Massacre. I'm not saying we could have saved everyone, but we sure could have done better than we did. So for this event, we want a much bigger set of Caretakers and medics from among the civilians; please start talking to your people about who's okay to step up for that."

"So I'm opening up the floor now," Magnum interjected. "We'll pass the mic around. Put your ideas forward."

"Can we change the Guardians' clothing?" Somebody called. "We don't want them to be so easy to spot and shoot."

Aidan wrote the suggestion down, and they were off.

The conversation went on all morning, and it would have gone longer if Billie hadn't gotten up on the stage.

"Ladies and…and gentlemen and…comrades," Billie was almost gasping the words out, and even across the room Aidan could see how hard she was fighting to stand and talk in front of so many people. She was doing so great, standing up there even when she was scared to death.

"Please make room for us to roll out the canteen tables, we'll be serving lunch in ten minutes," she eked out. Then she turned and scampered out of public view.

It wasn't so much making room as jumping up to help for most of the attendees; the next few minutes were a bustle of tables getting set, chairs getting rearranged and everybody finding seats. A few minutes later, Billie and her kitchen staff rolled a buffet on wheels in, and Billie stood in front of it with big eyes and a little smile.

"Please feel free to serve yourselves, everyone. There's enough for everybody."

Watching everyone work together to get organized and get lunch, it hit Aidan that they'd created a microcosm of the country. Lots of different people, lots of different attitudes, everyone agreed that they were going to get the necessities supplied for all of them and help out where they could. It really was something to watch.

"Hey big brother, you going to eat?" Naomi asked, knocking him out of his own head with a hand on the shoulder. He gave her a quick smile. "Yeah Omi, I'm coming."

"Where's the professor today?" Naomi asked as he joined her in line. *Man,* he wished she hadn't asked that.

He shrugged. "Out hunting, is what I know."

Naomi shot him a small smile. "Clandestine orders suck."

"Tell me about it," Aidan grumbled as he loaded his plate with amaranth and covered it in chickpea sauce. "Last call, he said he already got four of his targets: live arrests, nobody injured. Him and his team are doing good. It's just...I hate not knowing."

"I hear you," Naomi agreed. "Too bad he's not a loudmouth like the girls; every time they come home we get the whole story."

"Different kind of work," Aidan mumbled at his plate as they sat. "The girls are going after the more public CEOs; they get the ones who can get tricked into outing themselves and get arrested. Kevin and his team go after the ones who...can't."

Naomi said nothing, but she reached over and gave his arm a squeeze. Looking up, he gave her a weak smile.

They were nearly through lunch when Aidan noticed something going on; conversations were running up and down the table. People were leaning over to look at friends' tabs, pointing and grinning. A couple Union reps even got up, standing in a huddle. Aidan shot Naomi a look, and she gave him a subtle nod in return; she'd spotted it already, and she had eyes on the situation. Well, if it was a situation. Aidan had been so paranoid for so long that he wondered if he was falling back into that rut of seeing threats where there weren't any.

A beat later, the UN people walked to the main wall in front of the tables.

"Everyone, while we're eating, we'd like to let you know that the vote came in on our new flag and name! We're going to be known as the United Communities of North America, and we're going to wave this at the next march!"

The presenting lady tapped her tab, and a design floated up above their heads.

Looking up, Aidan set his fork down.

"Wow."

For a second, all he saw was a winding road under a starry sky. He could see the influence that the First Nation folks who'd been offered first design rights had on the final work. The bottom half of the flag was a red hemisphere, separated from the curve of dark blue on top by a thin line of white. Long, sweeping white lines formed a switchback road headed to the horizon. Overhead, eleven white stars gleamed. Each star had eleven points, and every one had a bright red center, making them look a little like stylized flowers.

A computer-generated image of what the flag would look like waving in the wind flew over their heads. At first, the room was quiet. Then the murmurs began. They built, and built, and then everybody was clapping and cheering.

Reaching over, Aidan gave his sister a hug, staring up at the new flag. There was a split second when he *wished* it was Kevin he was hugging the first time he saw this, and then he felt guilty as hell about that. He let the feeling pass, keeping his eyes on the flag. It showed everything: the long road they were traveling together, the land they stood on and the sky overhead. There were the eleven quadrants and all the people in them, the way they were all connected: everybody dealing with their own issues, sure, but nobody dealing with them alone. And there was the horizon. The future.

"It's perfect," he murmured.

"Yeah, big A." Naomi agreed. She rested her head against his for a moment. "Yeah. It is."

Event File 15
File Tag: Desired Course
Timestamp: 19:50-06-07-2162

Janice straightened up, stretched her back, and looked out over the little CAS subdivision with narrowed eyes. Around her, the solar panels spread across the rooftops gleamed blue in the sun. She nodded to herself. Yeah, it looked good. Only way to be sure it worked good, of course, was to switch it all on and see what did the job.

"Okay Pete, hit it!" Janice called down from the rooftop.

Below her, the lights on every home in the block went on. In the street, the impromptu block party that the solar installation volunteers had turned into set up a cheer.

Grinning, Janice hung off the flagpole atop the house, checking out her work. Yep, the neighborhood looked real good now.

Checking the clip on her climbing harness, she swung down to the dormer window and shimmied on inside. Her assistants met her with grins a mile wide.

"Great timing, dinner's here!"

"Yeah? The team get in from Four Aces?" Janice asked as she headed down the stairs.

"Took us a bit, but we got here." Now that voice was worth picking up the pace for. Janice just about dropped off the last step and into Milo's open arms.

"Well hey stud. Good to see you." She tipped her head up for a kiss, and he returned it, his locs tickling her temples.

"You too, beautiful." Milo wrapped his arms around her for a quick hug, then led her outside with an arm around her waist. "We brought a truckload of food in, got the table and chow line going. Abbie's at the table; she's got us some seats saved. You'll never believe the conversation we walked in on."

"Lemme guess, they're still goin' on about the sortition bit of the new constitution?" Janice asked with a snort. "Christ coming on a cracker. They keep goin' on like it's differential equations. It ain't that complicated." Shaking her head, she took Milo's hand. "C'mon, let's go see how far they's got this time."

"So let me get this straight," the nervy guy who'd been helping with the heavy lifting during panel installation was saying between bites as Janice took her seat, "we're going to have random people making decisions. Just…random? Like, anybody?"

"Well kinda, but sortition's more than just "random people make the decisions", Abbie was explaining. "See, under the new constitution, it'll go like this. Say we need to get the city budget together for Denver transit. There'll be a pool of people who know the work—engineers, street planners, garbage pick up guys, Go car programmers—and thirty of them'll be picked randomly out of that pool. Sixty citizens get picked to sit down with them. We all get alerts on the Common Ground if it's our turn. If we've gotta take care of a kid or go to the doctor or something, we put in when we're not available. The admins on the assembly sort out schedules until they have a forum—that's the sixty people and the thirty experts. Then we sit down for a week or two with the experts—"

"And we get paid for this whole time while we're sitting and not showing up at work?" the chubby lady beside her asked. Abigail turned a beaming grin on her. "But that's the thing, you *are* working right then! You're working for the community! And yeah, of course you get paid. Remember, everybody gets paid, that's what the clause about a national universal basic income is about. So you get that, plus all workplaces will have to pay your wages for doing your civic duty."

"Yeah, but who's going to tell us the right decisions?" the guy across from her asked. "I mean…what do I know about transit?"

"You know what it's like to use transit, and what it's like to get stuck or get left at night with no routes running that you can afford, yeah?" Abbie asked. "And you can talk to the people doing design about that. You sit in with the experts, you tell them the user experience, and they give you all the intel on the system design, and together you decide what makes sense," Abigail explained, grinning. "Between ninety everyday people who all use these roads, we'll get really common-sense stuff that works for everybody. And then the general population casts a final vote via the Common Ground for big stuff like laws. For everyday stuff like city budgets, it gets implemented after the assigned forum reaches a consensus."

"Yeah, but what if we make the wrong decision?" The nervous guy put in. Abigail shrugged. "Then we figure that out and we fix it. Together. Simple."

Janice leaned in. "Put it this way, fella. We ain't gonna do no worse than the Corps, are we?"

Slowly, the man across from Abigail relaxed. He even smiled a bit.

"That's a point," he agreed, taking a bite of his dinner.

"How's the vote on the Constitution goin', anyway?" Janice asked, taking another mouthful of her burrito.

"Pretty good, check it out," Milo offered, laying his tab in front of Janice's plate. She chewed thoughtfully as she looked over the votes for and against each clause, the suggestions for rewording and the ideas from around the country.

"So we got the bones all agreed on, everybody's talkin' through the finer points, that right?"

"You got it," Milo agreed, pointing out clauses. "The communities have all agreed to ratify the UN's Abundance Accords, and that'll be huge in the West, because it'll help us protect the groundwater and start gettin' the plant biome back together, and that'll help resurrect the Dust. Once the flora's reestablished, we can start on the animal ecology." He smiled softly. "Maybe we'll even get the Colorado River to flow again, one of these days."

"And in the meantime, we'll be running the communities of America on sortition-based referendums and citizens' assemblies, with a handful of elected positions at each organizational level keeping an eye on the general structure and making sure stuff gets where it ought to in their assigned areas of responsibility!" Abigail enthused. "It's going to work great." She put the period on the sentence by crunching into an apple.

Janice looked up at Milo, who was smiling fondly at their little supernova kid. Sitting there radiating confidence, their daughter was shedding light on all of them. She made this new system sound like it wasn't just going to work. Listen to her very long, and you were sure it was going to be the best thing ever.

And maybe it was.

Leaning back, Janice stretched. "Yeah well, I cast my votes already; while they finish hashin' out the constitution, I got another neighborhood to hook up for solar an' water condensers. Heat pumps too, if'n the truck from the fabrication plant's there when I get in. How long you here for?" She asked, leaning against Milo and slinging an easy arm around Abbie's shoulders.

"We need to head back day after tomorrow," Milo explained. "But we'll be back down again with a few other folks pretty soon."

"Oh yeah?"" Janice asked, leaning against him. He kissed her cheek. "Tell you in a bit."

"Kay. How's Jillian doin' on handlin' the system back home?" Janice asked as the conversation moved on around them. She did her level best to keep the question light, make it sound like no big thing.

Milo raised a brow at her, lips quirked up. "You getting broody about your base, mama hen?"

Janice sighed out a laugh. "Man, I spent so long mothering that fucking system, I ain't got no idea how to stop fussin' about it. 'Sides, Jillian's so damn new on it."

"Not as new as we thought, seems she did a lot more in those factories than she let us know," Milo said it like he was giving her shit, but Janice heard the way he wrapped the reassurance up in teasing. "And those pylons just about run themselves. Water's perfect. Isn't even giving the vanilla plants trouble, and you know how picky those are."

The little worry in the back of Janice's brain finally stopped gnawing on her. She smiled up at her partner. "Well ain't that somethin'."

"Ain't it just," Milo agreed, kissing her. Leaning against him, she enjoyed a long, slow stretch. "Whew, it's been a day. This guy got a bed for tonight, yeah?" she asked, glancing down the table at the neighborhood spokeslady. Jemmie gave her a quick grin. "Set aside that trailer back of Daniel's house for the truck drivers! Your girl can stay at the kid's dorm Nora's got going if she wants."

"Thanks much," Janice acknowledged with a quick wave. Standing, she put her plate through the recycler. "C'mon stud, let's get some down time. Abbie, you good?"

"I'm good!" Abigail agreed, waving from the circle of kids she'd ended up in.

Closed into the trailer Milo had been assigned for the night, Janice stroked one of Milo's locs.

"Good to see you."

"Same, beautiful lady," he murmured, leaning in for a kiss.

It was a while before they had much more breath for talking, or interest in anything but catching up on the physical side of things.

"Man, I needed that," Janice chuckled, resting her head on Milo's chest. His wide hand stroked her hair. "Same here."

"How long you down for?" She murmured, tracing his happy trail with one finger.

"A bit," Milo murmured. "Long enough to be part of the next big march."

"Next march?" The sheets rustled as Janice sat up. The light from houses around them outlined Milo's face, just enough to see by. In the gloom, he looked at her, cool as ice.

"They're shooting to run it on the twentieth. Big meeting's going on at the farm right now."

"Awful soon after the mess the last march turned into," Janice observed, stroking Milo's chest thoughtfully. "What're they doing to protect the protestors?"

"They're putting together a bunch of ideas," Milo offered quietly. "Me'n Abbie feel good about it."

"You'n Abbie? Milo!" She smacked his shoulder. "You ain't actually taking the kid!"

"She wants to go," Milo replied patiently. Janice rolled her eyes. "To where they're shootin' folks?"

"Nobody's getting shot at this time. The Force is gonna make sure of it."

"Says you," Janice snapped back. "An' if they miss a motherfucking trick, our daughter gets fuckin' shot! Or you get shot! Milo, you know what these flea-fuckers is like! I ain't watchin' you walk into a fuckin' meat grinder with our baby."

"Jan?" After her yelling, his voice was soft. "Abbie's not a baby. She's sixteen. And she's made a decision. The Corps shot her mom and dad both, different times. They killed her mom. Nearly killed her dad. She knows the risks. She wants to take them."

"And how about you, you want to take them too I guess?"Janice demanded.

Holding her eyes, Milo nodded. "This time, yeah. I do. Because it's worth taking. This march is special, lady. Know what it is?"

"I know you're gonna tell me, is what I know," Janice groused. Sighing, she flopped against him. "Well, go on an' tell me."

"It's going to be a memorial march," Milo explained as he stroked her hair back from her face. "Every attendee is going to bring a symbol of someone who's died or gone missing because of the Corps. Think an early Dia De Los Muertos, but this time the ofrenda is the whole march."

Janice blinked. "A walking ofrenda to the personas desaparecida and the muertos benditos…hunh."

"Something, ain't it?" Milo offered. "Abbie wants to carry Camile's picture in the march."

Janice nodded, mulling it over. Milo's first wife, Abbie's mom. A logistics girl who went down in the line of duty. A true Duster, one who gave up a cushy grid life to do what was right. Yeah, they'd want to honor her at something like this, and for good reason.

Still…

She glanced at him. "Milo…no shit, I'm freakin' out about this."

"I noticed," Milo agreed, amusement rich in his voice. Janice sighed. "It's one thing bein' in the Force an knowin' you're gonna get shot at, but this…it's like paintin' bullseyes on us and jumpin' around yellin' 'right here dickheads' at EagleCorp. It just ain't smart."

"Maybe not, but it's right." Milo murmured. "And if we let them scare us into hiding on our compounds with our guns now, when all the civvies are going to be out there? In my book, we let them win if we do that, Jan. I didn't fight this long to let them keep winning in my head."

Janice sighed. "Okay, I hear you, it's just…Abbie's so… I dunno."

"Hopeful? Innocent? Undamaged?" Milo suggested.

"All that, yeah." Janice agreed, waving a hand. "An' I don' wanna see all that thrown in the shitter and flushed with this march."

Milo's wide hand cupped her cheek.

"Jan. Look at me."

Janice raised her head, meeting Milo's deep eyes.

"She's my daughter," Milo offered. "She's Camile's daughter. And she's your daughter now too. She got strength from us, bone deep. She'll still be our sunflower girl after this. If anything, her roots will get stronger, even if it knocks some petals off."

"You sure?" Janice breathed.

Milo smiled. Reaching up, he pulled her into a hug. "Sure."

Janice sighed. "They got the action plan and the protection measures ready yet?"

"Be on my tab as soon as they finish hashing them out."

Sighing, Janice relaxed against him.

"So how're we gonna print pictures for this?"

"Okay, how's the list looking?"

Sarah grinned as she threw the screen up on the wall. "Denver officer in EagleCorp who willfully committed mass murder as part of running the EagleCorp "street cleaning" program, check. ArgusCo officer in charge of turning human remains into biofuel in Greely, check. Next up…Maxine Blanck. Wanted for knowingly buying shipments of biofuel made from human remains on behalf of ZonCom."

"Awesome," Yvonne exclaimed as the picture of a blue-skinned redhead with the most fashionable of ZonCom-approved mods flicked into the air. "We're sure it was with prior knowledge, yeah?"

"Human rights folks from the UN got proof," Sarah agreed, bringing up the reams of emails. "She knew she got a discount on anthropo…" She squinted at the word, then waved a hand. "Yeah, that thing, means human based products. She knew alright."

Sarah nodded, studying the screens. "So what do we know about her?"

"Hm." Yvonne went over the dossier that they'd helped put together. "Okay…she's a huge fan of eating original-flavor meat, like actual dead animal meat. Looks like pork especially. She spent…holy fuckballs that's a lot of money to spend on going out to eat…that's like a month's pay on a meal…on going out to eat some special kind of European wild pig. Weirdo."

"So…another round of the Housekeeping Act, do you think?" Sarah suggested. "Like, we swap ourselves out for her meat delivery people?"

"No, that'll get predictable and then we'll get dead…" Yvonne rolled on her back, watching her legs peddle in the air as she considered. "Really special dinners…pork…restaurants…there's gotta be something there…"

"Let's make some calls," Sarah suggested. "Talk to our Grapevine friends, ask what restaurants are the hardest to get into, or some special rare meal, or some meat farm or something."

"Kay, good call," Yvonne agreed, rolling back onto her stomach. She played with a few strands of Sarah's hair. "What if…what if…oh! Farms! Farming! But not Farming with an F, Pharming with a PH! Perfect!"

"You want to pharm her, for what? Her location?" Sarah asked. Sitting up, Yvonne shook her head with a grin. "No no no, not that! Look, we get into her computer, we put in some malware that redirects her to a specialty restaurant with some really rare pork thing, and she goes, and all us waiters and everybody are UN people, and we arrest her!"

Sarah grinned. "Ohmygosh baby, that's great! Okay, what's the first step?"

They got in through a faked thirty-percent off email from what looked like Blanck's most-visited restaurant. It took three days to get everything set up on her personal computer; then they had to wait another two for official approval on their plan, and another four to get personnel in place.

"Man, I hate how *slow* everything moves now!" Sarah groaned, pacing their room. Yvonne gave her a smile. "I hear you baby, I get it. But this is how it's gotta be if we want it to happen."

"I know," Sarah huffed, dropping onto the bed. "I know this is what cooperation looks like, I know it's better when we're organized and we don't just run around pranking and playing Russian roulette with EagleCorp. But it's *so boring*!"

"Cooperation is a lot less of a thrill than spray painting stuff and telling Peackeepers to fuck off," Yvonne agreed on a sigh. "But it works way longer." She patted the bed. "Come sit, let's watch some International Geographic."

They chose something about the woods of Central Europe, and the soothing voice of the narrator flowed over the sound of a wild boar snuffling over the forest floor.

"After nearly eighty years of international re-wilding efforts, these forests have reached full maturity. The ecosystem is rebalanced. Red deer are now bountiful in these woodlands. The genetically revitalized beaver populations ensure the health of the waterways. Wild boar have returned, as have the brown bears, Eurasian lynx, gray wolves, and wolverines. Once driven to extinction, numerous species of bird, insect and mammal have been genetically revived and released into this re-established ecosystem equipped with genes that allow them to thrive in the anthropocene.

"Each species was rigorously tested in the stations set up under the biodiversity section of the Zurich Abundance Accords of 2090, and the work done in these centers has renewed and enriched all of Europe. Once again, woodland stretches from the pine and beech forests of the Icelandic highlands to the rich oak forests of Spain, a state of natural abundance not known since two thousand BCE."

On the screen, deer ran with their fawns, birds flitted from tree to tree, and fish flashed like silver as they jumped from lakes.

"We are nearing the Abundance Accord's set goal of fifty percent natural ecosystem coverage across Europe and Africa," the narrator continued. "Sudamerica is quickly reaching the forty percent mark, and northern Asia has hit a milestone with fifty-five percent natural ecosystem coverage. In spite of its struggles, Canada has reached forty-two percent natural ecosystem coverage. What we have damaged in the past, human beings are in the process of healing today. Through our efforts, the European forest is rising renewed."

Sarah gave a long sigh. Glancing at her starry eyes, Yvonne squeezed her hand and smiled.

"Something good to dream about, hunh baby? Forests renewed?"

"Yeah," Sarah agreed softly. "Maybe that can happen here someday."

"It will," Yvonne agreed, giving her a squeeze. She kissed her girl's head. "Let's get ready for bed, kay?"

She woke to the buzzing of a tab in the morning, grabbing it with her eyes closed.

"Mmlo?"

"Civilian Action Advisor Flescher?"

Yvonne sat up. "Yeah?"

"It's Taskforce Officer Ngoma, Advisor. We've got Operation Carolina set up. We can launch as soon as the target accepts an invitation."

"Thank you, Officer, that's great news," Yvonne made all the right small talk. Hanging up the call, she squeed and landed on her girl.

"Ohmygosh it's on! We're on for Operation Carolina!"

Maxine Blanck received the invitation to the opening of a new Citizen Excellent Standing restaurant showcasing traditional slow-roasted pulled pork that afternoon. She scheduled her meal for two days out, in the early evening. Perfect.

Yvonne and Sarah got in just in time to get changed. Stepping in, they checked up with the UN team.

"We're getting personal protection on everyone," Ngoma offered with a quick smile that brightened his thin face. "You ladies shy?"

Sarah grinned back. "Not even a bit."

"Shirts off then, let's get these strapped," Ngoma offered with a grin as a female UN operative held out the personal protection belts and vests that would deflect bullets.

One of the two guys who were getting a pig carcass ready in what actually looked—and smelled—like a fire pit stuck into the middle of a stage on wheels looked away, his face almost the same color as his long carroty hair. The Black guy glanced at him, touched his shoulder, then glanced up and nodded at her. "Miss."

"Heya," Sarah agreed with a wave. Yvonne tucked her waiter's shirt back on and wandered over while she got the stupid little tie that contained her mic and recorder into place.

"You guys are the showcase performance, yeah?"

"Yes'm," the white guy agreed, "Azzie. Me'n Eber here fixed the delivery for a pig carcass so's it looks all good in the books; been workin' on this since yesterday. We're gonna show them out there what real Carolina Barbecue looks like, make the whole thing look real convincin' while you get the CEOs in your nets." He shot her a quick grin. "Dragon…I mean Ms. Lung asked us to come'n help out."

"And we're really glad you did, this looks amazing," Yvonne agreed. "I bet with you guys out there, the Corps assholes don't even look up till we slap on the handcuffs."

The white guy looked down and mumbled something that was probably "thank you, ma'am." The Black guy gave him the kind of look that told Yvonne everything she needed to know. Yeah, leave it to Tweak to find a couple of gay guys out of AgCo who could code *and* roast a hog, and who had every reason to bring this whole mess down. She found what they needed every single time.

"Bout ready," Eber noted, checking the thermometer he pulled out of the meat. "How's the clock?"

"That's fixin' to be ready too;" Azzie noted. "Best we move this out an' get settled for our show. Mr. Ngoma?

"Let's get you set up," Officer Ngoma agreed. "Ms. Blanck and her cadre will be here in half an hour."

The mark walked through the door of the faux-rustic restaurant like a model on a catwalk, barely even looking at Sarah and Yvonne in their waiter's uniforms with the dumb little bow ties. She was ushered to a seat with a couple other big fish that she'd brought along. Perfect, they could all go in the net together.

At the little staging area they'd set up, Azzie cleared his throat. They'd lit the fire under the pig again, with a little air-detoxifier hood right above the stage hidden in faux brick. Eber turned the spit smoothly.

"Ladies and gentlemen," Azzie began with a bit of a nervous twang in his thick Appalachian accent, "Welcome. Today, we present you with a Carolina tradition: old-style pit barbecue."

The CES types took their seats and made happy noises about the food. Around them, the bodyguards and aides they'd brought with them took up all the spots Sarah had predicted they would; good spots from strategic points of view, and perfect for the types of attack they were watching for. Good thing that wasn't the kind they were getting.

Azzie stood at the front talking through the finer points of roasting a pig in a dug-out pit. With a small smile, he wrapped it up and nodded at Sarah. "And now you'll have a chance to place your orders, before we move on to the next stage of the preparation: choosing sauces."

"Will you be having appetizers, ma'am," Sarah asked, proffering an actual analog menu the way she'd practiced. Blanck took it without a glance at her.

"Vanda, they've got crab croquettes! Mm, I'd love some crab."

"Isn't crab poisonous?" the icy blonde beside her asked. Blanck flicked blue fingers. "Not the farmed sort, dear. Only the stuff that actually lives in the ocean is contaminated." She looked over the list with pursed indigo lips.

"We'll take a bottle of the Fladgate Scion, and the crab croquettes to start. Charles? Anything you'd like to add?"

As the big-wigs went over the menu, Yvonne carefully checked the placement of the UN officers. Everybody was where they should be. Great.

Palming a remote, she hit the button.

From the ceiling, a dozen small darts shot. Each tranquilizer hit a bodyguard, taking them down before they could do a lot more than blink. *Nap time, boys and girls!* Yvonne giggled to herself. Stepping in, she took the blue hand holding out a menu and put a handcuff around it.

"Maxine Blanck. By the power invested in me by the International Criminal Court, I arrest you for the crimes of acting as a willful accomplice in genocide, profiteering from acts of human degradation and criminal obstruction in the aid of an ongoing act of human rights abuse. You are further charged with thirty counts of reckless environmental endangerment via emissions and purchase of environmentally hazardous goods."

"What?!" Blanck sputtered. "What is this? This is outrageous! This is…this is…manager! I want the manager! I want Peacekeepers! Get these people off me!"

As she threw her fit, officers cuffed her furious companions and read them their rights. Yvonne grinned as she pulled the woman out of her chair. Over by the roasting pig, Azzie and Eber gave each other a hug of what looked like sheer relief.

"You'll get lunch at the detention center, Ms. Blanck," Yvonne offered with a grin. "But it's not going to be pork."

One by one, they walked their prisoners out the door and into the waiting bus. Azzie and Eber helped the UN officers load the unconscious bodyguards in using the back ramp, dropping them on seats and clamping them there once they'd been checked and stripped of any gear that could allow them to escape. Up at the front of the bus, the CEOs were still yelling their heads off.

Yvonne smiled to herself as she watched the bus pull away.

"Alright!" Eber called as the Dusters and the UN reps filed in. "Everybody grab plates an' set; you done the Lord's work, you're settin' at the Lord's table for a feast!"

Kevin increased the brightness of his tab's projection, and smiled at Aidan's message.

> "We've got a new flag. There'll be one of these flying over the base when you get home. Take a look."

The silent video displayed a lovely new emblem; while retaining the color scheme that had stood for the United States since its inception, it had reconfigured those colors into a flag they could all stand beneath. Something worth fighting for. He tapped out a quick message in reply.

> It's gorgeous. I can't wait to see it in person. Should be home in a week or so.

He started to type 'I can't wait to see you', thought better and wrote 'I miss you', then deleted the whole thing with a scowl. What was he doing? He was a married man in his thirties, not a lovesick boy. It was true that being so far away from the place and the people he loved was wearing. He ached for the contentment of being around authentic people who meant well towards one another again. He longed to fall asleep safe in Aidan's arms at night, and relax with him in the morning. But he didn't need to say that. He traded his deleted statement for something less asinine.

See you as soon as I can,
—Kevin

"Your tab's a piece of shit," his contact observed tonelessly. Kevin gave a murmur of agreement as he shut the screen down.

"The fan has been getting rather loud of late. Sorry if it disturbed you."

The man on the couch across from him grunted a dismissal. "You got all the stuff for tomorrow?"

Kevin nudged the bag by his knee. "EagleCorp cleaning outfit, credentials, slick suit, restraining ties, clips for the tranquilizer gun, a disguise to put on after the operation. We'll wait until the Denver Commissioner is walking down the hallway to his office. I'll be in the maintenance cubby. One clean shot will tranquilize him. I'll wait until he's very close to his office door; when he collapses, you'll drag him into his office. We'll tuck him safely in the compartment of the automatic floor-sweeper that was retrofitted and delivered three weeks ago. At the end of its cycle, it's programmed to go down to the bottom floor for servicing. The United Nations officers are using a servicing van to remove their prisoner and place him under arrest. The surveillance feed is being handled by our technical people, as is the Commissioner's orders for a health-related leave of absence. We used your information on his credentials and health condition to code in a plausible cover story; a sudden stroke at home. Treatment at Cavanaugh Anschutz, under secure conditions due to threats against his life. No visitors. His disappearance will appear completely legitimate for at least two months. You and I will do our work, then return here to debrief after your shift. After I've done my part, I'll stay in this safehouse for two nights out of an abundance of caution. Then I'lll move on."

"And the UN says this is legal?" The man sounded gruff, but Kevin recognized anxiety in the repetition. Teddy had asked the question at least four times now. He pulled up the authorization documents. "Go ahead and give the orders a thorough check if you have any concerns; you'll find our mandate in order."

For a time, there was silence. Teddy flipped through the operation approval documents, but Kevin could tell that he wasn't engaging with the material.

Eventually, the powerfully built Peacekeeper leaned back, the muscles of his metal-plated arms gleaming in the glare of the overhead bulb. The man stared off into space.

"How come they want the commissioner alive?" He asked flatly. "How come they don't just want him iced?"

Another recurrent question. Kevin answered it with all the patience at his disposal. "What we need now isn't more death: it's accountability. We need the people giving terrible orders to be seen as they're held to account."

Teddy gave a snort of derision, looking away. "Rich to hear a Duster giving me a talk on law."

Kevin was so *very* glad he'd had some time to run through his meditation and mental-health exercises before he had to have this conversation.

"We're on the same side when it comes to justice, Teddy," he stated as he checked over his building schematics. "One of our main aims is making the law system substantively align with humane and compassionate justice."

"Yeah?" Teddy didn't exactly sound impressed. "And when's that gonna happen?"

Kevin sighed. "Teddy, if you feel this way, why are we working together? As I remember, you did reach out to us through the Guardian's Union. You're the one who made the offer of this opportunity; nobody's forcing you."

"Fuck you," the EagleCorp double agent snarled.

"Suit yourself," Kevin replied tightly. Turning, he got back to work on his planning for the next day. This was a huge opportunity; their first direct infiltration of EagleCorp headquarters. Not only were they making the capture of the Commissioner responsible for the Denver Metro area in his office on the fourth floor, but they were essentially doing a rehearsal for the operation that would one day capture the owner of EagleCorp in his office on the thirtieth floor of the same building. Perhaps they should have vetted this contact a bit more thoroughly before they agreed to a joint operation at such a valuable site. This fellow was bringing up rather uncomfortable memories of another fairweather ally. Kevin had disliked that contact for reasons he couldn't put his finger on as well, and he'd told himself to let it go in that instance. Suppressing that instinctive animosity had cost him the abduction and abuse of his husband. Aidan had endured days of torture in a Cavanaugh cell because Kevin hadn't vetted a contact with sufficient care, and he hadn't trusted his instincts. If this Peacekeeper turned triple agent, what would it cost him this time? Not too much, if Kevin put the right safeguards in place. He hoped. At least it was only him on the line this time; Aidan was safe at home. That was some comfort.

Kevin was well into a series of coded messages when Teddy gave a long, loud sigh.

"Look...all this is a shitshow. But I was outta line."

"Don't worry about it. It's easy to say something you wish you hadn't," Kevin replied after a moment, controlling his voice with care. "And...well, I've been told I can be a bit of an ass myself." He shot the other man a small smile. Teddy snorted. Kevin felt the tension fractionally decrease in the room, and was glad of it.

"I just want to make sure nobody's gonna get hurt," Teddy explained eventually.

Funny, you didn't seem to be thinking along those lines when you were abusing those who had absolutely no ability to defend themselves, Kevin thought in the silence. He knew it wasn't useful, but the sheer hypocrisy of an EagleCorp bully boy talking about people getting hurt after what Kevin had seen at the courthouse fell on his ears like acid. Then Teddy spoke again, and the words grabbed his heart and twisted. "I wanna look out for the guys, you know? My guys."

Carefully, Kevin raised his eyes and studied his companion. The man's face was a concrete wall, but the eyes…yes, there in the eyes, there was something Kevin recognized. Something he knew.

"Have you been with your unit a long time?" Kevin asked.

"Graduated the Academy at sixteen, joined 'em right outta graduation," Teddy agreed, crossing his arms as he leaned back in his seat. "So yeah. Long time."

And the story behind that brief statement was a tale that Kevin knew well. It was his story too. "Have you served under Commissioner Koonz that long?" he asked politely.

"Huh." Teddy made a face. "He decided he wanted to move his office to our floor five years back. Used to be way up top, almost where Mr. Hamilton has his office in the thirtieth-floor penthouse. Why, he decided he was taking us over? Search me. Been a pain for a while now, but that was nothing special. Not at first, anyway."

"And then it was, I suspect." Kevin suggested.

"What d'you know about it?" Teddy asked coldly, shooting him a glare. Kevin kept his own expression mild as milk. No sense giving this Peacekeeper the fight he was looking for. He wanted a fight because fighting was easy; Kevin knew that personal flaw all too well. A fight simplified things. A fight was nothing to be afraid of. It was baring your soul in words that was terrifying.

"I may have lived a version of that story, in my time." He kept an eye on his lexicon as he spoke; no sense speaking over this man's head and giving him a further reason for alienation. "A team you care about. A new unit leader screwing them up. Putting people you promised to stand up for in difficulties because one man likes his power. When it happens…well, you do what you need to do." He shrugged.

Teddy said nothing. Getting out a cloth, he went to work on his arms. For a long time, the man across from him worked in silence.

"Look…" The man drew a breath. "I know how you people talk about us guys in EagleCorp. And sure, we got our bad apples. But the guys, most of them are good guys. A lot of us—most of us really—we just want to make sure the normal people can go to work, and go home, and have a normal day. But there's assholes around, and bomb throwers, and freaks and bag-snatchers and car-jackers, and if we're not out there, who's gonna be there for the everyday Joes?"

Kevin kept his lips pressed tight. There was entire airport's worth of baggage to unpack in that little speech, but now was not and *could not* be the time. This man was already taking a huge step by reaching out and working with people he'd been taught to consider "freaks and bomb throwers" for the greater good. That was a big enough step, for today. If Kevin called him on his trash now, he risked stunting the man's future growth. And his allyship, for that matter. Not something to do on the night before a dangerous mission.

But Teddy hadn't finished. The silence had simply been a long pause for a man unfamiliar with the art of rhetoric.

"See, that's what we sign up for," he managed eventually. "A good, steady job keeping Mr. and Mrs. Normal and all the little Normals safe. And sometimes that means scaring people back into line, sure. But the other day…"

Another long pause. Kevin waited.

"We been scared shitless, everybody at the flagship office. Feels like the whole world's coming down around our ears," the Peacekeeper explained obliquely.

Your world, perhaps. Kevin thought. *Your stratified, caste-based world of landowners, sheep and sheepdogs. Yes. That is coming down. And good riddance to it.* But he knew better than to say it. He let the man talk.

"We been letting things happen that we never woulda before, because if we tried to take on things like those squatters in the factories around Five Points we'd have to burn the neighborhood down to get at them, and that's no good for anybody. But then Commissioner Koonz calls us up, and says there's a mob forming in the Argus Pavilion, and it's a terrorist rally. And we all think 'shit, this gets out of hand and we'll have nice High Standing ladies getting dicked and ganked by terrorists in the middle of Sixteenth Street. Nope. Not on our turf. We all kinda say, nope, they're not going to start shit downtown, period."

Kevin could feel the muscles in his jaw aching from the effort of keeping his mouth shut. Oh, how he *wished* he could call this small-minded product of corporate doggerel to account. How he *wished* he could call out Teddy's statements and their inherent assumptions. The crimes they were based on. The misery they produced. *Now is not the time,* he told himself firmly. *The man needs to believe he's not the bad guy. He can learn later. He needs to explain himself now. Let him talk. Keep your opinions to yourself. That is an order, officer. Mouth. Shut.*

"So Koonz gives us the kill order and calls the choppers; we're told that we fire at will on terrorists the minute we touch ground." Teddy continued, monotone.

Blood on the stairs. The image flashed behind Kevin's eyes. Blood on white marble. He hadn't realized that Teddy's cleaning cloth made a sound until it stopped moving on his plated arms. In one hand, the Peacekeeper balled the cloth up.

"So yeah. We hit the ground hot, and we've been talking procedure through all day, and we're all running on auto. Take out the threat. Execute terrorists. Only…only we get in there, and it's a bunch of kids and old people. And before we really put the pieces together, we've lined up Grandma and Grandpa Normal and blown them away." The cloth between the big man's fingers twisted until Kevin was sure it'd tear.

"Next couple weeks, a couple of my guys took themselves out. Gave their service piece a blow job, tried on a nylon necktie. Good guys, too. I mean, really *good* guys," Teddy continued hollowly. "The rest of us…Ever since the pavilion, we've been going downhill; some of the guys don't sleep right, they're getting into fights, some of them are just…I dunno, zombies. A lot of the guys're drinking too much, or doing other stuff. Hard stuff." He worked at an imagined spot in the gleaming chrome of his arm. "Some guys talk a big game. They tell each other the story a whole new way, say there were terrorists using the poor grannies as human shields. Say they had to do what they had to do. But I gotta think when I hear them, 'this is so you don't have to look in the mirror and say 'I shot a bunch of grandmas and grandpas because some schmuck in the office gave me an order', and live with that being who you are."

The Peacekeeper closed his eyes. "I done a lot of hard things in my day. But I never roughed up somebody who didn't deserve it before."

"An admirable statement," Kevin stated flatly, biting back a slew of acerbic comments on who, exactly, 'deserved' the abuse that EagleCorp's Peacekeepers doled out so generously.

The moment he'd made the statement, he wished he hadn't. The tone had been wrong: mocking and cool. Damn.

Teddy latched onto the affront like a lifeline. "What, like you never killed anybody?" He ripped out.

"A few times," Kevin acknowledged. "When somebody pointed a gun at my commander's head, I shot him. When someone held a knife to my friend's throat, I cracked his skull. I shot a bounty hunter who tried to take me in; I don't deny it. Sometimes situations move quickly, and it's kill or be killed. Defense of self, defense of the life of a comrade. Protecting others in a case of clear and present danger. Those acts are morally justifiable."

Slowly, Teddy nodded. "Yeah…yeah. Protecting others. That's my job…only…"

This time Kevin did the right thing and kept his trap shut.

"Only, right now, I gotta look in that mirror and say, "I shot a bunch of grannies, because I got given an order, and I was dumb enough to follow it." The man's voice had gravel in it. "And I'm a schmuck. And I'm gonna have to look myself in the mirror and be a schmuck for a long time. But the least I can do is stick it to the guy who knew more than me, who knew the whole picture, and *gave those fucking orders anyway.* Because I don't want to watch more of my guys go out the wrong way. So yeah. I want Koonz to go down for giving those fucking orders. For feeding us bullshit. He lied to us, and we didn't check the orders before we followed them. I didn't check the orders. I didn't check the situation for my guys, and I oughta. I broke the Peacekeeper's Oath and killed people who…we killed good citizens, because Koonz fed us lies and told us they were dangerous. If we have to live with that, and the families of dead citizens have to live with that, then he oughta pay for it."

Teddy swiped the cleaning cloth he'd been excruciating across his face and threw it down, almost resentfully. The microfiber cloth dropped to the floor with a sad, wet flop.

Kevin let the silence be for a moment, letting the man compose himself and regain his dignity.

"I'll make you a promise," he offered eventually. "I've planned this operation to the best of my ability. If it's at all within my power, what we do tomorrow won't harm anyone. Not even Koonz. Death solves nothing. Accountability. That solves things. That makes sure people like Koonz stop getting to do what he did to people like you. And me. And the innocents who died."He drew a breath, let it out. "Tomorrow we make a just and legitimate arrest. It will involve stealth and tranquilizers as a tactic, because this is the way we ensure the least physical harm to the suspect and the population. But he will be read his rights by a United Nations officer when he comes round. He will stand in a fair and impartial trial. And there will be justice."

Head low, Teddy nodded. "Yeah. Yeah." Slowly, he drew a shaky breath. Then his boxy shoulders squared once more. "Okay. Let's go through the plan again."

Kevin had never had an operation run as smoothly as the arrest of the Denver Commissioner of Peacekeepers did. With Teddy's information, he had absolutely no issue slipping inside as a new hire on the maintenance crew and displaying all the right credentials at the right times. He worked his way through several routine issues, slipping into the maintenance cubby in the appropriate wall just in time for the Commissioner's arrival.

Commissioner Koonz was surprisingly average in appearance: a nondescript man somewhere in his sixties. Nothing special. Nothing remarkable. Somehow the human psyche always balked at the banality of evil. It wanted outward signs of infamy to act as an external validation. But that wasn't how evil worked. Especially not the evil of the office and the system, which was so good at cloaking itself in layers of Just Following Orders and This Is The Way Things Are. The floor-cleaning machine ran its innocuous early-morning cycle down the hall. Koonz's hand was on the door. The dart caught him in the back of the neck, right above the collar. He slapped at it…wobbled…and collapsed against the doorframe.

Teddy opened the office door and pulled him inside. The cleaning unit whispered into the office. Kevin worked his way out of the maintenance cubby, and trotted over to assist. Five minutes of silent work later, the job was done.

"Well, that went beautifully," Kevin remarked that night. He flipped a screen up into the air, enlarging it so that he and Teddy didn't have to sit too close together in order to watch as Koonz was read his rights on camera. His tab's fan buzzed as the CPU was taxed with the effort of projecting a screen. Damn. He'd have to talk to Tweak about fixing that when he got home. Whenever that happened to be.

Blank-faced, Teddy nodded. "Okay." After a moment, he flicked a glance at Kevin.

"So…what's the plan from here?"

"For you, the plan is to work on your guys. See how many of them you can talk around to really wanting to protect the people, not the Corporate officers. If they want to become Guardians in the new union that's being formed, they'd be welcome," Kevin offered. "See who's ready to change."

"And the ones that can't?" Teddy asked blankly. Kevin shrugged.

"At some point, there will be large-scale arrests and disarmament of EagleCorp," Kevin explained quietly. "They can't keep doing what they've been doing. Maybe when Hamilton is arrested, more of them will see the writing on the wall. How much of the security for the upper floors can you get us?"

"Just about zilch," Teddy snorted. "Grunt like me's never let above Floor Ten, you think I know about the security at the top?"

"Everything helps," Kevin reassured. "Everything we do helps. Even if it seems small."

"Sounds like inspo-meme bullshit," Teddy scoffed.

Kevin acknowledged the comment with a small nod. "It does, but with intelligence operations, it's cold hard fact."

Teddy ran a hand over his crew-cut head. "All I know is, Mr. Hamilton has his own dedicated guard detail. He's got all the High Commissioner's offices right around him. Basically, you'd have to throw a huge disruption on that floor and put all of those people right off their game for there to be even a chance of an extraction without a fucking huge firefight up there. And that's if you can get in without fighting your way up thirty floors of us guys. If you sit down and talk to us in a room like this, sure, a lot of the guys'll talk about changing things. Some of us, anyway. But if you bust down the door of our office building, we're going to go with training. And training is, open fire on aggressors."

"I take the point," Kevin agreed. For just a split second, he considered the kinds of disruptions he knew his own team was capable of causing at a distance. Tweak's trick of overloading the battery packs in a given area and turning them all into small bombs came to mind. But no, that trick ended in offices that looked like slaughterhouses. That would simply add more bloodshed to a situation already soaked in gore. They didn't need more blood. They needed change.

Maybe some version of the disorientation devices they used for personal protection could be deployed? A floor full of executives vomiting as their inner ear and cornea was assaulted with debilitating combinations of noise and lights would be unpleasant, but it would be harmless long-term. That could work.

He pulled himself out of his plans when Teddy spoke again.

"Look…I never signed up to be this. I just want to do the right thing, go home, eat a good meal, have a beer, go to bed. But right now…right now I don't even know what that is, you get me? The right thing, I mean. Everything's a shitshow and I just…I don't know anymore."

The man who'd spent his life serving something he'd thought of as good shook his head. This veteran Peacekeeper had probably done things that Kevin would see as heinous in the service of EagleCorp. And yet he was simply this: a human being who'd made the choices he could, as and when they were available. This was the wonder and the horror of being human, Kevin reflected: they could learn anything. They could be taught anything was a normal and good way of organizing life and society, if you started on them young enough. And every one of them wanted to belong to something meaningful. Powerful people had used those human traits to twist men like Teddy into their tools since the human species had become bipedal. It took a hell of a lot of work to recognize what they'd done to you and choose to act differently. Kevin knew how hard a road that was; he'd traveled it before. Now this poor benighted soul was taking his second step on a rocky road to being a better person. That first step was the most jarring: the recognition. But the second step was more painful than the first: The disillusionment. The guilt, and the grief that came with the acknowledgment of past wrongs. Not many people talked about the second step. It wasn't as attractive as the first. But if it didn't come after the first, true change could not happen.

What could Kevin offer this man who was taking his second step on a road that must seem like it was made of broken glass? He could tell Teddy to take care of his men. But that would just be a platitude. Stiff upper lip, carry on. No, that wouldn't help. What *could* help? What could he say that would ease this terrible pain? For a moment, he had no idea. And then he did.

"Teddy? Do you pray very much?"

Teddy gave a snort, still staring at his hands. "Not like I ought to."

"What's your faith?"

"Just…normal go to church guy."

"Christian?"

"Yeah. Just normal, like I said."

Another statement with a busload of baggage that wouldn't get unpacked today. Kevin let it pass. *Long road ahead. He's only on the second step. Help him take it.*

"There's a prayer I know. It's right for a night like this. Will you pray with me?"

Teddy blinked, looking up. "Wait…you pray? I thought all you Dusters were…" He tailed off.

"Godless?" Kevin suggested. "Atheist?" He shook his head. "There are a lot more kinds of Dusters than an EagleCorp man might realize. And I suppose there are a lot more kinds of people doing Peacekeeping work than a Duster like me might be expected to assume. Am I right?"

After a moment, Teddy nodded.

"I'm a Jesuit," Kevin explained. "That's a kind of Christian. And I feel like this is a night to say a prayer. So, will you pray with me tonight?"

Teddy held his eyes for a moment, and there was a new spark there.

"Yeah. If you know the prayer…yeah."

From his pocket, Kevin pulled out his rosary and laid it on the coffee table between them. They both bowed their heads.

"O Lord, open my eyes that I may see the needs of others," Kevin began quietly.

"Open my ears that I may hear their cries;

Open my heart so that they need not be without succor;

Let me not be afraid to defend the weak because of the anger of the strong,

Nor afraid to defend the poor because of the anger of the rich.

Show me where love and hope and faith are needed,

And use me to bring them to those places.

And so open my eyes and my ears

That I may this coming day be able to do some work of peace for thee.

Amen."

"Amen," Teddy repeated, and his voice was hushed.

Looking up, the two men shared a smile.

"How's the printing of the placards for the march going?"

On the screen, Mx. Fredrickson of the Fabricator's Union gave Liza a thumbs' up. "We're printing gloss hardback signs as fast as people send us their image files, and stacking them up for the couriers to take out to the secure drops. We'll be ready for the twentieth."

"Is the protective gear printing going alright?" She asked, ticking off the item on her list.

"Mas o menos; I wrote a report, sent it to your tab so you can use it in your meeting today. Oh, your gal left a message before she headed out to Globeville this morning. Janice says quit fucking worrying and get to it."

Liza had to smile. "That's Janice alright. Thanks, Mx. Fredrickson. I've got a debriefing to get to and then a joint action meeting; your printing report will be reviewed as part of our discussion."

"Oh shit, am I going to get a grade?" The union leader asked, grinning. They waved a hand. "I'm just messing with you, but you know…we're on the same side. You Dusters gotta loosen up, yeah?"

Liza tried for a smile. "I'll keep it in mind. Thank you for the report, and all your hard work."

Once the call was over, Liza let her smile fall off. Loosen up. *Civilians.* Oh well. Let it go.

Standing, she headed for Tweak's office.

"How're we doing on our setup for the infiltration and neutralization of EagleCorp?"

"Great," Tweak replied, spinning her chair from side to side to soothe the little girl strapped to her chest as she typed. Glancing up, she gave Liza a grin like the glint on a knife blade, the light of her screens gleaming on her scaled arms. "They n-never found the infiltration c-c-clamps I put in when we took out the Citizen Standing s-s-Scores. I r-retrofitted them to b-bounce signal through the Mesh, so now I can use them l-long distance. I've got an easy in for their s-system from here."

"How long have you had that access?" Liza asked, blinking. Tweak gave one of her little shrugs. "I c-coulda s-s-screwed them any d-day since the m-mesh got going."

"And you held onto it this long?" Liza asked, amazed. Tweak shrugged. "Eh. I p-played with it. B-backed up r-r-random t-toilets. Shut off the hot w-water. Stuff like that. When I got b-b-bored. Shut off their AC after the c-c-Courthouse. But I didn't want to w-waste our in. G-gave the w-w-word to Aidan and the b-brass. They said s-s-save it. For a b-big d-d-day. When we need it. We've been setting up. The same thing. In every one of their s-stations. In the country. Ever s-s-since. Got them all. Now."

Liza nodded, hoping she looked a little less shocked than she was. Was this competent, strategy-minded woman really the feral girl they'd taken in a few years ago?

"So what're you planning to do with that?" Liza asked, taking a seat. Tweak's grin widened into something truly dangerous.

"I g-got full access to all their b-building c-c-climate and infrastructure c-c-controls. We're going after the Sixteenth Street office f-f-first, yeah? I'm g-g-gonna put a c-couple of the b-blockage gates down in the w-water pipes that run through the ceilings of the top six floors and turn the p-pressure sensor off. Pipes get b-backed up, pipes go b-bang, water goes s-splat everywhere! They call in the m-maintenance team, Kevin's on that, and he puts in all the d-d-dis...the things. For screwing Eagle." Tweak swallowed, glancing down at her nursing daughter. "Gonna be good. Nobody'll l-look too close; the civvies're gonna r-run a d-d-decoy thing with our people while it happens. N-not a r-riot like the f-first time we got in there. Gonna be s-spray painting the s-s-side of the buildings, any s-squad cars around, and r-r-running. Chucking b-bottles. That kind of stuff. We're hoping p-p-pissed off Eagles will c-chase them, and so n-nobody'll look r-real close at people fixing some b-broken pipes for a c-couple d-d-days."

"Sounds good," Liza nodded. "Who's going in to help from our team?"

"Omi and b-Bird are gonna r-run the d-d-distract while Topher and Kevin g-go inside," Tweak replied, her voice quieter now. She stroked her daughter's ears. "I'm g-gonna stay on the mic with B-bird, track v-vitals for everyone else on their t-t-tabs."

"Sounds like a plan," Liza agreed, watching the other woman. She knew Tweak was anxious about her partner, and she wished she knew how to actually reassure the girl. But she'd never seemed to be able to do that quite right. "He'll be okay, Tweak," Liza offered finally. It wasn't great, but it was something. Tweak cuddled her baby close for a moment. Then she raised her head, staring at her screen, and nodded.

"Yeah. Everybody w-will. I'll w-watch. Make sure."

Then her unblinking eyes flicked to Liza's face, and she grinned. "I'm g-good, L-liza. You got a m-m-meeting. Today. Yeah? Tell them, we're good to g-go. We're g-g-gonna fry these b-birds like KFC."

Liza grinned. "I'll pass it along."

Back in her office, she laid out the chairs and the holographic projectors, and settled herself for the meeting.

At fourteen-hundred on the dot, the projectors flicked to life.

"Good afternoon, everyone," Liza began. "We have UN people here, we have Unions, we have civilian action groups. And we have our final slate of protective measures to go over. So let's stay on topic." She brought up her windows. "The plan is for a nation-wide nine-evening marching period that has been dubbed the March of Memory, beginning June twenty-fifth. Given the heat, it's safer to march by night. Each evening, participants will gather and march down the planned routes carrying pictures of the missing and the dead. They'll be informed of the routes two days prior, via the Common Ground app. In each area, our people on the ground will maximize visibility and disruption while minimizing threat to the civilians participating via the blocking of Go vehicles, route planning, and use of local conditions. The Unions will be focused on maintaining group cohesion, leading collective action, and handing out protective gear and supplies to their people. The UN will be tasked with documentation, medical care as needed and oversight. The Democratic State Force will be acting as the buffer between Corporate forces and our allies. We intend to set up a number of measures to prevent another death."

She flicked up her screens, still amazed at the way people listened these days. Nobody interrupted her. Nobody called bull. Nobody said she was out of line. She could get used to this.

"Given that EagleCorp's executive office is situated on the lower portion of a main artery in downtown Denver, the main focus of units in our sector will be rendering the head office of EagleCorp ineffective. Best case scenario, we take and defuse the building as part of this push. Worst case scenario, we maintain civilian protection and keep EagleCorp and their contractors too distracted to do anything."

"I read up on your plans," one of the UN people, a Finn if Liza remembered right, asked. "Aren't you depending slightly too much on the reactivity of EagleCorp? You're expecting them to come out and chase your decoy teams because they start spray painting the EagleCorp office and levering up the statue at the front door. Couldn't they simply shoot their tormentors?"

"They could," Liza agreed, "but we've planned to prep and protect our teams with that in mind, and we're well versed in EagleCorp psychology. Even if they're ordered to stay inside, a fairly large number of Eagles will come out to confront people they see as insults to their authority. They enjoy giving a good beating, so they'll chase in hopes of doing that. And the decoy teams are only one layer of our solution to the problem. An infiltration team is carrying out an operation to implant disorientation devices on the top floors of the building. Those will effectively incapacitate the leadership without causing physical harm. With most of the senior leadership out of order and the lower ranks chasing our decoy teams, the military branch of our operation should be able to take the building without too much trouble. We currently have full access to their building's system AI and its maintenance programming, so we intend to add in a layer of confusion beyond our implanted supersonic emitters and light diodes by flickering the lights, overflowing the toilets, turning on the fire alarms and the sprinklers on every floor. A full plan is attached to the briefing packet. While Eagle is watching their nest come down around their ears, we'll be making sure our civilians march and get home safely every night. Everyone in the Denver Metro has been supplied with heat protection, food access and water production tools at this point, so they'll be alright whatever sanctions the Corporations attempt to impose.

"We've set a general schedule of three weeks for local planning. On the twenty-fifth of June, we stage the March of Memory across the nation. So, what details do we need to go over?"

"Let's talk more about the layered security we're going to use nationally," one of the union leader piped up. "I want to hear details about what me and the media folks will be handling."

"Communication mostly," one of the UN folks explained, grabbing a diagram. "We've got EagleCorp's channels, but we need you guys on the propaganda-refutation side of the work. We've worked up some possible approaches that get to the underlying psychological appeal we need; we can list off facts to people who aren't involved all day, but if they don't *feel* like the information is true, they'll keep buying what your corporations are selling. Tell us about how you're subverting the communication channels."

The meeting went like that the whole time, their little group hashing out details that each one would take back and spread to their part of the movement. A few disagreements came up on tactics and approach, but overall Liza was pretty satisfied by the time she turned the projectors off and stored them back on their chargers.

Meetings completed, she began her base duties for the day. Checking her tab, she nodded to herself; no disciplinary writeups today. Good. She did a tour of socialization and work areas, keeping an eye out for issues before they rose to the level of reports. There were the usual small interpersonal things that came up in any communal living situation, but Four Aces Farm was turning out to be the kind of community that settled their problems with very little fuss. Liza found herself becoming more of a resource officer than anything lately. In the tour of the base, she directed a man whose battery pack for his prosthetic leg was giving trouble to the technical hub Tweak had set up, got a lady who needed toothbrushes set up with Billie's base service team, and sent someone asking if he could help outside to Milo's team. A ferrety little man slipped past her as she opened the new med-bay's door, shooting her a sidelong look. Liza suppressed the knee-jerk urge to turn around and watch him. It was going to take a long time to get her used to all these strangers around the base.

Farm, she reminded herself. *It's a farm now.*

"Who was that?" she asked as she came level with Alice. "I thought I'd met everyone on the latest intake."

"He's Marshall," Alice offered with a smile and a shrug. "Just got his intake checkup. How're things?"

"Good," Liza replied with a quick smile. "I wanted to drop by and check on the behavioral cases you're working with. See if anybody needs community support."

Alice nodded thoughtfully. "Well, Cameron's in again; he's gotten into a habit of hitting himself when Jenny cries for a while, and he's started hitting the floor and hurting the bones in his hands. Damian's with him in cubicle three."

"He's not hitting his kid, is he? Or his wife?" Liza asked carefully.

"Oh, no, no, it's not like that," Alice reassured, giving a quick wave of both hands. "He doesn't have an abusive bone in his body; the self-harm is a maladaptive stress reaction, that's all. If you can help us keep an eye on his stress levels, it'd be good."

"Noted," Liza agreed. "Who else?"

"We need to do some work with Dolores, she's having panic attacks when she tries to help out in the finance department. And Matt's still on our high-needs list."

"Any more violence?" Liza asked, flashing back to the young man who'd been so knife-happy on arrival.

"Nope, but he's…" Alice trailed off. Then she shrugged. "He's a little like Tweak used to be. Take it easy on him, okay?"

Liza gave her a smile. "I'll put him on our extra support list. I got him a room, didn't I? He's not still bedding down in here?"

"Sometimes he comes in here to sleep with other people around, when he's had a rough night." Alice replied. "He's in right now, actually. Down in cubicle fourteen. We just got him set up with a therapy app, and he's learning to use it here before he goes back out."

"Think it'll be alright if I check on him?"

Alice eyed her for a moment. Then she nodded. "See how he does. Back off if he gets intimidated, alright?" Liza nodded. "Roger that."

Stepping down the med bay, she moved the curtain of the cubicle to one side. "Matt?"

The boy looked up, and so did the man sitting beside him. Kevin gave her a smile. "Well hello." Standing, he shook Matt's hand. "Thanks for the idea. We'll talk later, alright?"

"Yeah," the boy on the bed agreed. It was amazing how different his face looked when he wasn't wearing a terrified scowl.

Closing the curtain behind him, Kevin gave Liza's shoulder a quick squeeze, a finger pressed over his lips. They stepped quietly away.

"Anything in my department?" Liza asked when they'd reached the privacy of Damian's office. Kevin gave her one of his softer smiles. "Oh, I think he'll be alright. You shouldn't see a recurrence of aichmophilia from him."

Liza gave him a cockeyed look. "I'm going to assume that means he's okay."

Kevin chuckled, giving her a quick sideway hug. "Very much so, dear girl. Now, what about…" He glanced up at a giggle, and blinked as Damian stepped into the office behind Alice, bent his head and gave her a quick kiss. The door gently clicked shut. Kevin cleared his throat. "Erm…Damian? Alice?"

Damian's head snapped up. Liza got the impression that, if he could have blinked, he would have.

"There is no privacy in this unit," the doctor stated flatly.

"Afraid not," Kevin agreed ruefully. "But at least you won't suffer a Touchdown Party. Anyway, we've overstayed our welcome."

"That's putting it mildly," Damian stated in measured tones. "Out, people. I want my office."

"Many apologies, we were just leaving," Kevin agreed, almost skittering for the door. Liza followed him out. Once the door closed, Kevin caught her eye, grinned, and snapped his fingers. "Damn, now I owe the betting pool five dollars."

Liza sighed. "I can't believe you guys still run a betting pool on who's dating who. When did you get in?" "About an hour ago. I'm home to help organize our handling of the EagleCorp headquarters. Got time to fill me in?" He pulled the bag from his shoulder. "I've got a bottle with our names on it in here."

Liza raised a brow. "We're on duty."

"*You're* on duty," Kevin agreed with a wink. "*I* just finished quite a long run and have a day's leave. So one of us can and definitely will have a drink. Come along."

Liza couldn't help but smile behind his back as he led the way.

Kevin lounged into his office chair. "So, when do we infiltrate Sixteenth Street?"

"Tweak's got everything set up for the fifteenth, well ahead of the public action," Liza explained. "You and Topher will be inside team, Naomi and Inyoni on the outside team doing distracts. I've touched base with the other units helping out on this; everyone's ready."

"Please tell me Tweak's not using overflowing the toilets as our way in?" Kevin asked, sounding like he expected it was. Liza flashed him a smile. "Burst overhead pipes in the executive offices."

"Thank you God and all His hosts," Kevin exclaimed, laying a hand over his heart. "What a relief! I was dreading a few days knee deep in sewage."

Liza chuckled. "Tweak's not *that* bad anymore. So will you stick around for the March of Memory?"

"Mm, still deciding," Kevin explained as he popped the top in the whiskey bottle and pulled a glass from his desk drawer. "It depends on where my targets situate themselves at any given time."

"How many more do you have still?" Liza asked, watching him pour. His hands were steady, and his eyes were normal. Good. He'd been really good about leaving the stimulants alone in the last few years, but Liza always checked when he got stressed. Just in case.

"I've nearly finished," Kevin replied quietly. "I've got two more targets in Cascadia. Didn't make it to Tidewater quite in the nick of time, so the Tidewater missions have been scrapped. There's three targets in New Netherlands to take care of, and one in the Midlands. And Harrington, of course. I'll finish my work with him."

Liza didn't like the way his face changed when he said that. She didn't like the way his body language shifted.

"And you'll bring him in alive." She hadn't meant to give an order, but that was the way the words came out. "We need human rights criminals alive to stand trial."

Kevin raised his eyes to hers as he drank.

"There will be justice, Liza. My word on that."

"But not vigilante justice, Kevin," she retorted. "Swear to me that you're not planning to kill him."

"You know, I don't remember you having a heart to heart on vigilante justice with Naomi," he observed casually, studying his glass. "And I know for a fact that she's shot people in the line of duty. You never sat down and tried to extract a promise of nonviolence from Lazarus either, by the way."

"Low blow, Kevin," Liza stated flatly, controlling the surge of hurt at the way he'd tried to get around her using their buddy's name.

The man across from her cocked a brow. "And also accurate. Feel free to elaborate."

"Naomi can pull a trigger without wrapping her heart and soul up in doing it," Liza explained with exaggerated patience to match Kevin's. "She does it because it's the next thing to do. And Lazarus used guns like a marksman. He was nuts most of the time, true, but when he was handling munitions he aimed at targets, not people. You're not thinking about taking out a target in the line of duty, Kevin. I'm going to just say it, because somebody on this base needs to call you out; you're thinking about committing a revenge murder. I know what it'd do to you to kill someone because you hate them. So do you."

For a beat, it seemed like the air had left the room. Kevin held Liza's eyes, swirling the amber of his drink so that it flickered around his glass like light in a forest.

"My infiltration and arrest plan is filed with Command. Death of the target isn't the objective I wrote down."

Liza shook her head. "Not good enough, Kevin. Give me *your word*."

Kevin's eyes were blank silver coins behind his glasses. When he spoke, his voice was toneless. "I've given my word already, Liza. I won't do anything that isn't just. I made that promise. I'll keep it."

Liza didn't love that. But she wasn't going to get anything better out of Kevin right now. She let out a long breath. "Alright. Then let's get some work done, I guess."

Event File 19
File Tag: Constructive Placement
Timestamp: 06-13-2162

"Okay. Bird. Ears. Up."

Inyoni raised his ears as Tweak ran the wand over the sides of his head. Tweak nodded. "Kay. Ears. Down. Arms. Out." She added, running the wand further down him. It never actually touched, but Inyoni kept getting the feeling that he could sense a prickle on his skin when the wand passed over it. The light out of it made his tattoos flare extra bright.

"Turn. Round." His woman instructed.

He was really, really glad they could do this in their room, because standing naked like some weird doll while Tweak ran a wand all over him was one of the freakiest, most weirding things he'd ever done. Yeah, okay, he'd gotten strip-searched before. But the thing was, when you didn't like the guy patting you down, you could kind of protect part of yourself by calling him an asshole. When it was your lady going all over you, it wasn't the same. When you really cared about the call the person with the magnifying glass made, it kind of hit different.

Lucky for him, Tweak wasn't judgy about looks. She did look down and grin once, because he'd gotten a kind of half stiffy when she'd been down there and her breath had done stuff. He grinned back at her, feeling like a dumbass. "Sorry."

"Jackass," she teased, stepping in and standing on his feet so she was tall enough to kiss him. "We do that. L-later. Get d-dressed, we g-go over these r-readouts. My office. B-better s-s-screens."

"Sure. Wanna grab Bao Li from the crib while we're at it?"

"Sure."

The unit had gotten in the habit of calling it the crib, but it was really a block of rooms where all the farm's kids got looked after before they were old enough for education programs and mentoring. There were about a dozen toddlers and young kids running all over the place, and Billie checking on her childcare helpers in the middle of it.

"Hey guys," she waved, smiling. "You in for Bunny?"

"Yeah," Inyoni agreed, trying to smile for his woman's bestie. He still kind of hated it when people called his little girl Bunny; it was too much like the times they called him Donkey or Jackass and they didn't mean it nice. But he worked on rolling with it; everybody around here had nicknames. Didn't mean anything.

Billie smiled up at him. "She's next door. C'mon, I'll show you." The surfaces had been softened up with all kinds of cushions and stuff in the next room, and that's where the babies were. Bao Li was over in a bed of pillows, propped up and chewing on a soft rabbit. It made her look like a little cannibal, because her ears were about the same size as the toy's. She looked up and smiled as Tweak knelt beside her. Then she spotted Inyoni, and started giggling and making grabby motions with her ears straight up in the air. Tweak looked up at him, grinning. "She wants to g-grab your ears again."

"Yeah, I know." Inyoni sighed, smiling. "We gotta get her to stop doing that." For now, he pulled off one of the bracelets that helped him know if he was bleeding or not, and held it out. It was too big to fit in Bao Li's mouth, but she grabbed on and started chewing on the side.

"Eh. Baby. They grab." Tweak replied as Inyoni knelt and picked his kid up. She could already hold her head up by herself now. Tweak squeezed his arm. "C-c'mon. R-r-readouts."

Settling into their chairs in Tweak's office, Inyoni snuggled Bao Li as Tweak got her rig running. She was right; it was easier to look at complicated things in her setup.

"Okay, see?" Tweak pointed at the schematic of Inyoni's body. "Here's your d-density m-m-map. There's your sex-health implant, your holo, all your b-bones. N-nothing weird."

The next image showed his body picked out like a city at night.

"Electrical m-map," Tweak continued. "Lemme look…okay. Here's the b-brain, heart, n-nerves, all good. No r-random c-c-clusters of EM action. That means, no n-n-nanoid implants."

"What's that really bright mark around my neck?" Inyoni asked. "Looks like a collar."

"That's the energy r-running your holo," Tweak explained. "Skin's thin around your n-n-neck. Conducts the p-power until it thickens up."

"So…I'm good?" Inyoni asked. Tweak nodded. "Only thing I can see with p-p-power is your holo. And I saw inside that. And it's good. So yeah. You're good."

It was hard to explain just how much he'd been freaking out on the down low about the idea that all the people who'd bit it were because of him. Chilling out felt like every muscle in his body loosened up at once.

"Thanks Dragon," he murmured, putting an arm around her. She leaned against him. "It's cool. We're c-cool."

"Yeah. We're cool," Inyoni agreed, leaning in for a kiss. In his arms, his daughter gave an adorable little yawn. It was hard to believe things could get this good.

Too good. The fear socked him in the chest, the way it always did around now. This was all too good. It was too perfect. Good things didn't last; they got taken away.

"When're you going in?" Tweak asked against his ear.

"Goin' in on the fifteenth," Inyoni murmured. "Be home by the twentieth. Going back out on the twenty-fourth. March starts on June twenty-five."

Tweak nodded. "You're g-gonna wear the m-molar mic I f-f-fitted for you. This time. Y-yeah?"

"Still feels weird, having something stuck inside my back teeth," Inyoni sighed. "I keep worrying it'll come loose and I'll swallow the thing."

"Safer," Tweak replied. Her scales glinted gold as she shifted to snuggle in close. "They d-don't look for b-bone conduction m-m-mics so often. And it's easier on your ears."

"You're not wrong," Inyoni agreed, laying his head back against his chair. There was a pressure, and a sideways tug, and he opened an eye. Bao Li had dropped his bracelet and gotten ahold of his ear again.

Tweak chuckled against his shoulder, and reached over to detach Bao Li's little hand. The baby grabbed her finger instead, and so they sat like that for a while: Tweak with Bao Li's fingers around one of hers, both of them snuggled up to him.

So good.

Too good.

"Ready to go?" Kevin asked a few days later as they suited up in the garage.

"We're good," Topher agreed, pulling on his riding gloves and snagging his helmet. Inyoni stopped running his tongue back and forth over the mic tucked up behind his back top teeth. Man these bone-resonance things felt weird.

"Inyoni?"

He blinked. "Wha? Oh. Yeah."

"Getting used to the molar mic?" Kevin asked with a quick smile. Inyoni blinked. "How'd you know?"

"Sarah looks the same way you do when she has to wear them. Like a dog chewing a caramel," Kevin replied with a pat for his shoulder. "You get used to them, don't worry." He shot Inyoni a grin as he took his fixed-up riding helmet off the hook in the garage and passed it over.

"How about a reason to enjoy the mics?" Kevin suggested.

"Yeah?" Naomi asked.

Kevin pulled out his tab and brought up something on the physical screen.

All the sudden, a guy was singing loud and happy in what felt like Inyoni's ears.

Beside Inyoni, Naomi snorted, rolling her eyes as she pulled her helmet on. "I should know better by now," her voice grumbled in his ear.

"Oh for f-fuck's sake," Tweak's voice cut across the music. "Old shit? S-seriously, k-k-Kevin?"

"Bon Jovi can raise anyone's spirits!" Kevin sounded all defensive in the mic, but he was almost laughing too; Inyoni could hear it. He heard it when Tweak kind of laugh-sighed, even over the sound of the music. "Yeah. Yeah," Tweak came back through the mic. "Bird. Double check. Sound quality. Okay?"

"Sounds great," Inyoni agreed. "And it'll stay in touch all over?"

"Supposed to, y-yeah," Tweak's voice agreed. "k-Kevin and Topher got them in too, so we're all s-staying in touch. N-not having the c-c-courthouse happen again."

"Inshallah," Topher agreed quietly.

"Heaven forefend," Kevin muttered, doing that crisscross thing with his hand across his chest that he did sometimes.

"Kay, you're good," Tweak's voice added in his ears. "Go 'head. I'll check in. Sometimes."

"You got it, Dragon," Inyoni agreed.

"And. All of you. Come. Home. Soon," Tweak added tightly.

"As Her Majesty requires," Kevin said as the garage door rumbled up.

Tweak's voice sounded the way it did when she was working not to laugh.

"Can it, CES. Go k-k-kick ass."

Kevin laughed as he kicked his bike into life. "Roger that. Inyoni, Topher, in line with me. Let's go."

It was getting easier to be on-grid these days; between the helmet's hearing protection and the tricks everyone had taught him, Inyoni could keep the noise out of his head for the most part. Today was supposed to be easy, too. At least, that was the plan.

They all split up at the train station to head for their safe houses; they'd do the thing tomorrow around sunset. Today, they'd fly under the radar by staying with some civvies.

He passed an ad for some lady playing a cello in a big show in Seattle and the newest chill vests, winced at a sudden blat of promotional music and pushed his way through a hiring ad to get a look at the street. Outside the protection of the station's climate-control windows, the air sizzled on the Denver pavement. Good thing they were doing all the active stuff at night. Way too fricking hot out there for running.

"Hey Tweak," he murmured without moving his lips, the way they'd shown him. "You there?"

"Here," Tweak's voice agreed in his ear. "You good?"

"Long as you got my back, yeah," Inyoni agreed. "You know these people I'm staying with?"

"S-sorta. People. In the m-movement. Civvies. S-scared. But nice. Checked their b-building. C-c-cleared out the s-s-surveillance. It's cool." "Thanks."

"Course," Tweak agreed, voice calm and soft. "I got work. I'm g-gonna stop t-t-talking. But if you n-need me, I'm listening. Kay?"

"Kay," Inyoni agreed.

He made it to the little CAS apartment in the ZonCom neighborhood. Pulling up the contact he'd been given, he wrote "here".

The door cracked open a second later, and he slipped inside.

"Hey."

"Hey," the person with hair dyed yellow, green and blue smiled at him, waving him inside. ""C'mon, Sherry's got dinner ready."

Inside, a lady who looked like she might be from the same part of the world as Topher turned, crinkly black hair bobbing. "Hungry?" She asked, holding up a plate with a little smile. "Amp said you've come a long way."

"Kinda," Inyoni agreed. "Call me Bird."

"Sherry," the lady replied as she set his plate on their little table. These two had grabbed what looked like an office chair for him to sit on; their table only had two chairs that matched it. "And the rainbow child here is Amp."

"Thanks for letting me crash," Inyoni offered. "Dragon checked in, let you know she cleared all the bugs out for you folks?"

For the first time, Sherry grinned, and it really made her pretty. "Yeah, she did it for us two months ago. Pulled all the surveillance out of our buildings, our personal devices, everything. And she taught Amp's affinity group how to do it for themselves. You can't believe how nice it is to just *talk*."

"Yeah I can," Inyoni replied with a grin. "Pretty new Duster, me. Still getting used to how cool it is to say whatever."

"We're going to see a lot more of that coming up," Amp added with a smile for Sherry. "People are saying the Corps will come down by the end of the year."

For a second, Inyoni saw fear in the woman's eyes. Then she swallowed, straightened up in her seat and took a bite of her dinner. "And we've already got food and water set up through non-corporate sources. And the plans are already in place for a government and a way to run the city after."

"Yep, the plans and the infrastructure are all there. There's going to be enough food and water and stuff for everybody," Amp agreed. Inyoni could hear one of those conversations that go back and forth between a couple; he couldn't tell how, exactly, but it was something in the way they talked and the way they looked. Old running conversation between these two. Definitely.

He ate a bit of the ravioli he'd been served. "So, yeah, my officer said you were running the civvie part of the distraction? Me'n my teammate are gonna be your liaison, call any problems into the Dusters or take care of them on the fly for you."

"Cool," Amp agreed. "I've got a team ready; tomorrow night we'll sneak up to EagleCorp's perimeter. When the verbal warning stops working, that's our cue to go ahead." They nodded at the bag by the door. "Got all the paint we need in there."

"I'll serve everyone a meal when you get done and come back," Sherry tacked on.

"Really appreciate it," Inyoni agreed between bites. Glancing between them, he saw how freaked they still were. How vulnerable they looked. Maybe he could help, if he didn't leave them feeling all alone in that.

"Hey uh, I want to save some power on this," he lied, tapping his holo. "I got some gamma stuff going on under this holo; you guys cool?"

Amp smiled. Flexing their arm, they showed off the scaly brown patches where their skin was more lizard than human. Not as impressive as Tweak's look, but definitely gamma.

"We're cool. Let it all hang out," they encouraged.

Inyoni laughed, and tapped his holo off.

They watched a couple movies to kill time that night, nothing heavy. In the background, the couple's water condenser bubbled.

Around eleven, Sherry yawned. "I'm going to call it."

"Good plan," Amp agreed. "Bird? We put a mattress and stuff down for you in Sherry's office. Down here."

Leading Inyoni down the little hall, Amp pointed into a cute little room where a roll-away mattress had been laid out on the floor. Inyoni walked in and started to mess with the bedding, and something smacked his head. He felt the pressure, but he didn't get knocked over or feel dizzy, so it was probably something light.

"Crap, let me fix that." Amp stepped in, grabbing the board that had been leaned against the wall. For a moment they held it awkwardly, looking around the room. "I guess we'll stick this in the bedroom till the march. Not really a lot of room in here." Inyoni tipped his head, getting a good look at the placard that'd smacked him. Amp followed where he was looking, and gave a funny little smile. "This is my picture for the March of Memory." They held it up. "My affinity group and me, with our cooling shelter. We're part of the Caretakers' and Resource Distribution Workers' Union. We built this shelter for our neighborhood, with folks from the Builders' Union." They kept their eyes on the picture as they spoke. "The Corps took it apart. A bunch of people in my group got arrested when it happened; we haven't seen them since." They underlined the words 'gone but not forgotten' with a finger.

Inyoni looked up. "Man. That sucks. I delivered the stuff to build that cooling shelter. Saw it go down in the news."

"Yeah," Amp agreed, "it was bad." They shrugged. "But it's gonna change, right? And if we're going to help it change, we need some sleep." They held out their hand. "I'll wake you at sunset; sound good?"

"Sounds good," Inyoni agreed, shaking hands with a smile.

The sun was down a long time when they all gathered in the Wynkoop alley that gave them a clear view of EagleCorp.

"Okay, here's the plan," Amp whispered. "Carly, Earl, you're dressed pretty regular; walk by and see if the perimeter warning barks at you."

"Right," the whisper replied in the dark. Someone slipped back up the alley. A few minutes later, the guy called Earl walked by like anybody on his way to a job. He crossed the gold line around the EagleCorp building like probably a million people did a day; casually, without paying attention.

"Citizen, please help us maintain this building by leaving the area around it clear," a neutral voice blatted out of the imbedded speakers.

With the usual surprise-and-irritation expression of somebody pissed off by the pointless security warning, Earl hurried off. He was back with them a few minutes later.

"We wait half an hour," Naomi whispered. "Then we try again."

"Got it," Amp agreed. "Next time, Carly, you're up."

When Carly's turn came, she took the clueless teen approach, bopping along to her headphones with her eyes half open. She stepped on the gold line in the cobblestones.

"Citizen, please…." the recording began, and then it died away as if the program was drifting off to sleep.

"You're clear!" Tweak's voice said in Inyoni's ear, making him jump. "Tweak?"

"Y-yeah. K-k-Kevin and Topher are inside. You're clear; perimeter's safe. Go for it."

He grinned.

"Dragon says we're good to go!" He whispered loud enough for everyone around him to hear, pulling the mask he'd brought up around his nose and mouth. Everybody had put camera-block on already; with the masks and the reflective cream on their skin, they were set. They streamed across the space between the statue of a foot crushing a demon and the building, crossing the golden line. There wasn't a peep out of the perimeter warning.

Grabbing his bag, Inyoni flicked his holo off, pulled a can out and started to spray.

YOU ARE MURDERERS, he started. Then he wrote names. He knew them all; all seventy five people shot at the courthouse. Sixty three adults. Twelve kids. It took a while, but he had time tonight.

Around him, other people wrote other things.

"Capitalism is organized crime and we are all the victims", one guy was writing. Amp was going with the simple, "FUCK THIS NOISE!"

Inyoni grinned as he sprayed. Man, did it feel *good* to lay it all out here, all public like this. He wrote and wrote, getting out everything he was feeling. The names of the dead. A stick figure of a Peacekeeper beating the shit out of somebody on the ground with a big red circle and line through it. Huge letters that read WE'LL STOP RESISTING WHEN YOU STOP ATTACKING!

"Hey!"

"Time to go!" Naomi hissed, eyes bright. All of them took off together, high as a kite with Peacekeepers who'd never catch up behind them.

"Oh baby, you look so good!"

Yvonne went up on her tiptoes and twirled, her long blue dress flowing out around her.

"And I'm not the only one!" She laughed, looking at her perfect wife in that green off-the-shoulder sheath that made her look like some kind of fantasy. "We should take pics, we'll never look this good again!"

"You bet we won't, because I'll never put up with another hair and nails and makeup session like that again," Sarah agreed with one hell of an eye roll. "I'm scared to touch my own hair right now, not to mention yours. And with how good you look, that totally sucks."

"After the show, sweet girl," Yvonne reassured, kissing the tip of Sarah's nose. Pulling her tab out of her evening purse, she checked it. "We've got forty-five minutes, one car trip and one ferry ride to get there. Let's go."

Benaroya Hall was on its own island in Seattle's Union Bay, with the island holding the Space Needle visible in the near distance. The cute little retrofitted houseboat that gave them a lift via a rideshare forum that had been set up on the Common Ground app wobbled as it stopped at a dock, paid the fee and docked in.

"Thanks!" Sarah called down to the guy who'd given them a ride. He waved back.

"Careful," Yvonne murmured as they walked up the dock. "High Standing types don't talk to the help."

Sarah rolled her eyes. "Okay, gross. But it's a point. I'll be careful."

"Won't be for long," Yvonne whispered, giving her hand a quick squeeze. Coded into the system as Excellent Standing high-ups, they got their seats in record time. Being inside Benaroya Hall was like being inside a really expensive red pillow. The walls were all red, the fittings were cream, and the accents were brass and real, actual wood. Yvonne reminded herself that her persona would see stuff like this every day. She couldn't make a fuss. She couldn't look around.

Up on the stage, Nicole Ma and the rest of the orchestra were already getting warmed up. People worked their way along and into their seats. Glancing up and to her left, Yvonne spotted Marcus Z and his girlfriend of the week taking seats in their private box. In the contacts she was wearing, he was outlined in yellow, along with every one of their targets. The security details with them were outlined in white for easier pinpoint. She shifted, feeling her dart gun against her thigh. The guests in the hall were screened for weapons, of course, but the UN had done all the negotiating to make the arrest with the venue; luckily the staff had joined a union already, and they were totally onboard for this. They'd still appeared to get screened, but their weapons had been marked as permitted.

With the grace of a swan, Nicole Ma swept to the front of the stage.

"Good evening, honored guests. It's been almost a century since a member of my family has visited this country, and I'm honored to be here at this time and in this place."

She lifted what looked like the gigantic bow in her hand. "In recognition of this history and our hopes for the future, my first piece will be a multinational arrangement of Concertino No. 3 in A Major, by Jean-Baptiste Breval."

A wave of appreciative clapping rippled through the room. Yvonne looked at Sarah, who gave her a subtle shrug. It definitely meant something, though, if everyone was clapping. So they clapped too.

Nicole Ma grinned up on the stage. "With the performance of the first piece my great-grandfather played when he performed before John F. Kennedy as an immigrant child, I hope to usher in shining days of opportunity, artistry and excellence for America in the years to come."

Amid the applause of the crowd, the performer turned, took her seat, and began to play.

At first, the piece was…Yvonne was no expert, but it was pretty. It was like sitting by one of the ornamental fountain-and-stream setups in a park on a day when Peacekeepers didn't move you along, just listening to the nice, orderly, reliable melody.

But then somebody started on a snaky violin, and the music started to change. Now there were layers and levels. Now it was alive, with a wood flute somewhere in there, and drums, and now the cello was all snaky and alive too. Now this was the good stuff.

Yvonne flicked a glance up at Z's box; the contacts automatically zoomed in. Good, he was focused and into it. Okay. She flicked an eye around the room. Their own people, tagged in blue through the contacts, moved and changed seats as if they were dancers moving to the beat.

In her ear, she heard the coded command.

"Brahms Lullaby."

Yvonne grinned. All around her, Corporate bodyguards were getting a dose of tranquilizer. It wouldn't feel like anything when the painless darts sank tiny needles in, but it'd do the trick. They'd feel like they were just gently…nodding…off…to the music. The only ones who'd get fast-acting darts would be Z's direct guard detail; those goons would get tranqued backstage as they waited for their boss.

On stage, Nicole Ma leaned into her cello as if it was saying something she wanted to hear, her hands dancing across the strings and bow. The song eddied around them all, filling up the world.

When the music ended, the applause was a waterfall of sound.

"And speaking of a hopeful future for America, we'd like to do something special tonight." Nicole Ma said, smiling at the crowd. "Mr. Zuckerberg, would you join us on the stage?"

Around Yvonne, there was a rippling little "ooh" of excitement.

In his box, Marcus Z stood and waved. His box was an elevator, and it lowered him right to the back-stage area. He came out from behind the curtain with a smile on his weird, smoothed-out face.

Nicole Ma put out her hand to shake his. He took it. And she snapped a handcuff around his wrist.

"Marcus Zuckerberg the Fifth, you are under arrest," a UN operative stated, coming out of the wings and cuffing his other wrist. He was at least twice the corporate head's size, and the guy who came up on his other side matched him.

"By the power invested in me by the International Criminal Court, I arrest you and your subordinates for the crimes of acting as a willful accomplice in genocide, profiteering from acts of human degradation and criminal obstruction with the aim of concealing numerous ongoing acts of human rights abuse," the UN guy on the right stated calmly. "You are further charged with one-hundred and sixty three counts of environmental degradation and willful neglect of emissions control."

On the stage, the orchestra set down their instruments and began to clap. In the crowd, little yelps and spurts of cussing went up as corporate officers and tranqued bodyguards got cuffed. Yvonne caught Sarah's eyes, and they grinned at each other. Standing, they both began to applaud.

People looked up at them, wide eyed. But someone started clapping, and then someone else. And then the hall was ringing with applause as the CEO whose family had run the shipping and consumer goods sectors of the country's economy as their private money farm for generations was taken away in handcuffs.

"Oh my god! Oh my god, we just did that!" They tumbled through the door of their room in a fluff of expensive dresses, hugging and jumping around.

"We just did that! Oh my god! Oh my god!"

Sarah laughed, tipping her head up to kiss Yvonne. "You bet your ass we did! Holy shit, the way it went down!"

"The way everybody clapped!"

"The way they started cheering!"

"Let's turn on the news. Where's the channel the Media Union took over?"

"Channel sixty-four."

They flipped the screen up into the air over their heads, flopping onto the bed. The elderly person on the screen waved.

"Hello everyone! I know we had a food-crop cultivation show scheduled for right now, but National Public Reporting has just gotten something that you're going to want to hear. Everyone, it's official: Marcus Zuckerberg the Fifth has been taken into custody by a joint team of the United Nations and the Democratic State Force. The ZonCom executive, guilty of policies that have caused massive mental and physical health damage to our people as well as supporting ecologically harmful shipping and manufacturing practices, is the third of seven corporate heads to be removed from their positions and arrested. Only Bob Walton of ArgusCorp and Jack Hamilton of EagleCorp remain in their positions. We reported last week on the death of Steven Evers, who was found dead in his bunker in North Carolina with about sixty members of his inner circle in an apparent mass suicide. Currently, we don't know where Theodore Harrington, owner of Cavanaugh Corporation, has gone to ground. The UN and the Democratic State Force are actively searching for him." A picture of the owner of Cavanaugh flashed on the screen, and then the presenter was back with a smile. "I imagine everyone hearing this is as excited as we are here at the National Public, but let's remember that we've all got responsibilities as part of these changes. If you haven't voted in your local administrative representative's sortition pool, do that now on the Common Ground. The Regional, Quadrant and National votes will show up on your apps later this month. If you know anyone whose shipments of food or household supplies have gotten lost in the chaos as ZonCom's leader is taken to stand trial, get them in touch with the organizers at your nearest Equal Standing Space or unionized ZonCom warehouse. If you're in a rural area and your shipments have been disrupted, write the handle at the bottom of the screen that corresponds to your Quadrant, and you'll get help. Let's keep taking care of each other as we go through these changes; together, we can do this! And now, here's some footage of what happened in Seattle today."

Yvonne flicked the screen off and rolled over next to her wife, grinning. "We can skip that, we saw it first hand." Snuggling up to Sarah, she kissed her.

"We're really doing it."

"We really are," Sarah agreed, stroking her hair.

"We really got a Corporate owner arrested," Yvonne breathed.

"We really did," Sarah replied, kissing her softly. Her skin was starting to tingle.

"We really gotta celebrate," Yvonne kissed down Sarah's throat, sending shivers all through her. And that was when both their stupid tabs went off.

"Dammit," Yvonne groaned, rolling back and grabbing her tab. Seeing her commander's handle, she flicked the screen up. "Hey Aidan!"

Aidan grinned, half the Wildcards packed in behind him. "Hey guys! We just saw the news!"

The crew cheered, waving behind their commander. Aidan waved a hand to settle them down. "Heads up girls, you aren't done yet. How fast can you get home?"

"Why, what's going on?" Sarah asked, leaning up on her elbows.

"We're taking out Eagle back here," Naomi cut in with a sidelong grin, shoving her bangs back out of her face as she leaned closer. "And we figured you two would want in on that. So how fast can you get here?"

Yvonne and Sarah glanced at each other. They said the next word so close together that they sounded like a chorus.

"Fast!"

It took some tricks and some trades, but they were pulling into Four Aces Farm twenty-two hours later, desert stars shining bright over their heads. Yvonne cut the motor and leaned over to kiss her sleeping wife's cheek. "Sarah girl, c'mon honey. Let's go inside."

"Mmmrwehome?" Sarah slurred, eyes cracking open. Yvonne couldn't help but smile at how soft her girl looked trying to wake up. Reaching over, she stroked Sarah's black-feather hair. "Yeah hon, we're home. Let's go inside. Keep it down, it's oh-two-hundred."

"Yeah," Sarah agreed through a stretching yawn. "Sounds good. C'mon." They slipped down the hall into their room, closing the door as quietly as they could. All the same, it slid back open before it'd even closed the whole way. Tom rushed inside, hugging Sarah tight, then turning to squeeze Yvonne so hard her ribs creaked.

"Hey Tommy," she whispered, kissing his forehead.

"Glad you're home," Tom whispered in the dark. Then he pulled away. "Did you get food on the way in? I asked Billie if she could put cold plates together for you and leave them in the fridge."

Yvonne had to smile at her little officer, always on top of things and taking care of people. "That sounds great. Come sit with us, and we'll tell you about how we landed Zuck and the shmucks."

In the dim night-cycle lights, Tommy's eyes sparkled as he grinned.

"Ready for this?" Milo asked, giving Janice's hand a squeeze.

She sighed. "Guess I better be."

"We're gonna be good," Abbie reassured, fingers wrapped tight around the poster of her mother as she smiled. "Mom'll watch out for us."

Janice ran a gentle hand over her daughter's bright orange 'fro.

"Yeah hon." She raised her eyes to her partner's, and smiled, holding his hand tight as they waited in the sweltering dark. They were supposed to get moving by twenty-one hundred; the civvies had all been told to be there and ready in César Chávez Park by nine pm. From here, they'd march down the hill in a more-or-less straight line, an hour's walk down Federal Boulevard and Colfax that'd block one of the city's main arteries. That'd get some attention. At the end of their walk, they'd converge on Byron White Courthouse and turn the steps into a memorial to the dead. EagleCorp had tried to take a piece out of them with the massacre on those steps: they were about to have it crammed down their throats that their tactics hadn't stopped jack. Janice hoped they fucking choked.

"Hey," a kid with bright green eyes in a dark face asked Abigail, "You got an affinity group? You got your contact handles writ on your arm? Amp told us you gotta do that."

"Don't bug people, Benny," the twenty-something with dyed rainbow hair and a sky-blue getup that practically glowed in the dark suggested, ruffling the kid's mop. They glanced up and smiled. "We taught him to be careful at events. Amp, by the way. Caretakers' Union." The youngster nodded back at a group of folks, and the dark-haired girl beside them gave Janice and Milo a smile. "You guys got backup, yeah?"

Janice poked a thumb over her shoulder, where thirty folks who'd come in from Four Aces to be part of the march stood waiting. Yvonne raised a picture of Lazarus, giving a little wave.

"Janice, this's Milo, an' our girl Abbie. That's our bunch; Four Aces Farm. We're good to go."

"Looks like it." Amp agreed. They smiled down at Abbie. "You ready?"

"Yeah!" Abigail exclaimed. Her throat felt like it had a knot in it, but all the same, Janice had to be a little wowed by the kid. The steel-girded guts of this little one, ready to go in spite of everything.

"Okay then." Amp handed the placard showing a smiling crowd in front of a cooling shelter to their girl.

Behind Janice, Yvonne checked her tab.

"Time!" She kissed Sarah's cheek and handed her the poster of her cousin. Trotting over to the lamp post in front of most of the gathering, she shimmied up it faster than Janice could believe. The amplification collar against her voice box worked like a loudspeaker as she called out.

"Everyone! Thank you for answering our call! For the next nine nights, we're going to honor our missing friends and family! We're here to remember our dead and our lost, everybody who died or disappeared because of corporate greed and corporate garbage!"

A cheer rose, posters and placards of the smiling dead held over people's heads.

"We're going to make the Corps remember their names this week!" Yvonne called. The cheer was twice as loud this time.

"And we're going to make sure that nobody else dies to make a buck for the Corps!" Yvonne's voice trumpeted from her lamp post.

The crowd roared their affirmation.

With a laugh, Yvonne waved the hand that wasn't holding her onto the lamppost.

"Okay! Remember your drills: follow the directions of the Caretakers, they're the ones in blue! If you need anything; extra water, a snack, where to go to next, find the caretakers! If there's trouble, if you see assholes starting fights or EagleCorp trouble, get the Guardians! They're in orange, with hard hats! And remember, the Corps want you to fight so they can label you thugs and shoot you without anybody complaining! Don't fall for it! Don't let them fool you and make you fight down at their level. Blood washes away! We want more than blood! We want change!"

"We want change!" The crowd called back. "We want change!" "We want change! Let's go make it happen!" Yvonne yelled, sliding down the lamppost. "Come on!"

The crowd moved like one gigantic animal, and Janice moved with it, swept along. She glanced down at a beaming Abigail, and smiled for her. "Showtime, girly!"

"Showtime, guys"

Tweak typed. She stretched her fingers, adjusted Bao Li in her nursing sling, and pulled up her screens. Front and center, the communications window showing the rest of the Code Monkeys gleamed in the half-light she preferred when she wanted to focus.

"Denver march is moving."

"Anchorage march started moving twenty minutes ago," Deniki reported.

One by one, the team listed cities on the march.

"New York's moving."

"Seattle's on the move."

"Chicago's going!"

"Here goes Baton Rouge."

"Temp just dropped down off a hundred and twenty, Phoenix marches in an hour."

"Pueblo's marching," Tweak added. **"Buffalo...Salt Lake...yeah! Everybody's on time."**

"Same!" LaQuan agreed.

"Like clockwork!" Fatima agreed as Lulu cheered.

Tweak grinned as she typed.

"Okay awesome. So, plan is, we all focus on our areas, check back in an hour?"

"You got it, Dragon," Deniki agreed with a smile. She grinned at him.

"Luck, Moose. Luck, everybody."

"Same, Dragon." Rhin agreed. "See you on the flip side!"

One by one, they disconnected from the voice chat to focus on their cities and their immediate responsibilities. The conversation quieted down to the occasional typed comments.

Tweak checked Bao Li, who was completely passed out in her sling. Smiling, she pulled up her headset.

"Stay hydrated, people!" Yvonne called, glad that she had an amplifying collar now instead of the bulky bullhorn she used to carry. "Steady pace! No rush!" She jogged back along the line. A new chant went up as she passed a group of First Nation ladies with red handprints across their faces. All of them carried pictures of smiling young adults.

"No more stolen sisters! No more stolen brothers! No more crying fathers! No more weeping mothers!" Jogging further back in the crowd, she entered into a different chant.

"We will resist! Until we can exist!" this chant leader was calling, and the part of the crowd around them called it back. From the pictures, Yvonne recognized an affiliate group made up of all gammas. It was great that they were feeling secure enough to be out here in the open.

"Give back our children!" A group of women were chanting, holding pictures of babies and toddlers with terms like "not an aberration!" and "my baby was not a drain on resources!" Cavanaugh moms. Kids must have gotten taken under the Perfection Mandate. Yvonne wanted to hug every one of them, but there wasn't any time.

The more she moved up and down the crowd, the more chants she heard. And wow, what a mix they'd turned out to be. Everybody was representing here. Down a ways, AgCo field workers from the plains towns held up pictures decorated in all the colors of Dia De Los Muertos. "Se busca! No mas!" They chanted in Spanish. AgCo might try to ban the language, but it lived on these people's tongues.

"You clocked them in alive at nine! Give them back alive at five!" a team of factory workers chanted; they carried images that were before-and-after shots of people mangled by industrial machines and processes. Man, that was a wakeup call right there.

""We will never stop searching for you!" A group holding posters of people EagleCorp had taken and never released chanted, waving their images high.

One group had dressed up like masked pall bearers and were carrying an actual fricking coffin, with a band playing jazz behind them. Yvonne grinned as she trotted past. She nodded to Caretakers and Guardians, who flashed her a thumbs' up. Everything running smooth. They were nearly down off the hill that led from the Tennyson neighborhood into Downtown. Pretty soon they'd be on Colfax.

Dog-trotting back up the line, she fell in with her own people. They weren't chanting anything in this part of the crowd right now, but everyone held their pictures high. Janice carried a pic of that first boyfriend she'd had as a teen, the guy who got bombed by a drone. Abigail held the poster of her mom's smiling face over her head. Milo carried a pic of little Henrietta. Sarah carried the placard of Lazarus propped on her shoulder. With him grinning in the pic, it was like he was beside them. Yvonne grinned at the placard.

Sarah caught her eye, and smiled at her. "Stunt this big, he'd give us hell if we didn't make sure he got in on it too."

"Yeah," Yvonne agreed, feeling tears prick behind her eyes as she smiled.

Tapping her tab, she made a quick call.

"Hey Tweak! Inyoni! Get ready, here we come!"

A new chant rolled back to them, and Yvonne joined in, pocketing her tab without waiting for an answer.

"An injury to one of us!

An injury to all of us!"

It felt like the entire crowd joined that one. Chanting the words, they marched under the shadows of the downtown skyscrapers.

"Hey b-Bird. You hear?" Tweak asked. Her guy's voice sounded good when he came back. "I hear. They're coming our way; we're ready!"

The vitals from his tab looked good; his heart rate, blood pressure and biochemistry was okay, and he didn't have any signs of blood loss. Better to ask though.

"You good?"

"Good," her guy's voice replied. "The distract is going great. We're tagging their prowl cars," Inyoni explained "They're gonna spot us any time now; fact they haven't noticed us yet tells us just how busy they…oh man, here we go."

"What's your cross streets?" Tweak asked, and Inyoni answered fast.

"Sixteenth and Wewetta, right on the other side of the Station."

"Kay." Tweak brought up her camera feeds, zeroing in on the coordinates in her guy's tab and activating her ins to the surveillance drones in the neighborhood. Now she had eyes. "Okay…yeah, I see you. Okay. You g-got Eagles behind you, some on your l-l-left. Go right. Grab your people. Alley."

"Got it," Inyoni agreed, breathing heavy in the mic. She turned the sound down when he raised his voice to talk to the other people, studying the readouts and crunching numbers. Through four drones she was controlling now, she watched her guy and his team, watched the EagleCorp goons on their tail.

"B-b-bird. Break your t-t-team into three," she stated into the mic. "One up c-c-Chestnut. One heads for T-t-Tennyson. Your team. D-down the alley. Straight ahead. Fire escape. Onto the r-r-roofs."

As she spoke, she opened the back door that'd get her into the EagleCorp's chatter. Most of it was just noise and cussing, so she tuned it out.

"Up onto the roofs," Inyoni's voice said in her ear. "Tweak? How close are they?"

"Hundred f-feet b-back," Tweak replied. "M-m-move."

"Got somebody stuck. Working on it."

Shit, Tweak thought, hissing between her teeth. She reached for her eardrum-shatter program, getting it ready to inject into the helmets of the EagleCorp goons just in case she needed to—"

"Team three, disengage," the EagleCorp comm channel crackled. Tweak blinked. Disengage? What?

She zoomed her drone cameras in, watching the Eagle unit at the mouth of the alley. They were peering down it, but they weren't moving. The fire escape ladder was still rattling with the escape going on above, and they were stopping?

The Eagles were as weirded out as she was, sounded like.

"But sir, we can…"

"Are you deaf, Briggs? I said disengage."

"But sir!" the guy whined. In the camera, he was fidgeting like a dog being told he couldn't pick up the treat on the floor.

The commander turned away. "Orders from the nest, Briggs. Not the guy with the ears; it was in the briefing. He's one of ours. We'll try to bag the ones who went up Eighteenth."

And Tweak's world stopped. It just…stopped. Everything froze. Even her breath.

For a few seconds, everything was glass. Frozen. Brittle. Ready to shatter.

Then she heard Inyoni's voice. It was tiny, and it sounded so scared.

"Tweak…I…Tweak. They just said 'not the guy with the ears.'"

Tweak swallowed.

"Y-y-y-you heard that?"

"I always hear their mics," Inyoni almost whispered. "Can't help it. Tweak…they said…they said I was…"

Tweak closed her eyes.

One of ours.

That's what they said.

One of ours.

"They said I was theirs," Inyoni gulped. "Tweak…what the fuck's that mean?" In her coding chair, Tweak curled around their baby, eyes squeezed shut.

"Tweak?" Inyoni sounded freaked as hell. "Tweak. Dragon. Talk to me. What the fuck? What'd they mean?" He sounded an inch from panic. She felt the same. All the pieces fell into place like a truck full of bricks spilling down on her.

Tweak gulped down a breath, shoulders bending under the weight of putting it all together.

"They m-m-mean…" She had to lean in and breathe in the scent of her daughter before she could whisper the words.

"They mean you're the s-s-sleepw-w…w…"

She couldn't get the word out.

"Sleepwalker," Inyoni whimpered. "They mean I'm the Sleepwalker. Oh…*fuck*."

"You ready for this, lad?" The man beside Kevin whispered through his mic. Inside his slick suit's helmet, Kevin grinned.

"My friend, I've been ready for this nigh on a decade."

United Nations Taskforce Officer MacBeth gave a little laugh. His Scottish accent burred over the amusement in his tone. "Man, man. Not going to mince your words about it, are you now?"

"As a great poet once said: let us not talk falsely now. The hour is getting late," Kevin stated. What had begun as a joke seemed far too solemn once it was said.

"Shakespere again?" Taskforce Officer Gu asked on his other side.

Kevin shook his head. "Bob Dylan, actually."

The man from Hong Kong laughed. "I mix all those old guys up."

"Cut the chatter," the sharp voice of Commander Hall stated in their ears. "Red team. Red one. Position?"

"Main doors, covering," a woman's voice replied. "Security measures disabled. Ready to deploy."

Kevin listened as the teams forming a noose around the house jutting out of the side of Mount Elbert sounded off. In her position as mission control, Commander Hall methodically went through her operatives.

"Check. Red team. Red two. Position?"

"Kitchen window. Security measures disabled. Ready"

"Team five. Red five. Position?"

"Rooftop entry three," Kevin replied into his mic. "Security measures disabled. Ready to deploy."

His blood pounded in his ears. They'd spent more than two weeks watching the property. They'd learned the routines. The security. Kevin had drawn a map of the interior based on memory, and they'd fleshed it out via observation.

They were ready.

"Black team. Black one. Perimeter check."

"Perimeter clear. Fence disabled.'

Kevin glanced down at the gate that he'd once been driven through as a privileged guest, his HUD telescoping as he focused.

"Black team. Black four. Perimeter check."

"Perimeter clear. Fence disabled."

Kevin ran his eyes along the fence from checkpoint to checkpoint. The electric sizzle was gone from the metal as far as the eye could see. The fence was inert. Perfect.

"All teams," Commander Hall's crisp tones rapped across the ear. "Prepare for deployment."

Crouched on the roof beneath his slick poncho, Kevin felt his muscles tense.

Wait for the command...

Wait...

"Deploy."

Kevin's muscles uncoiled. He snicked open the lightwell he'd prepared beforehand, motioning the two people he was responsible for to follow as he uncoiled the rope, secured it to the rooftop with their help and shimmied down. It was coated in the same fiber optic mesh as the slick suits they wore, and a distracted mind could take amusement from the appearance of glass hands moving over a glass rope. But now was no time to be distracted.

All of them left their slick ponchos above; from here, flapping cloth would be a liability. The slick suits they wore beneath would be more effective.

"Through here," he murmured into his mic as they landed cat-footed. "Security room."

"Roger," his team agreed.

Tranquilize the security contractors in Harrington's employ before they had time to react. That was the first step. Kevin took point; high-standing reflexes paid at times like these.

They moved slowly, lest the flicker of a slick suit against the patterned wallpaper gave them away to watching human eyes via any number of cameras. But they moved with purpose.

The guard's break room. Here. Perfect. Kevin took a quick reading through the door. Eight heat signatures. Easy enough.

Drawing the prepared compound from his pouch, he peeled off the wrapper and tucked the cloth in the crack under the door. The colorless gas it released under pressure wouldn't take long to effervesce into the room. He only needed the contractors to be sluggish, not completely unconscious. The darts would finish the job.

"Prep darts," he murmured into his mic, drawing his own dart gun.

"Roger," MacBeth affirmed.

There was a thud, and a confused murmur.

"Now." Palming his dart gun, he opened the door, knelt and shot. His teammates shot over his shoulders. Eight contractors crumpled without more than a whimper or two.

"Red five, reporting," Kevin murmured into his mic. "Security group zero out."

"Red one, reporting," another voice murmured in his ear as he and his team were finishing the restraint of the off-duty security team, laying them in the recovery position just in case. "Security group one out."

Security group one. That was the team watching the cameras in their little office upstairs. Perfect.

"Red four, reporting," Kevin heard as he headed down towards where he remembered Harrington's lounge room to be. This late on a Saturday, surely he'd be trying to relax. It wasn't as if he could do much business in lockdown.

If only Harrington's home weren't so carefully shielded against surveillance, they could check where he was through the biological surveillance nanoids in his body. But if the home weren't so carefully shielded, he wouldn't be Harrington.

Carefully, Kevin stepped up beside the office door. "Red five reporting. Snakehole one. Hole plugged," he reported with an irritable twist of the emotions. Of course bloody Harrington would line the door to his lounge to make heat-sensors ineffective. Not unexpected, but irksome all the same.

"Can opener," Hall's voice stated.

"Roger," Kevin agreed. He opened the door slowly, then shoved it open and swung his arm in an arc, covering the area.

One poor maid dropped to her knees, covering her head. From a distance, Kevin checked her for weapons signatures or anything else. "Snakehole one. Civilian. Unarmed." He stated. "Request escort."

"Black three. Escorting. Five minutes."

"Roger." Kevin knelt beside the woman. She looked up at him with terrified eyes. Opening his helmet's visor, he smiled at her.

"It's going to be alright," he murmured. "You're not in trouble, and you're not going to get hurt. Someone's going to come up and take you outside. Please stay quiet until you're out there. They'll have food and water for you. We heard you haven't been getting paid your wages? We've got a stipend set up; everybody gets paid tonight. Don't worry about your family; we've already made sure everyone in the barracks at the bottom of the mountain are safe."

Swallowing, the woman nodded jerkily.

With another small smile, he pressed a finger to his lips and stood, securing his helmet. At the door, his relief held up a hand. Kevin gave a thumbs' up.

"Red five, moving on." The wine bar, that was his next best guess. After that, he'd try Harrington's home office.

The door to the wine bar was open, and the room was empty. Kevin waved his team forward.

"Snakehole two. No snake," he stated into his mic. Narrowing his eyes, he studied the wall. Harrington had remodeled since Kevin's days as a visitor, replacing the faux-log aesthetic of the former winebar with a more rugged red sandstone veneer. But…yes, the concealed door to the wine cellar was right where he remembered.

"Down under," he murmured. "Permission to proceed?"

"Permission granted," Hall agreed. "Proceed."

Kevin waved his companions in. Stepping forward, he closed his eyes and remembered.

The trick lock. You found the little metal ball just here with your fingers. Mr. H had let him do it as a treat, when he and Tim and Marty had wanted to play down in the rock tunnels. And the little ball followed the maze…right…left…left….right again…and down into its burrow.

Snick!

The door came away from the wall. Kevin nodded to his men, and stepped onto the stairs. Good thing they'd already taken the security room and disabled it. He could see the infrared sensors on either side of the stairs; if they'd been at work, the act of stepping on the first stair would have broken the beam.

"What is this?" MacBeth asked.

"Wine cellar and vehicle storage area, dug into the mountain." Kevin explained. "There's four bays. We'll start on the left and work our way across. Each bay is a room roughly sixty by sixty by twelve."

""Meters or feet, yank?" Macbeth's voice burred in his ear. Kevin had to smile. "Feet, sorry. The Corps keep us on the Imperial system, because of course they do. Visibility is low in the wine cellar; there's racks of wine bottles. Careful."

"Roger," Gu agreed, sweeping his weapon in a slow right-left arc as they exited the stairway.

Luckily, the slick suits masked their movement sufficiently that they weren't sensed by the automatic lights. It wouldn't look good if the room suddenly lit up without reason. But cutting the power to Harrington's home would have given too much advance notice. They needed to catch the snake in his hole with as little warning as possible. Otherwise, he'd strike, or he'd slip between their fingers.

"Down under," he reported. "Snakehole one. No snake. Investigating snakehole two." He nodded to the men in his charge, switching frequencies to speak to them alone. "Gu, take the right. MacBeth, the left. I'll go down the center, start at the back wall and work forward."

"It's a plan," MacBeth agreed. Gu nodded.

"Right." Kevin stepped into the wine cellar, switching frequencies and listening in on the other teams.

"Red one. Snakehole five. No snake."

"Red seven. Snakehole twenty. No snake."

"Red two. Snakehole eight. Four civilians."

"Black six, escorting. Five minutes."

"Roger."

Kevin reached the back wall. His fingers wandered across it…and yes. The little stone marble was right where it had always been.

Behind his helmet, he bit his lip for a moment. *I wonder…*

It would make sense…

I should call it in…

I wonder if the combination is still the same. Let's see.

Right…left…up…right…right again…and down into the hole.

The door must have been maintained; it didn't make a sound as it cracked open.

I really should call this in.

I really should.

But if he's there…

Slipping inside, Kevin closed the door silently behind him, and turned off his mic.

I have to.

He hung his helmet up on the hook on the wall, still there in the place he remembered. In unadulterated darkness, he deactivated his slick suit, following his feet and his memory to the hidden den they'd called the Book Nook as children.

Light grew as he navigated a switchback in the tunnel. Ah. So his psychological analysis had been accurate after all. Mr. H. had always been a man who considered possibilities and took precautions accordingly. Under stress, that tendency could become paranoia. Apparently it had in this case. The cozy secret library revealed as Kevin stepped out had been converted into a tiny home; a bed against the wall, a door to what Kevin assumed was a pantry based on the crumbs near it, and another that most likely lead to a small commode. In the place it had always occupied, Harrington's ancient desk stood foursquare. Comfortable reading lamps encircled it in cozy light. Along every wall, well-stocked bookshelves rose to the ceiling. A simulated fireplace was merrily burning. Harrington was in his reading chair behind the desk, sipping at a glass of wine.

Kevin stepped out of the dark. "What a cozy little scene. I think I'll join you. Why don't you pour a glass for me, Mr. H."

The CEO of Cavanaugh Corporation started, spilling wine across expensive green leather and fine wood. He stared up, the blood draining from his face as Kevin sauntered in and took a seat.

"It's been some time since I've joined you for a sip," Kevin remarked with a thin smile. "And we do have a great deal to catch up on."

Harrington swallowed audibly. "Kevin…"

"Indeed." Kevin inclined his head. "It's been a long time, Mr. H. No, I'm afraid I can't permit you to leave your seat," he added calmly, pulling his service piece and covering the older man in one smooth movement. "I want a word."

Harrington sank into his chair, staring at Kevin's hand. At the gun. "Kevin…don't do this. You're not a…you were a good boy."

"You're right. I was a good boy," Kevin agreed, feeling his nerves singing. "To be accurate, I was a compliant child. Obedient. Conforming in every particular with Cavanaugh Corporation's expectations of me. Devoted to my future at the head of this Corporation. I was Kevin Craydon. I am Douglas Craydon's son. I am the heir to everything the Cavanaugh Corporation has been, and to what it *could* have been," Kevin stated, every word measured. Leaning in, he dropped his voice to a murmur. "And more to the point, I was the son of a man you called 'friend'. I used to be the boy who wanted nothing more than to be just like him. Just. Like. *You.* I was the boy you patted on the shoulder while the coffin of the woman you gave the order to *kill* was put in her crypt. Remember that?"

Slowly, the demon he'd come to exorcize shook his head. "It wasn't that simple. There were levels of complexity you were too young to—"

"Spare me," Kevin snapped. "And don't bother to continually push that button in your pocket. Your security forces have been neutralized. We won't be interrupted while we wrap up our loose ends."

Harrington licked his lips. "Kevin, son. Put the gun down. Your father and I were always trying to make people better. So were you. You remember. You're Cavanaugh. You're too good for this kind of behavior."

"Oh, on the contrary, this kind of behavior is exactly what Cavanaugh Corporation bred me for," Kevin rejoined. "The best people for a better future, isn't that our motto? Survival of the fittest in the most stringent eugenic tradition, in other words. And I am certainly not *your son.*" Standing, he took a lounging seat on the edge of the desk, avoiding the spilled wine. The hand he wasn't using to brace himself toyed with the gun. "I'm the son of an honorable man whom *you murdered* in order to take this position. I'm the son of a woman you ordered *beaten to death*. However, you make an apt point. You took my parents from me. You took my future. You ripped everything of worth out of my life. The people who took me in put something else back." Leaning over, he brushed the gun barrel under Harrington's chin. "And while I was out there living on ration bars and prairie dogs, you sat here in the seat of a company that was dedicated to healing—in my seat, in *my father's seat*, with *his blood* on your hands—and allowed the people we were entrusted with caring for to *suffer and die*. Oh, you tormented and killed your enemies, par for the course—"

"Now that's a blatant slander, I have never killed a single—" Harrington cut in, voice pitched to fill the room. Kevin was having none of that. He jammed the gun barrel into the thin skin under the older man's chin. "*Do not* bluster with me at the moment, Harrington. And *don't you dare* to try to plead non es factum with me. I know *all* about the things you do to people in little rooms far from the public eye. You put people I care about in those rooms, and I'm tempted to kill you slowly on those grounds alone." With care, he pulled away, point made. "And I know about the bio-weapons. You remember, don't you? The ones my father banned and *you* resurrected? I watched friends *suffer and die* because of your pet monsters. *I watched children die* because of you." He stared down at the man behind the desk, his soul scintillating with fire and ice.

"But they're 'the enemy', fair enough. You, though." He shook his head in mock- admonishment. "You did worse than that, didn't you? So much worse. You killed *your own citizens*, you meretricious viper. People you promised deliverance from their pain died in *agony*. Those who didn't die lived in drudgery. You chained millions to debts they could never pay off. Contracts they could never live up to." Leaning in, he tipped his captive audience's head up with a gun barrel under the chin, ever so gently, so that Harrington had no choice but to look him in the eye as he spoke. "You have buried millions of people in holes of degradation and despair. You spoke of the sanctity of life and the improvement of the human condition before the cameras. You repeated our slogans. Cavanaugh, the *caring* company. The best people, for a better future. And all the while you were turning babies who didn't fit your genetic specifications into *dog food*. You crawling, mendacious, fork-tongued *worm*." His finger tightened on the trigger. Harrington swallowed. "Kevin, please," the CEO gasped, chin tipped away from the metal of the gun barrel. "Don't do this. I know how it seems, but I had to make hard decisions in hard times. I'm not your enemy here! I can help you! Please, just give me the chance!"

"You had that chance sixteen years ago." Kevin stated flatly. "Before you killed *my mother*." Slowly, he leaned back. Moving with deliberate care, he turned his service piece this way and that, watching the firelight play on the gun barrel. "What's that old board room joke? We make good men and better women? Ironically enough, you achieved your goal with me. Not as you intended, of course. But if you hadn't done what you did, I'd probably still be a compliant corporate puppet upholding my responsibilities in a system that is *evil*. I believed it was the best way to help people, as a boy. I knew of no alternative to the way things were, before you ripped everything out from under me. I've learned so much since then."

Harrington's eyes flickered as Kevin allowed himself the luxury of speech, taking in exits, angles, possibilities. Running the calculus of survival. Kevin lounged back, balancing the gun between two fingers. "So, Mr. H. The best people for a better society. Survival of the fittest. How does that motto stand up in praxis?" He was savagely pleased to see the panic in the man's eyes as he toyed with the weapon. "For example, which one of us is most fit to survive, Mr. H.? Can you tell me that?" Smiling to himself, he spun the gun by its trigger guard, watching Harrington. There it was. The tell. The tensing of muscles. Any minute now. Any…minute…

Harrington uncoiled from his chair, lunging for the gun. He was fast, endowed with all the genetic advantages of their station in the company. Yes. He was fast. But he wasn't fast enough. Kevin had all the same advantages, twice the training and half the age. He easily leaned out of the way and viced the back of Harrington's neck in one hand, pressing the gun to the back of his head as he slammed the older man's body down across his desk. "Now, according to the Cavanaugh playbook, this is the point where the fittest survives, the winner takes all, and I blow your brains out." He ground the man into the puddle of spilled wine, leaning in. "But we're not playing by those rules today, because those rules are pernicious drivel and they always were. I'm not going to shoot you, Mr. H. The people around me and the life I've lived actually *did* make me a good man." He tucked the gun in its holster and pulled the older man up with a grip that yanked his wrists against his shoulder blades. Technically, he ought to put the cuffs on the prick now. But he couldn't do that yet. Not just yet. A hunter's grin pulled his lips back from his teeth.

"But they didn't make me a saint." Spinning the weaker man to face him, he allowed himself one punch, just one: a fist driven hard and fast into the bastard's solar plexus. His bete noir collapsed in a retching heap at his feet. Standing over him, Kevin took in the sight of Harrington thrashing like the crushed serpent he was. "That's for *my family*, you son of a bitch." And it was for his family; all of them. For his parents, brave and true to the very end. For Commander Taylor, so strong and so incredibly kind. For wonderful, crazy Lazarus who would always be his brother in arms, and for gentle, generous Andrea. For little Henrietta. In the name of everyone he'd lost too soon, this crawling excuse for a man would live to be held accountable. Leaning down, Kevin pulled the flexi-cuffs he'd brought from his inner pocket and handcuffed his prey, yanking the deposed CEO to his feet. Let it never be said that a prisoner had been abused while in custody; after all, Kevin had gotten his own in before the cuffs went on. Fair play, according to the rules. "By the power invested in me by the International Criminal Court, I arrest you for the crimes of genocide, deprivation of physical liberty, enslavement, persecution against vulnerable populations, and natural resource destruction. You have the right to remain silent. You have the right to humane treatment under the UN accords regardless of your choice to speak. Anything you say can be used against you in court. You have the right to have a lawyer during questioning. If you decide to answer questions now without a lawyer present, you have the right to stop answering at any time."

One hand in the small of his prisoner's back and one hand gripping his bound wrists, Kevin forced him to walk.

"Down under. Snakehole two. Snake caged," Kevin stated once he'd situated his helmet again. "Havers man!" MacBeth's Scottish accent had thickened into something Kevin had never heard outside a movie. "Where the divil are you? I cannae see you!"

"Hidden room on the back wall of the wine cellar. Coming out now," Kevin explained calmly, pushing the door with his foot. "Walk," he ordered Harrington. The other man twisted to stare at him. "You really think this three-ring circus of yours changes anything?" He hissed waspishly.

Kevin returned his sneer with a feral smile. "I think it changes everything, Mr. H. At least, it does for *you*. Now walk. Here!" he called, raising his voice. "He'll need his rights read to him on camera."

"We called the other teams!" Gu called down the aisles of wine bottles. "What happened? You went out of touch."

"Rock down here blocks signals sometimes," Kevin deflected. "It's probably why he made his bolthole down here."

Harrington began to say something, still glaring at Kevin over his shoulder. But then he looked from one UN taskforce officer to another, and his shoulders went rigid.

"I want my lawyers," he stated icily.

"They will be contacted," Commander Hall agreed calmly, marching down the aisles of bottles. "Until then, you will be remanded under my authority and placed in humane conditions in the United Nations Facility of the Western Quadrant, pending your shipment to the Hague. You will be supplied with the means of contacting your legal council as soon as we reach a secure facility. My officers will escort you to the transport. Please comply with their instructions, sir."

Harrington growled a little in the back of his throat, a sound of pure balked ego. But he walked with dignity between the two UN officers.

Slowly, Hall glanced from the open door to Kevin, and back again. One eyebrow rose.

"Stone blocked the comms signal?"

"Ma'am," Kevin acknowledged mildly, hands clasped behind his back. He was so overwhelmed by the moment that he barely felt his feet on the floor. For a breath, Kevin wasn't sure which way the moment would go. Then Hall smiled, the scar in her cheek pulled into a shape like a star.

"A very neat capture, Officer McIllian-Headly. Absolutely by the book. My congratulations." Kevin nodded his head. "Thank you, ma'am."

"Prisoner escort will be leaving in twenty minutes," Hall continued briskly, turning away. "The property has been secured. Officers will remain to maintain and catalog the contents." Kevin nodded automatically, numb with elation. Harrington. In custody. On his way to face justice. Cavanaugh's stranglehold. Broken. The demon, exorcized. It was over. So many years, so much work. So much agony. Now it was done.

His mind was smooth, flat expanse of euphoria. Silly fragments of thought bounced and wandered across it like happy little drunkards as he paced at his superior's side.

It's over.

It's finally over.

I am so lucky that worked.

I am such an idiot.

Thank you, Lord, for helping me make that work.

I've done it. I've brought Harrington to account for…everything.

And I still have a soul afterwards. Isn't that nice.

Thank you Lord.

Thank you.

"McIllian," Hall continued, "an e-plane will be landing in ten minutes. You're required in downtown Denver. The central office of EagleCorp is our next target, and they have taken numerous hostages at this time…including a member of your unit. A specialist named Inyoni Amanzi."

Kevin's head snapped around. He'd been happily drifting on endorphins, but that little statement brought him down to earth like a netted sparrow.

"Situation, ma'am?"

"Apparently he walked up to their front door and surrendered himself to the Peacekeepers the morning of the second," Commander Hall turned, that brow cocked again. "Is this some plan you Wildcards have been cooking up?"

"Not that I know of, ma'am," Kevin replied, bewildered. "I'm needed for covert extraction?"

"Nothing covert this time," Hall replied dryly. "You're needed to help knock out that wasp nest in a controlled manner. If we can keep the casualties to a minimum, that's preferable. But that place comes down."

Kevin saluted. "Orders received."

"Hey!" Inyoni shouted. "Hey, assholes!"

He rolled on his back and used both feet to bang on the metal wall of his cell. Not like they were going to answer, or even pay attention. He knew that. But what else did he have to do in here?

He flopped back onto the cot once he ran out of energy. Two fucking days. Two fucking days he'd been in here. Nobody had done more than shove a plate and a gallon of water through the door once a day.

He wondered how hot it was in this little oven of a room. It felt hot but okay, but the way the light sizzled on the floor told him it was probably not good. He had the feeling an Alpha would pass out from the heat in here. At least the toilet flushed.

He wished he could reach Tweak. He hadn't heard her voice since he stood in front of EagleCorp with his hands up. They hadn't found his molar mic; they'd been so jumpy that all they'd done was pat him down and take stuff like his bracelets and his tab. Hell, they hadn't even found his contacts.So he still had his mic, and that was good. But if he talked, they'd know he had one. Tweak wasn't saying a word, and that made him feel like shit.

Were they really just going to leave him in here until…when? Until the March of Memory was over? Until this place got taken down?

Forever?

He sighed, closing his eyes. At least here, he wasn't getting anyone else in trouble. In here, he wasn't feeding Eagle information that got people around him killed.

That second when everything clicked had felt like a bone breaking inside his head. Why hadn't he seen the pattern? The Corps always got perfect intel from the Sleepwalker when he was on grid, because the bug that must be in his holo somewhere had all the signal strength it needed when he was in the city. They stopped getting his GPS when he was at home, because the slick tarps blocked that stuff. But they still got recordings of what people said and did around him. Any time he was in the Dust, they had a read on him and uploaded all his recordings. That's how they'd gotten Sky House.

And it hadn't just been Dusters he'd gotten nabbed. The surveillance chip had to have been installed when his holo was. He'd always been thrown by how often people he'd been on the streets with had gotten nabbed, but that'd just been…life. It'd sucked, but he hadn't known no different. It'd just been the way things went.

Turned out it wasn't. Turned out it'd been him getting people nabbed all along. No, not him exactly. His holo. He ran his fingers over the little disc, feeling his heart beating too fast. His holo. He'd gotten it so he could be safe. He'd gotten it so he'd have half a chance at a real life. And the Corps had even used *that* against him. They'd used his only way to be safe and even a little comfortable to make him the reason for other people getting hurt and killed. He squeezed his eyes closed, breathing hard. Fuck. He'd never had no good choice to make, had he? Just a bunch of different shitty options. And the Corps had decided what options he had, every step of the way. He'd never really had a choice at all, had he?

The door of his cell banged. There was the thud of boots on concrete. The clack of guns being cocked. "Up. Now," a voice barked.

Inyoni opened his eyes. Four Peacekeepers were standing over his cot, weapons aimed.

"Hands out," the lead Peacekeeper snapped. "Get up."

Inyoni blinked at them. "Man, if you're gonna shoot me, just do it here, okay? Don't feel like movin'. Too hot." Truth was, he hurt too bad to care if they shot him, right then. That was the thing people didn't get: when he said he didn't feel pain, he meant on skin and bones. The feels, that was something else. That could hurt. That could hurt bad.

Two of the EagleCorp assholes grabbed him and yanked him off the cot, snapping cuffs around his wrists. One of them gave him a hard shove in the middle of his back. "Walk, freak."

Inyoni sighed, and walked. Least it was cooler in the hallway. So much cooler that he got the shivers.

"Junkie," one of the Peacekeepers sneered. Inyoni snorted, but he didn't bother answering. Not worth it.

They piled him into an elevator, and rode in silence as they climbed floors. Ten. Fifteen. Twenty. Right up to the top. Hunh.

The floor they got out on was still metal and concrete, but it was *classy* metal and concrete: up here stuff was fancy, polished. Brushed, wherever it could be. Up here everything had smooth sharp knife edges. It was like being on the inside of an expensive gun, Inyoni thought while his feet moved on automatic.

Through a couple more doors, past a bored secretary, and into a chrome and concrete office. Inyoni was slammed down into a cold metal chair. Guns clicked as they were trained on his back. Across the table, a big white guy was sitting with his legs splayed, staring at a handful of holographic cards with a pile of projected chips in front of him. He was the kind of big that told you there was muscle under there, and he was dressed all kinds of nice: a fancy brown and black cooling jacket lay over a brown three-piece suit with blood red cuffs and a red tie. His greying buzzcut had been expertly faded on either side, two lines shaved right and left making him look slick. Looking up, the man studied Inyoni. His eyebrows moving like two fat black caterpillars who wanted to get together. Under them, black eyes glittered.

Inyoni knew that expression. He'd seen it on the vids often enough, when Hamilton had been giving some talk about security and his Corporation's work. Across the desk, Jack Hamilton smiled, relaxing back in his chair. He got rid of the card game with a wave of his hand. "Time for the bird to come home to roost, hunh? I hear they call you Bird. Or do you like Sleepwalker better?"

Inyoni stared. He shifted in the cold chair. Play dumb, that was how you handled assholes like this. Play dumb, they loved to show off. "What?" He asked, blinking slow.

The man crossed his arms behind his head, grinning now. "What, you still don't get it? We really *did* do a good job. Even that freak you screw didn't catch on. Didn't any of you dust-brained dumbasses wonder how we got such good intel?"

Inyoni's gut knotted. He shook his head. "I ain't a spy, an' you ain't made me one, neither. You ain't been in my head."

The man's sneering grin widened. "Oh buddy are you ever wrong. You been one of our best sources of intel in years."

"No," Inyoni muttered past the lump forming in his throat. His hands started shaking; he pushed them together so hard his wrist clicked. "No, I ain't. I ain't done nothin' for you."

"You fed us everything we ever wanted every time you got in range." the man leaned forward. "Get it yet, dumbass?"

"How?" Inyoni asked, his voice small. "How'd you do it?"

Grinning, the man tapped the side of his neck. "Your little buddy. You're not the only ones with hackers, bub. Eagle works with Techo to keep the pipeline for personal masking tech nice and tight. You thought you went to some cut-rate CPS mech'n'tech who was on your side because you paid him?" He snorted a chuckle. Standing, he walked around Inyoni, put his hands on Inyoni's shoulders from behind and spoke right beside his ear.

"What you don't know is, those mech'n'techs charge so cheap because they're getting paid by *me*. I have them all on the payroll. And when things like you come in trying to hide, well, they've got their orders.

Every holo projector that gets implanted has a little surveillance setup stuck to the back of it. It gets implanted *inside* you, and you never see it. But we hear everything you do, and we *always* know where you freaks are. We want to get rid of you, we can pinpoint you any goddamn day of the week." He chuckled. His breath made Inyoni's ear twitch.

The asshole pulled his fancy-ass desk chair out and sat it down right in front of Inyoni, man-spreading like no other. He smiled, shaking his head. "I mean, you *really* thought you could run around my city without me keeping tabs on all your kind? We've *always* known about you. We've *always* watched your kind. The freaks. The perverts. The antisocials. We *always* track you. And when you get uppity, we *always* knock you back down. You thought you got to break those rules, did you, Birdie?"

"Inyoni Amanzi," he stated quietly. Just like they taught him on base. "Inyoni Amanzi, logistics specialist. I invoke my rights as a citizen of this State under the International Bill of Human Rights."

"Rights?" Hamilton laughed. "Your *rights*? Boy, you don't *have* rights. *I own you* and everyone like you. We decide if you live or die on a given day. See this?" He pulled a fob from his pocket and hung it on the chain that closed his jacket, patting it like a pet. "This is the control for your handcuffs. I'm holding your freedom in my hand, literally. And I always have been. All your weird, ugly little life, me and the men like me have been holding your leash. We decide what you buy. What jobs you work. We decide what you're *worth*. So don't even start with that *rights* shit. We're sending you back to work in a bit, so pay attention. Now that you're not just a passive source, we're going to need a lot more cooperative behavior from you."

Inyoni blinked, one ear flicking disinterestedly. "Back to…work?"

Hamilton sneered at him. "Poor birdie," he mocked. "Your brain's all fried from the heat, isn't it? Never seen somebody do so well in the Hot Box before, I'll give you that."

Man, I'm a fucking Gamma, Inyoni snorted silently. *And you're a fucking dumbass.* But he kept up the stupid act.

"What do you mean, you're sending me back to work?"

"You need to show me some respect when you talk to me," Hamilton came back. "You call me 'sir', got it?"

"What do you mean, you're sending me back to work?" Inyoni repeated patiently. One of the Peacekeepers slapped his head. "Sir," he tacked on.

"I mean, you're going back to that little farm of yours, and you're keeping your eyes and ears open." Hamilton replied, grinning all over his big fat face. "We got a lot to do to get back to normal around here. You're going to help us get some law and order back around here, by telling us what the Dusters are doing."

"And why'm I going to do that?" Here it came, head smack. "Sir," he added, getting done with this whole thing real damn quick.

Hamilton stroked the fob to Inyoni's cuffs. "You're going to do that because we've got an infiltrator on your base. And he's on orders to place a bomb in your hydroelectrics room. You cross the line, he sets it off, and your cute little house on the prairie setup goes boom."

Inyoni shook his head, ears gone flat. "I don't buy it." But his voice gave him away.

Hamilton smiled, slow and…yeah, evil, Inyoni decided. That was what evil looked like. Pulling out an expensive tab, he placed a call. "Yeah, Marshall? Deliver that package. Take a picture. But don't open it." Leaning back in his seat, Hamilton tapped his tab on the arm of his chair. "Like I said. Boom. Farm, wife and friends go bye-bye. Now, that's only what happens if you step out of line." He leaned in, smiling. "You toe that line? Well, then you get to go home. You go back to your wife. You get to see your baby grow up. You save the lives of all your friends. We get this country back to normal and calm everything down, that's all. We get everything back in order. And if you toe the line, well, then you and your wife and kid, you'll be just fine. Maybe you'll be even better than fine. We can do a guy a lot of good if he's a high-performing employee." Lifting his tab, Hamilton sprayed a fan of screens showing all kinds of adverts out around them. "You can have all of this. A good life. A normal life, once the country is settled down again. Move out of that rathole in the Dust, into a nice house. Drive a nice car. Get surgeries and genetic treatments for you and that little lady of yours. You'll have nice, normal lives, and you'll be secure for the rest of your days. We'll even make you Citizen Secure Standing. You'll watch your kid grow up safe and happy," Hamilton murmured coaxingly. "And all you have to do is keep doing what you've already been doing for years without knowing it." He leaned back, hands clasped. "So. What do you say? We got a deal?"

Inyoni blinked at him once, real slow. "I'm gonna say...I'm gonna say nah. Hell nah. NOW Tweak!"

Leaning back in the chair, he kicked with both feet, putting one foot on that fob, one foot right into Hamilton's gut.

Around him, the world went dark, and then it went apeshit. Every fire alarm, every sprinkler, and all those disorientation devices that Kevin and Topher had planted so carefully worked together to make the team of guards at Inyoni's back into a team of entries in the World Chunder Wheel Competition. All of them were either throwing up or reeling in seconds. Inyoni grinned as the cuffs on his wrists came undone, reared back in the chair and kicked Hamilton again. He was rolling out of the chair before the guards knew what was happening. A couple of them remembered their training and tried to go for him, but they just went straight down with their inner ears telling their brains that the floor was on the ceiling. Guns clattered as they fired, but the men aiming them were too slow, too slow to hit a Gamma when they were barely holding onto gravity and their lunch. Something pretty hot ran along the outside of Inyoni's forearm. Might have been a bullet. He'd check later. The head of EagleCorp sort of roll-fell out of his fancy chair, wheezing. "Shoot him, you idiots!"

"Fuck all y'all," Inyoni snarled, standing tall. Tweak and that doctor pal of Janice's had set him up with the little implants deep in the funnels of his ears to act as internal hearing protection, and those plus the contacts Tweak had gotten for his eyes were on point. He was the only one in the room who wasn't a complete fucking mess from the disorientation devices emitting supersonic tones and hyper-flashing lights to totally screw over a baseline human system. He turned his back, but Hamilton wasn't done yet. Lurching up, the big guy grabbed for Inyoni. "Fucking gamma freakshow! C'mere!" He shouted some racial shit and more shit about gammas too, almost lost in the wail of the fire alarms. His hands grappled for Inyoni's shirt. Inyoni let the asshole pull it off over his head. No big loss. "My name is Inyoni Amanzi," he called over the noise, stepping to one side and kneeing the son of a bitch in the gut. "Not Gamma! Not Citizen Fucked Standing! Not Freak! Not Bum! You hear me?! Inyoni Amanzi!" Hamilton threw up on him, but those giant hands still grabbed Inyoni's arm and tried to break it, felt like. Turning, Inyoni used their momentum to swing the bigger man across his desk on his belly. He didn't have time for this, and there was probably only one way to get an idea through this entitled bastard's head. Inyoni grabbed hold of Hamilton's skull and banged his head hard into the desk. Every word was underlined with the smack of human on wood.

"My!" *Thunk* "Name!" *Thunk* "Is!" *Thunk* "Inyoni!" *Thunk* " Amanzi!" *Thunk* "And! You! Don't! Tell! Me! What! To! Do!"

Finally, Hamilton stopped moving. Breathing hard, Inyoni looked around. Okay. Hamilton out of the way. Guards down and groaning. The room was still hazy with falling water from the sprinklers. He was good, but he needed his out.

"Bird!" Tweak's voice cried in his ear. He grinned for just a sec at the sound of her voice, before his heart twisted. "Dragon. You hear all that? You on base?!"

"Heard!" Tweak agreed breathlessly. "Bomb. Here. Eagle. Spy. Here. Omi's. On. It. You! Roof! Now! Plan!"

"You got it," Inyoni agreed. Stooping to pick a couple things off the belts of Peacekeepers and the floor he thought he might need, he booked it out into the hall. The plan. Okay, from here, he just followed the plan…oh, and the green arrows Tweak was projecting onto his contacts, showing him the right way to go. "Nice arrows," he muttered. "Focus," Tweak snapped.

It'd taken them a whole night of silently typing conversations back and forth once they got what must be going on and how they'd missed it. But the plan was perfect now. He passed some guards, but one was in the fetal position in a corner and another three were throwing up with their heads leaned against the wall. Stopping for a second, he grabbed a first aid kit off a wall; he'd need it.

The hardest thing about booking it out onto the roof of the EagleCorp building was the way the water for the sprinklers made all those nice smooth concrete floors into a giant slip'n'slide game. He nearly skidded off the stairs and went flying at one point, but gamma reflexes and the railing saved him.

The roof door snapped open ahead of him, and he was out, the night wind whipping roof cinders over his bare skin.

"Plane! For you! Ten m-m-minutes!" Tweak piped in his ear. He nodded. "Great. But I gotta do something 'fore I get in."

"What?"

"I gotta get rid of this bug they put in my holo. There's auto-pads here. It's no big." Inyoni laid what he'd grabbed out on the cinders. A tactical knife. A pack of autopads and a giant thing of disinfectant liquid out of the first aid kit. That'd be enough to do this.

They'd used him. They'd used the one thing he'd had to defend himself with and twisted it into a corporate tool. He'd betrayed the people he loved because of this thing. Fuck them. Fuck every last one of them. He slapped one of the autopads on his arm where a bullet had grazed. He prepped the second one, but didn't put it on just yet.

"G-get r-r-rid of it?!" Tweak yelped in his ear. "B-b-bird, I d-deactivated it!"

"And they'll reactivate it sometime," he replied, not sure if he was calm or crazy right this second. He lifted his knife and traced the edge of the holo in his neck; not hard enough to cut, just enough to get a feel for the spot. "Could be five seconds. Could be five days." He doused every bit of the knife and his hands in disinfectant, rubbing more on his neck. "Damian will g-get it out for you here, where it's c-c-c-clean and s-s-safe, you ass!" Tweak just about yelled in his ears.

Inyoni shook his head. "I can't come home with this in me. Can't wait. They used me, Tweak. Through this thing. I want it out tonight. I want it out *now*."

"Bird," Tweak demanded, "don't be a—"

"I gotta," Inyoni let the knife slide in as he interrupted his woman. "I gotta do this, Dragon. They used me. They don't get to use me anymore. I gotta fix it so they can't."

The knife slid and squelched. He dug in a careful circle, cutting the small metal disc out of his flesh. There. He had his fingers around it. Gave a good yank. The holo made a strange sucking sound as it came free, dangling by the wire that connected it to his heart. He sliced the wire. Something tight and weird happened in the middle of his chest, but he was still breathing okay, so he figured it was fine.

Dropping the bloody silver disc to the rooftop, he crushed it under his heel.

"My name is Inyoni Amanzi," he repeated. "I decide who I take orders from. They don't own me."

In his ear, his woman sighed. "Your. Name. Is. Jackass. K-k-Kevin and his t-t-team are c-clearing the b-b-building under you. I'm t-telling them. To come. Help you. Stay there. Don't m-move!"

"Thanks, Dragon," Inyoni murmured. Feeling a little loopy, he took a seat and situated the auto pad he'd gotten ready across the hole in his neck. "Love you."

"Don't. Even," Tweak's voice snapped back at him. "I'm so m-m-mad at you r-r-right now! Fucker! You b-b-bleed out, I'll k-k-kick your ass! Don't d-d-die! You hear me?" "I hear you," Inyoni agreed, closing his eyes. Down below, the sound of chanting marchers filled the night. Listening, he smiled.

Cursing, Tweak slammed from one communication window to another. "K-k-Kevin! In there! Deets?"

"If you mean how's the final dismantling and arrest proceeding, beautifully!" Kevin replied happily. "Once you let us know the situation with Inyoni's holo and the plan you'd laid down, the Force and the UN got a more than adequate contingent mustered. We're clearing the building floor by floor, but in reality we're scraping two thousand completely disoriented and demoralized EagleCorp people off the floor and shoveling them into their own prison buses!" Tweak could always tell when Kevin was happy, because when he was he wouldn't shut up. "The same thing is happening at every other EagleCorp station in the country. These poor saps couldn't beat the skin off a pudding at the moment; the few scuffles we've seen so far have been pure comedy. How's Bird?"

Finally, he gets to the fucking point, Tweak snarled in her head. "On the r-roof!" she managed, squeezing her throat and hoping like hell her stutter would fucking wait. "B-bleeding! Neck! Cut!"

"Oh damnation," Kevin griped, coming down off his high a little. "Alright, I'll grab a medical team and head up there. We've made it as far as the twentieth floor; we're close! Is he bleeding heavily?"

"Y-Yeah!" Tweak replied tightly. "Go go go!"

"I'm going!" Kevin called back.

Tweak flicked back to the drone camera she had on her guy; he looked mostly okay, lying on the roof with a big stupid grin on his face. She snorted. Moron. Thought he was in some kind of movie, pulling that big "cut this out of me" stunt. She was *so* making him feel that later. But he was going to be okay. Kevin would take care of him.

Slamming her coding chair back, she grabbed her tase knuckles off the wall by her desk and took off down the hall.

The hydroelectrics room had its door open when she got there, and Dozer and Cameron were circling some scrawny little asshole with an electro-knife. Naomi's feet were sticking out under the main hydroelectric pump.

"Omi!" Tweak skidded to her knees beside the woman. Please please *please* don't let her be dead. "You g-good?"

"I will be when people stop interrupting me while I'm trying to defuse a bomb," Naomi said patiently. "I got the remote detonation taken care of; now I just need to take the rest apart. Help with the infiltrator." She sounded as calm as ever. Yeah, she was fine. Tweak pushed off, going for the guy with the knife. She came in on his blind side and crashed her tase knuckles into the arm holding the electro-blade. The blue-buzzing knife skittered on the ground, sparking, as the asshole turned on her with a snarl. He swung for her; she ducked and kneed him in the balls. Bad move; didn't guard. He clocked her hard across the side of the head, and she went down. He should have gone down with her, she thought as the world spun. Damn, that usually worked. He should've gone down. He must be wearing a cup. At least he bent over though, and Dozer got ahold of him.

And then Dozer got a knife in the arm off the asshole's non-dominant hand. Blood sprayed.

"Fuck!" Dozer hissed. The weaselly guy twisted free of hands slick with blood, kicked Cameron hard in the gut and booked it, backup knife in one hand and dead arm hanging at his side. Tweak scrabbled to her feet. At the door, Jillian skidded into the weasel. "You asshole! You stop right—""

"Knife!" Tweak screamed. But it was already in Jillian's gut, already being dragged up and twisted through her. Beside her, Cameron let out a roar like a bull hit with a cattle prod. The EagleCorp asshole glanced back, had a kind of "oh shit" moment on his face, and booked it. Cameron took off after him like a rockslide with a grudge.

Dizzy, Tweak grabbed out her tab.

"WE NEED A MEDIC IN HYDRO NOW!!!"

She tapped out fast as she could. "Docs c-c-coming!" She yelped at Dozer. "M-med kit! W-wall!" Then she took off. She had to jump over Jillian, and that felt like shit, but she was no doc. She couldn't help a cut up woman. What she could do was kick ass. So that was what she'd go and do.

"Clear!" She shouted, taking off down the hall after the sound of Cameron's feet slamming on the floor. They were heading for the garage; the asshole must be thinking he could get out on a bike. And he probably could, with Dozer bleeding back in the hydroelectrics room and Janice off-base. Dammit!

She skidded to a stop as she came around the corner and into the straight hall that led to the garage. That was where Cameron had caught up with the infiltrator. He was still stamping on the ribcage when Tweak made it there; the weird crack of ribs inside a body made her want to hurl. It definitely wasn't a living body anymore though. Cameron had beaten the guy's head into something like hamburger with rice in it. Teeth. That rice was teeth. Tweak did lose it then, dry-heaving as Cameron kicked the body he'd broken up and down the hall a few times. Tweak didn't know what made him stop, but he wound down after a while. Standing over the corpse, he breathed hard, spattered in blood. Then he walked over to a corner, curled up in it like a giant kid, and started to sob.

"Tweak?" She looked up as Aidan knelt beside her.

"You okay?" He asked quietly.

She nodded, wiping her mouth just in case. "Fine. Dozer? J-Jill? Bomb?"

"Naomi took care of the bomb," Aidan reassured. "We're safe. Dozer's going to be fine. They've got Jillian in surgery."

Tweak nodded. Swallowing, she nodded down the hall.

"Cam?"

For a beat, Aidan closed his eyes. Then he opened them, and gave her a tired smile. "I'll take care of Cam. Go tell everybody to leave us alone in this hall for a couple hours. Give us some space. Then go get a shower, kay? You've got blood on you."

Tweak nodded. "Kay."

The hot water felt like the slap that brought her back to reality. She changed into clean clothes. She checked her screens, but everybody had already handled the things that needed to be handled. All she had to do now was chill. And that was the hardest thing to do.

She went down to the crib. In the quiet softness, with babies and toddlers playing, Billie wrapped her up in a hug.

"You okay?" Billie whispered in her ear. Tweak shook her head.

"Hang out here?" Her oldest, best friend asked. Tweak nodded.

"Cool. We got snacks," Billie agreed. A couple seconds later, there was a plate of crackers and chocolate by her hand, and Bao Li was being settled in her arms.

Tweak stared down at her baby, feeling the tears that she couldn't get rid of itching behind her eyes.

Inyoni had just cut his own neck open like a pack of sandwich meat. Like a crazy man. She knew she had the crazy in her, right under the surface. She'd lost it so many times on people who touched her or messed with her head. And Cameron had so much crazy it came out his ears. He'd just kicked a guy to death. Actually kicked a guy to death.

If that was what gammas could do, what would her daughter do one day?

Had Bao Li gotten born without the crazy in her genes? Or was it just waiting to explode inside her too?

The tears came now. Tweak wiped them on her baby's blanket. She didn't know how long she sat there in the soft quiet with her kid. She gasped when a shadow crossed over them, but it was just Billie sitting beside her.

"Aidan wants to come talk," Billie offered quietly. "It okay if he comes in?"

Swallowing, Tweak nodded.

Softly, Aidan took a seat beside her.

"Hey."

"Hey," Tweak agreed. "Whazzup?"

"Inyoni's safe; he's getting treated down in Denver. Jillian's in surgery," Aidan offered. "Cameron's sedated. Dozer's arm looks good. The base is safe. Everything here is secured. And now they want me down in Denver. Apparently I got chosen in the first sortition for a committee tasked with putting the city back together." He made a face. She cracked a watery little smile. "Poor b-bastard."

"You're telling me," Aidan agreed. "I thought I'd finally get to take a fucking break after all this." Closing his eyes, he relaxed back against the pillows. "Dammit, I thought I was almost done." Then he cracked an eye, and sort of smiled at Tweak. "But I didn't come in here to bitch and moan; I came in here to say, since they need me down there anyway, I offered to drive a supply truck of food and stuff down. You want to ride down to Denver with me? We pretty much own the city now. We can go check on Bird if you want."

"Yeah?" Tweak asked, swallowing.

"Yeah," Aidan agreed. "You want?"

Drawing a breath, Tweak nodded.

Aidan checked over the big supply truck on automatic, helping the agriculture team make sure the boxed produce in the back was secure. He hadn't been this tired in a long time. The constant adrenaline hits of the last couple weeks made him feel like crawling under a blanket and staying there. But they were almost through this part. Almost done. Almost. Almost done.

"You're ready to go!" One of Milo's guys called out cheerfully, slapping the side of the truck as he hopped out. Aidan gave him a smile. "Thanks Al. Be back in two days. Seeya."

Tweak got into the truck on the passenger side, silent and ready in her big black leather jacket. He knew better than to try to make her talk. If she wanted to, she would.

A couple hours, and they could drive right into town. The road was clear; they could go straight to the fabrication plant where Janice, Milo and Kevin were staying with Inyoni until he was safe to move. And then he could fucking *rest*. At least, for a little while.

It came to Aidan that Tweak might be a little freaked out by what her guy had done to himself. Granted, he couldn't feel it, so when Inyoni cut himself it wasn't the same as what Aidan used to do to himself. But when he'd done it, Kevin had been just about scared stiff. Was Tweak going through that now? Was that why she was so quiet?

"Inyoni's okay in the head, y'know," he started gently, "not just the body. I know what he did looked scary—and don't get me wrong, it was *stupid* — but I don't think he's going to go the way Cameron does."

Tweak glanced at him for a moment. Then she rolled her eyes.

"Missed. The. Point. Boss."

"Okay. Want to tell me what I got wrong?" Aidan offered. Tweak snorted. "We're in the m-middle of a w-w-war and you're still talking like a psych-bot?"

"Nobody needs psych help as much as people in a war, Tweak," he offered quietly as he navigated over a rise. "I think we both know that. So come on and talk to me."

Tweak gave a teenager-worthy sigh, and dug out her tab.

"Look, I'm worried about Bao Li," Tweak's voice came out of the device in her lap as she typed. She'd really nailed that program; it sounded exactly the way she would without a stutter. Aidan nodded. "What about her?"

"I'm worried that one of these days, it'll be her turn to go crazy. Gammas go crazy. I beat up Damian that time. Inyoni cut his own neck open. Cameron just kicked a guy to death. What if she got that?"

"You think that's a Gamma thing?" Aidan asked quietly. "Can't say I agree."

"What's that mean?" Tweak asked. Aidan worked his way down a tricky wash as he talked. "I used to cut my legs open when things got bad. Kevin went crazy a couple different times. Lazarus *was* crazy, pretty much all the time. Naomi knocked me over and whaled on me a bit once. Gammas don't have the monopoly on crazy, is what I'm saying. And your kid? If we raise her so she's not dealing with so much bullshit pulling her down, maybe she won't have to go crazy just to survive what her own head and heart are doing to her."

He spared a moment to look over at one of his best people and smile. The little woman smiled in return, swallowing hard. She typed without looking down.

"Thanks Aidan."

"Hey, it's what I'm here for," Aidan reassured, looking back at the landscape out ahead of them.

The ride was pretty quiet after that. Aidan didn't bother with the radio; either they'd hear stuff they couldn't do anything about right now, or they'd get a bunch of chatter and music. What they needed right now was quiet. So they drove in silence, passing stalled vehicles of all kinds in the ditch.

They were halfway down the I-70, and Aidan was really starting to relax. Things were looking good. Aside from all the random vehicles in the ditches, the roads were clear. Maybe this wasn't going to be so...

FUCK. Aidan slammed the brakes as a bunch of guys stepped out from behind a pulled-over semi and aimed guns at him. The truck brakes squealed, skidding them to a stop.

"Oh you have got to be fucking kidding me," Aidan groaned.

"Should've k-kept d-d-driving!" Tweak hissed.

"And then they would have shot us," Aidan murmured back, eyes fixed on the men ahead. "Stay in the truck, Tweak."

Carefully, he got out of the truck, hands up.

"We're unarmed!" he called. "Food and supply transport! Humanitarian aid!"

"This vehicle is required by ArgusCo!" one of the guys with guns barked. "Stand aside!"

Aidan glanced at the truck in the ditch. Two tires out. Three guys in suits waiting in the cab with a cooling system running.

"You mean those guys?" He asked, tipping his head towards the truck. "Because ArgusCo doesn't exist anymore. The United Nations froze all the assets of all their officers, you hear about that? They can't pay you."

"Shut up!" One of the men barked, leveling his weapon. "On your knees."

Aidan shrugged, and got on his knees. "Your loss," he sighed as he put his hands behind his head. No sense doing anything else, with this many antsy trigger fingers around.

For a moment, the hired men were silent, hesitating.

"What do you mean, they can't pay us?" one of the men asked. The guy in the middle of the line swung his weapon at what Aidan guessed was his subordinate. "Shut it, Longstreet."

"I dunno cap, I want to hear this. We're three weeks back on our pay already," A guy on his other side stated. His tone was neutral, but Aidan could see the way these guys were leaning. They were already frazzled and pissed.

The one who was probably leading this protection detail pointed his gun at Aidan. "Explain."

"The United Nations declared the corporations to be criminal entities. They've frozen the assets of all the corporate officers," Aidan explained calmly. "The Democratic State Council has been declared the legitimate governing body, and the Democratic State Force is their army.

So yeah. It's official." He nodded at the truck. "You can run with those guys, but they can't give you anything anymore. And they're not going to get very far. So, at this point, you guys can steal my truck and take food meant for little kids and old ladies for those guys over there to eat, and you can keep driving for the border, and you'll probably end up like the extras in a bad action vid." He shrugged, getting to his feet. "Or you can let me call in for an arrest detail to pick up those guys in the truck, we can leave them some food and water, and you can get in the back of the truck with me. We can ride down to Denver, have a snack, and we can start finding you guys some new gigs. Free food, free housing. Not watching your back every second. Not taking orders from shmucks who think they're a higher life form. How's that sound?"

"And get arrested for complicity?" one of the protection detail snarled. "Oh, yeah, no thanks."

Smiling, Aidan shook his head. "No arrests, unless you do a crime now. Only the Corporate brass, the big guys, are getting arrested on sight. You guys had a job you got hired for, and you did a job. Now it's time to change jobs. Most people are going to be changing jobs; no big deal. Unless you shoot somebody in cold blood? You're just another American now. And we need hands to help us unload all this food. So yeah. You take off the helmets, you pull the ammo out of these guns and leave them behind, you're just more hands to help us out. And we need everybody's hands. We'd be glad to have you."

"Enough of this shit," the lead snarled, pulling up his gun.

Well, I tried, Aidan thought, staring down the barrel.

BANG!

Five guns went off. The lead man of the security detail was dead before he hit the road.

The air rang with echoes. The world froze.

Carefully, one of the security detail set his gun down. With both hands, he reached up and pulled off his helmet. Underneath, he was a haggard man well into his sixties. He glanced from the body of his former leader to Aidan.

"Self defense?" He suggested. Aidan gave him a smile of acknowledgement.

"Definitely self defense. Can I call in this arrest?"

A man who was barely more than a teen pulled off his helmet and gave Aidan a nod. "We'd appreciate that. Thanks."

The drive down into Denver was surreal. Aidan had expected tension. But no, there was a giant half-party-half-cleaning brigade going on as he came down Broadway. People were scraping up broken glass here and there, waving at each other across the street, hanging the new American flag up from street signs and anything else that held still long enough. Getting off the main streets, Aidan headed the truck down into the warehouse district, flashing his credentials on the truck's HUD as they approached just in case people were feeling nervy. Not like they didn't have a good reason to be.

It was Janice who opened the door of the unionized fabrication hub. Planting a hand on her hip, she grinned at them. "Well look at you two. And who's all them?"

"Hands to help us unload the truck," Aidan explained. He waved at their new allies. "Bring it in here guys, they'll show you!" Then he got out of the way as Tweak almost elbowed him aside.

"Jan. Where's. Bird?"

Janice grinned. "Thought you'd ask. C'mon this way. Aidan? Those new guys need beds?"

"Yeah, and everything else," Aidan agreed. Janice nodded. Turning, she cupped her hands around her mouth. "Milo! Abbie! Food truck!" Then she turned in another direction "Kat!" she bawled. "You holla?"

"I holla!" Someone down the floor shouted.

"Newbies! Need the goods!"

"You got it!"

Janice nodded to herself. "Kat'll take care of them. C'mon you two," She continued in normal tones. Aidan resisted the instinct to rub at his ears as he followed Janice. *Man,* could she yell.

A back room of the warehouse had been retrofitted into a medical unit. "Don't lay into him too hard," Janice suggested as she led them down the line of cots. "I did that already."

"Roger that," Aidan agreed. Tweak just snorted.

On a chair beside his bed, Inyoni was sitting with a tab in his hand. He looked ashy, but his big long ears were perked, so he was in a good mood. He glanced up, and a slow smile of wonder blossomed like a flower in his face.

"Dragon!"

Tweak stopped in front of his chair, little fists on her hips and head on one side.

She stared down at him with unfathomable black eyes. Inyoni swallowed hard as he looked up at her, his ears going down like deflating balloons. "Hey…guess you…uh, made it in okay, huh?"

"Yeah. I did." Tweak stated quietly. "Bird. Stand up."

Inyoni stood up carefully, leaning against the table, his ears pinned back. "I in trouble?"

Tweak nodded, studying him for a long, long moment. "Yeah. You are. You ok? No lie."

Inyoni smiled weakly. "Yeah. I'm okay. They gave me a blood transfusion, so I'm okay. Long as this doesn't get infected 'fore the new skin attaches." He tapped the autopad on his neck. "Long as it stays clean, I'll be good."

"Good." Tweak nodded. Then she slapped her husband, hard. The slap came adder-fast and completely out of left field. The crack made Aidan flinch. "That's for freaking me, you s-s-stupid twat!" Tweak snapped out. "Thought I was g-g-gonna l-lose you. Jackass!"

"Sorry," Inyoni muttered, his flat ears making him look like a kicked dog. At his sides, his hands fluttered helplessly, giving the illusion that the feathers tattooed on his arms were rustling. "I…didn't know what else to do. They were killin' our friends 'cause of me."

Aidan felt for the kid there. Maybe he should step in, but—

"Stupid." Tweak spat before Aidan had more than two seconds to think. In the blink of an eye,she'd stepped in, stood on Inyoni's feet, grabbed one of his ears in either hand and yanked him down for a hard kiss. Carefully, Inyoni's arms slid around Tweak's waist and pulled her close. Aidan blinked a couple times. Talk about a quick turn-around.

"That's 'cause you lived." Tweak stated when the two of them came up for air. "Never s-scare me l-like that again."

"Won't," Inyoni promised gently, kissing her again. "Nothin' to do that's scary no more."

"Good." Tweak whispered, her gold-scaled arms picking up the light of Inyoni's shining tattoos and gleaming with them. "C-c-can't lose you. L-l-love you..."

"Same," Inyoni muttered.

"They really are sweet, aren't they, love?"

Aidan's heart danced in his chest. Turning, he grinned at his husband. Kevin held his arms open, and Aidan fell into them.

"Not sweet," Tweak put in, which kind of threw the moment. "Sweet. Can. Fuck. Off. Kevin."

For the first time in way too many days, Aidan heard his husband's laugh again. Damn that was a good sound.

"You're a cretin, you know that?" Kevin retorted, arms holding Aidan close as he teased Tweak.

"Man, I don't even know what that is!" Inyoni grumbled.

"My point exactly," Kevin came back.

Tweak snorted, rolling her eyes. "Get. Lost. CES."

"As her highness demands," Kevin chuckled, his slim fingers interlaced with Aidan's. "Come on love. Let's find a quiet corner of our own."

After the last couple days they'd had and the way Kevin had showed how happy he was that they were together again, Aidan slept like the dead. He only woke up because Kevin's fingers brushed his hair, pulling him awake.

"Come on, love," Kevin coaxed. "We've got a committee meeting to get to."

"Yeah," Aidan groaned in acknowledgement. "I know…" Rolling over in the bed they'd been given in a back office, he reached for his tab. "Time is it?"

"Fourteen hundred, we've got two hours to get ready and get over to Capitol Hill," Kevin murmured, kissing his cheek.

Aidan scrubbed at his face with both hands. "What's the word from the base?" He asked through a yawn.

"Liza and Naomi report good security, Milo's team reports that the crops are healthy and that the new gene-modded native seed mix is doing splendidly." Kevin pulled off his glasses, polishing them.

"There is some unfortunate news as well. I'm afraid…well, I'm afraid Jillian didn't survive."

Aidan winced, closing his eyes. "Fuck."

"Indeed," Kevin agreed softly. "Billie's got Cameron set up with childcare support. He's out of sedation; he's…well, Damian says he's a wreck. They're beginning therapy."

"I hate to ask," Aidan admitted, "but it's my job. Is he going to be a danger to the team?"

Kevin shook his head. "No, he won't be a danger to our crew. Nor to himself. Damian and Alice have it in hand. We've scheduled the memorial for a week from now."

Aidan sighed. "Okay. Good to know. So how dressy is this event?"

Perching his glasses on his nose again, Kevin held out a hand. "I've got suits for us. Come on."

Aidan blinked at him. "Suits? How'd you pull that off?"

Kevin chuckled and wiggled his fingers. "Logistics, it's my forte. Now, let's get you ready."

An hour later, Kevin looked down at him with soft grey eyes. "You know, you look rather gorgeous in a suit." Kevin had done him up in a deep blue suit and blue-grey tie that, yeah, did make him look good. Kevin had dressed to compliment him in a classy blue-grey double-breasted getup and a tie that matched Aidan's suit.

Aidan sighed and adjusted his tie. "I feel like I'm wearing a costume. This's weird."

Kevin gave him a patient smile. "Welcome to legitimacy?"

Aidan went on fiddling with his tie, just for something to keep him occupied. "Sorry. Just…ugh." He didn't have words for the way his gut was twisting up, the way his head was starting to get staticky. He could handle a base full of friends and comrades, but a committee full of total strangers? Making sure they could rebuild the country in a way that was good for everyone? That was totally different.

Or…was it? Wasn't this exactly how he'd felt seven years ago, when he was riding over to meet the Wildcards for the first time? And that had turned out okay. So maybe…

"Hey." Kevin tipped his chin up with two fingers, and kissed him softly. "Don't wander off now. This is what we fought for." He followed up with a kiss for Aidan's brow. "I love you. And I'll be there with you."

"Love you, too," Aidan muttered. Despite their nice, new suits, he stepped forward and wrapped his arms around Kevin in a tight hug. Kevin's arms enfolded him, gently stroking his back. He took several deep breaths, breathing in his husband's scent as he muttered, "What if we fuck it up?"

"Then we'll learn from it." Kevin murmured, gently stroking Aidan's hair. "And we'll be better than we were. Have faith, love."

Aidan nodded weakly, and forced himself to step back. He smiled as best he could, twining his fingers in Kevin's. "Well…I guess we should go face the music."

Kevin nodded, and squeezed his hand so that their wedding bands clicked together. "Carpe diem."

Aidan nodded, trying for a smile. "Let's hope it's what you think it is…"

"Pessimist," Kevin teased as they opened the factory door.

The temperature wasn't too bad today, and people were holding another day of their general block party. Pulverized concrete crunched underfoot as the two men walked up the street. The sound of laughter, push-brooms and people cleaning the streets mixed together in the cooling wind. Kevin caught his eye and grinned, and Aidan couldn't help but grin back.

All the ad holos were turned off, and without their noise and color, you could really see how pretty the gold of the afternoon light was. They crossed a bunch of little side streets and headed along Colfax, which had so many tables laid out on it that it looked like a big buffet. Up ahead, there was cheering, whoops and hollers.

Hand in hand, they entered the plaza in front of the old Capitol building just in time to see a flag raised on an aluminum strut in front of the big marble obelisk. It had been showcasing a couple of corporate logo flags before. Now, what was going up was their flag. The new American flag. It gleamed in the golden summer light.

"Holy shit," Aidan whispered, staring wide-eyed at the celebration around him. He'd known, logically, that something like this might happen, but he'd never really expected to see it. Now, somehow, here he was. *They'd won.* They'd brought down the Corps, for good. All around them, people were laughing, hugging each other. jumping up and down. Hands waved. The cheering was deafening.

Aidan glanced at his husband. Kevin was staring at the flag as if it was…Aidan didn't know what. As if it was the Holy Grail, maybe. There were tears on his pale cheeks. Slowly, moving like he didn't even know he was doing it, Kevin put his hand over his heart. His voice was soft at first, quavering, but it rose in those gorgeous tenor tones of his, and people turned to watch him sing.

"Oh, say can you see by the dawn's early light
What so proudly we hailed at the twilight's last gleaming?"

Aidan had to smile, shaking his head. The old American anthem. Of course Kevin would dust that old thing off and start singing it today, big sap that he was. What Duster didn't know this song, the one you sang after a few beers when you were talking about old times and dead buddies?

Around Kevin, veteran Dusters grinned. Other voices joined Kevin's.

"Whose broad stripes and bright stars through the perilous fight,
O'er the ramparts we watched were so gallantly streaming?"

The song had started out thin, but it swelled as people shared the words with each other on their tabs. Now the song was something new. For the first time in who knew how many years, this song wasn't a lament: it was a victory hymn.

"And the rocket's red glare, the bombs bursting in air,
Gave proof through the night that our flag was still there.
Oh, say does that star-spangled banner yet wave
O'er the land of the free and the home of the brave?"

By the middle of the song, more than half the crowd was singing or humming along, Aidan right there with them. He turned and wrapped his arms around his husband, holding him tight. He wasn't even sure what to feel—happy, proud, anxious about the future, relieved that the bloodshed was over, some strange mix of all of it. But he knew that right here, right now, this was right. Closing his eyes, he raised his voice and sang.

"And the star-spangled banner in triumph shall wave
O'er the land of the free and the home of the brave!"

Kevin's face was wet with tears when he finished the last note, laughing and crying at once as he kissed the top of Aidan's head. "Aidan. We've...we've won. We did it..."

"I guess miracles do happen," Aidan whispered into Kevin's neck. He stepped back with an anxious grin. "Now we just have to make sure we don't fuck up the next bit."

Kevin cracked up laughing, tears still shining on his cheeks. "You horrendous discrutator! I ought to—"

"Commander Headly-McIllian?" A skinny Duster stepped over. She saluted, then held out her hand to shake. "Great to meet you, heard about you, anyway we're needed at the committee. This way. By the way, it's June," she added. "Figure we all might as well get used to first name basis; we're not soldiers anymore."

Aidan grinned at her. "Sounds good. It's Aidan."

"Oh, I think everybody knows your name,"June laughed. "Your unit's a legend. If I'm right, you're going to be a guest of honor at the dinner after the first committee meeting."

Aidan bit back a groan at that and raked his fingers through his hair. He glanced at his husband. "Is it too late to back out now?" He asked, only half-joking.

"Most definitely so," Kevin retorted gently, putting a hand in the small of his back and pushing him forward softly. "Come on, love. Time to reap what you've sown so diligently."

Aidan groaned, but let his husband usher him forward. When he saw the number of people gathered in the rotunda of the old state capitol, he wanted to crawl into a hole. So many strangers. So many *eyes*. He took a deep breath and walked into the crowd with as much dignity as he could manage. He felt like an actor who hadn't prepped for his part. He felt like a fake in the suit he was wearing. But Kevin squeezed his hand, and he kept walking.

Whispers started up like a wind in dry grass, the name "Aidan Headly" being passed from mouth to mouth as people turned to stare at him. Hands slapped him on the back, people called out greetings. "You going to give a speech?" someone called from the back. Aidan looked pleadingly up at his husband. Why was everyone looking at him? He wasn't a hero. He wasn't any more impressive than any of these other commanders, certainly not the Quadrant Commanders, who had more on their plates than he'd ever had. And here they all were, treating him like some kind of icon. It made him want to shake all of them until they saw sense.

"All right, all right!" Quadrant Commander Oray called, stepping into the middle of the gathering. He wasn't wearing his Duster BDUs, or even his formal Force uniform. He'd dressed as a Ute tribal chieftain today, the feathers of his war bonnet framing his face and his beaded vest showing symbols of his acts as a leader gleaming in the overhead lights. Aidan had never seen this side of his Quadrant Commander. Man, and here he'd been intimidating in his BDUs. In the regalia of leadership for the Ute Nation, Commander Ouray was a force of nature.

"We all know what we're here for!" Commander Ouray called. He held up his tab. "We've got our mandate from the United Communities of America. We've got votes on first priorities for Denver, and for the West. Everyone, take your seats. Let's get to work, we got to get this country back on its feet!"

Amid thunderous applause, the first committee of the United Communities of America took their seats.

"Bao Li, you silly girl! What are you doing up in that tree?" Kevin called teasingly, looking up at his impossibly precocious daughter.

"Swinging!" The five-year-old called down. And indeed, she was swinging by her knees from a sturdy branch, her kinky red-brown hair haloed out around her head. Kevin tipped his head, meeting her eyes with a grin. "But it's not swinging time, little treasure! It's language time! Are you going to come down?"

"Nope!" The little girl giggled. "I can language inna tree!" The wide, rabbit-like ears that had so quickly given her the nickame 'Bunny' were perked in joy as she swung, enjoying the sight of the world upside down.

"Yes, but it's easier to talk when you're down here," Kevin coaxed. "Come sit with Jenny and sing the cabbage song!" Jenny sat beside him at the trunk of the tree, singing like a bird. For a six-year-old her French accent was fairly good.

"Savez-vous planter les choux?

A la mode, à la mode!"

Up in the tree, Bunny threw her arms out and joined in.

"Savez-vous planter les choux?

A la mode de chez nous!"

Kevin smiled up at his little treasure. Well, let her practice her French in the tree; it wasn't hurting anything.

"I see Mama!" Bunny sang out, and scrambled down to run to Tweak. Kevin had to laugh as Tweak picked the girl up and joined him. "Oh, of course she gets out of the tree for *you*."

"Yep," Tweak agreed with a quick smile, boosting their daughter up onto her hip and looking up at the tree. "How's the c-crop?"

"Coming along," Kevin acknowledged easily. "And how about the new work roster? Did that algorithm bug get fixed? I couldn't schedule anyone yesterday without it throwing a bloody error code a minute."

"Done," Tweak chirped. "I l-loaded deets. Of the fix. Up on the c-c-c-Common Ground. We're good."

"Wonderful," Kevin enthused, "Then you can join Aidan and Milo and I for a picnic and a native plant class. We're giving a talk on our native forbs to a bus full of visitors up from Denver."

"Cool," Tweak agreed, her scales glittering like metal in the filtered sun between the leaves of the fruit tree. "Milo's gonna do the t-t-talking?"

"Indeed," Kevin agreed. "Billie's got the lunches packed. Treasure? Jenny? Do you want to go outside the pylons today?"

"Yeah!" the two little girls shrilled, jumping up and down.

"Well then!" Kevin laughed. "Let's go get cooling jackets and hats and sunglasses! Jenny! You need sunscreen! Allons-y!"

Inside, Aidan met them with a tab in one hand and a picnic basket in the other. "Ah," Kevin teased, lifting the tab out of his hand and tucking it in his own back pocket, "You're going with us to take a break, love. Not to work. Did you put on sunscreen?"

"Yeah I did," Aidan agreed with a sheepish smile and a peck for Kevin's cheek. "Are we good on time?"

"As long as the little ones don't take a week to get dressed, we are," Kevin agreed.

"I got them dressed," Inyoni called, coming down the hall with Bao Li on his hip and another basket in his hand. "Um…they kinda told Mo, and the rest of the crib, so…" A cadre of the farm's children trotted happily behind him, Billie appearing like a Madonna among the children with her gentle smile. At Inyoni's heels, Jenny was walking hand in hand with four-year-old Miriam, who looked up at Billie with Topher's smile and Billie's own dark eyes. Everyone called her Mo these days, and Kevin had to wonder what she'd think of *that* as she aged. But then again, everyone on this farm had a nickname. Perhaps it wouldn't matter.

Aidan glanced up at Kevin with a wry smile. "So now we're taking all of them?"

"That we are," Kevin agreed, a mix of joy and chagrin in his voice. He loved the children dearly, but they were more than a handful outside the pylons. Or inside them, for that matter.

"I'll come along and watch the kids," Billie offered.

"I'll give you a hand!" Liza called, trotting down the hall with a backpack full of what Kevin was sure would be extra hats, sunscreen, and probably a first aid kit. "I heard there was a class, and Del's got everything taken care of in our department." Aidan gave the two women a relieved grin. Kevin could almost read "oh thank God" written across his forehead. He still marveled at this quirk of his husband; this incredible diplomat who had proved that he could talk any arguing rabble into a smoothly working committee time and time again was, all the same, terrified of watching the kids from his own community by himself. It really was adorable.

"Thanks guys," Aidan acknowledged. Then he raised his voice. "Okay, everybody hold hands, we're going to the gate! Stick with your group when we're outside!" The happy crowd of children became a more-or-less orderly daisy chain at the words of their compound custodian.

Up on the gate, the two men Dozer was training waved, and Kevin waved up at them as they opened the main gate out onto the prairie. Fewer people called it the Dust these days, and for good reason.

Outside, gramma grass and junegrass waved green-gold in the nearly tolerable heat of late afternoon, stretching as far as the eye could see. The drone seeding program was going incredibly well. For more than two hundred square miles around Four Aces Farm, the land was prairie again. They'd start reintroducing animals fairly soon; the official vote on biome improvement was next month, and after that, they could begin to grow the embryos.

Genetically adapted buffalo grass cushioned every step, sweetly springy under Kevin's feet. Taking his husband's hand, he headed out to meet the visitors from the city, his daughter running ahead of him.

For a moment, Kevin glanced back at his home. Over the gate, the flag of the United Communities of America flew in the golden sky. He smiled, feeling his heartstrings give a twang. Even now, sights like that could catch him off his guard and bring everything into a clarity so sharp it hurt.

I am so very, very lucky.

We all are.

"Kev?" His husband asked, looking back with a smile. "You coming?"

Kevin adjusted his glasses as a cover for the wiping of his eyes."Of course. Let's go." Kissing his husband's brow, he strode after his running daughter and the other children, eager to see what they'd learn today.

A Note From The Commander

If you're ready to make changes, you're not alone. Reach out. Get connected.

Hi. Aidan here. So yeah, we just won our country back and changed the whole game. And you're thinking that's because it's fiction. But you know what? In your world, there's people making big changes too. A bunch of them are listed off here. You want things to get better in your life, your country, or your world? These people can help. Reach out, connect up. Get involved. Change happens slow, but every day matters. Take it day by day, and together we'll get there.

   —Aidan.

WorldCat

WorldCat.org is a great resource for locating unique, trustworthy materials that you often can't find anywhere except in a library. And by connecting thousands of libraries' collections in one place, WorldCat.org makes it easy for you to browse the world's libraries from one easy search box.

Check it out at https://search.worldcat.org/about

IndieWeb

The IndieWeb is a people-focused alternative to the corporate web.

It is a community of independent and personal websites connected by open standards and based on the principles of: owning your domain and using it as your primary online identity, publishing on your own site first (optionally elsewhere), and owning your content.

Check it out at https://indieweb.org

Climate Justice Alliance

Climate Justice Alliance (CJA) formed in 2013 to create a new center of gravity in the climate movement by uniting frontline communities and organizations into a formidable force. Their translocal organizing strategy and mobilizing capacity is building a just transition away from extractive systems of production, consumption and political oppression, and towards resilient, regenerative and equitable economies. They believe that the process of transition must place race, gender and class at the center of the solutions equation in order to make it a truly just transition.

Read more and get involved at https://climatejusticealliance.org/

Sprout Distro: How To Start An Affinity Group

This zine is a basic overview of how to form an affinity group. Goes over the basic components of affinity groups: assembling a group, developing and carrying out a plan of action, and consensus.

Check it out at

https://www.sproutdistro.com/catalog/zines/organizing/how-to-form-affinity-group

How to Start a Tenant's Association

A group of tenants can collectively exert more pressure for their views than an individual tenant can on their own. Tenants try to work together for a common goal, to make their lives and living situations better. While the landlord may find it easy to ignore individual tenant demands, a group of tenants speaking with one voice may be harder to ignore.

Read more at:

https://homelinemn.org/organizing/form-a-tenant-association/
and http://tenant.net/Organize/Lenox/lh-1.html

Rebel Steps: Community Support and Mutual Aid

When people first set out to make a difference, they often gravitate toward charity. Yet charity has existed for eons, and the poor are still poor. Learn about the difference between charity and mutual aid projects. Check it out at https://rebelsteps.com/episodes/5-support-your-community.html

How To Start A Union

If you and your coworkers are interested in organizing together, CWA will help you build majority support during your campaign. CWA will provide you with support and guidance after you and your co-workers take the first steps to forming your union.

Here's a brief summary of where to start.https://cwa-union.org/join-union/how-organize

It's Going Down

It's Going Down is a digital community center for anarchist, anti-fascist, autonomous anti-capitalist and anti-colonial movements across so-called North America. Our mission is to provide a resilient platform to publicize and promote revolutionary theory and action. Check them out at https://itsgoingdown.org/

Tips for Protesting Peacefully and Safely

Every person has the right to protest against the injustices marginalized groups face every day, so the Human Rights Campaign has compiled tips for protesting safely and peacefully. Get geared up and learn the tips and tricks at https://www.hrc.org/news/tips-for-protesting-peacefully-and-safely

Make Change: How-To's for Effective Peaceful Protest

Taking to the streets in peaceful protest is a sacred right of all Americans, enshrined in the First Amendment to the Constitution. Here's how to make what you need for safe, peaceful, and effective protest. https://commonslibrary.org/make-change-how-tos-for-effective-peaceful-protest/#Introduction

KNOW YOUR RIGHTS: Protesters' Rights

The First Amendment protects your right to assemble and express your views through protest. However, police and other government officials are allowed to place certain narrow restrictions on the exercise of speech rights. Make sure you're prepared by brushing up on your rights before heading out into the streets.

https://www.aclu.org/know-your-rights/protesters-rights

The Bail Project

The Bail Project strives for a more perfect justice system, one that works for all people no matter their race or wealth.

Get help at this link: https://bailproject.org/help

Get involved at https://bailproject.org/donate/

The NAACP's Legal Defense and Educational Fund

The NAACP's Legal Defense and Educational Fund uses litigation, advocacy, and public education to work towards racial justice and equality for all Americans. The organization is fighting to protect voting rights, reform the criminal justice system, and improve equal access to education, among other civil rights causes. https://www.naacpldf.org/

Fair Fight

Voter suppression is widespread and endemic in this country, and an election year is yet another reminder that our government cannot make progress until people of color are not disenfranchised at an alarming rate. This organization, founded by Stacy Abrams, is working to ensure free and fair elections. https://fairfight.com/

Doughnut Economics Action Lab (DEAL)

The one doughnut that's good for you! Doughnut Economics Action Lab (DEAL) is part of the emerging global movement of new economic thinking and doing. The organization's aim is to help create 21st century economies that are regenerative and distributive by design, so that they can meet the needs of all people within the means of the living planet. They call this Doughnut Economics.

The organization works with changemakers worldwide – in communities, education, cities and places, business and government and more – who are turning the ideas of Doughnut Economics into transformative action and aiming to bring about systemic change.

Check it out and get involved at

https://doughnuteconomics.org/about

A Guide to Degrowth: The Movement Prioritizing Wellbeing in a Bid to Avoid Climate Cataclysm

The current economic system sacrifices both people and environments at a time when everything from shifting weather patterns to rising sea levels is global in scope and unprecedented in nature. How do we handle it? By living better with less.Check out the basics of the idea at:

https://www.cnbc.com/2021/02/19/degrowth-pushing-social-wellbeing-and-climate-over-economic-growth.html

The Circular Economy Action Plan

The European Commission adopted the new circular economy action plan (CEAP) in March 2020. It is one of the main building blocks of the European Green Deal, Europe's new agenda for sustainable growth. The EU's transition to a circular economy will reduce pressure on natural resources and will create sustainable growth and jobs. It is also a prerequisite to achieve the EU's 2050 climate neutrality target and to halt biodiversity loss. Read up on it at:

https://environment.ec.europa.eu/strategy/circular-economy-action-plan_en and check out an American version that's being planned at https://www.circularcolab.org/us-circular-economy-report/

Providing Decent Living with Minimum Energy: A Global Scenario

It is increasingly clear that averting ecological breakdown will require drastic changes to contemporary human society and the global economy embedded within it. On the other hand, the basic material needs of billions of people across the planet remain unmet. Here, the authors develop a simple, bottom-up model to estimate a practical threshold for the final energy consumption required to provide decent material living

to the entire global population. Check the plan out at
https://www.sciencedirect.com/science/article/pii/S0959378020307512

Degrowth: A Theory Of Radical Abundance

As the climate crisis worsens and the carbon budgets set out by the Paris Agreement shrink, climate scientists and ecologists have increasingly come to highlight economic growth as a matter of concern. Growth drives energy demand up and makes it significantly more difficult – and likely infeasible – for nations to transition to clean energy quickly enough to prevent potentially catastrophic levels of global warming. In recent years, IPCC scientists have argued that the only feasible way to meet the Paris Agreement targets is to actively scale down the material throughput of the global economy. Read about the theory and its praxis at https://href.li/?https://static1.squarespace.com/static/59bc0e610abd04bd1e067ccc/t/5cb6db356e9a7f14e5322a62/1555487546989/Hickel+-+Degrowth%2C+A+Theory+of+Radical+Abundance.pdf

Democratic Lottery — A Guide to Sortition

In this book the idea of sortition is one of the main new governing mechanisms. According to some experts, 'sortition' could eventually replace elected politicians altogether. In reality, it is already in use alongside elections – quietly revolutionizing the way political decisions are made. But what exactly is it? Find out at https://democracy-technologies.org/getting-started/democratic-lottery-a-guide-to-sortition/

Democracy Without Elections

Democracy Without Elections is a member-run 501c3 nonprofit that promotes the use of democratic lotteries. In a democratic lottery, legislatures or groups of leaders are selected by lottery from the common people. Read up on the ideas at https://democracywithoutelections.org/

Free Heirloom Seeds

Free Heirloom Seeds is a grassroots effort to empower individuals & communities with the resources necessary to provide for their basic needs without chemicals or corporations. They send free heirloom food seeds upon request. It is their hope that through their efforts more people will begin to save seeds-

~ Ensuring biodiversity on earth.

~ Reducing pollution by producing more goods locally & with sustainable practices.

~ Increasing planetary health by giving more people affordable access to fresh local foods.

~ Reducing the relevance & impact of biotech & corporate "food" producers.

~ Empowering individuals & communities to be self sufficient.

You can reach them at Free Heirloom Seeds c/o Stone Spirits, 865#B Arcata, CA 95521, at https://www.freeheirloomseeds.org/about.html or FreeHeirloomSeeds@gmail.com

Garden For Wildlife

Founded on the belief that everyone can enjoy and protect wildlife where they live, work, learn, play, and worship, the National Wildlife Federation's Garden for Wildlife programs provide simple steps and resources to create beautiful spaces that make a big impact for local and migratory species, from small window boxes to vast habitat corridors. Standing seven million people strong, Garden for Wildlife is America's largest, longest-running movement dedicated to helping local wildlife and wild spaces.

Check it out and get involved at https://www.nwf.org/garden

Kill Your Lawn — A Homeowner's Guide to Navigating Regulations and Ordinances to Strengthen Localized Sustainability

Urban sprawl, human convenience, overpopulation in regard to resource availability for any living creature, colonization, and capitalism all have had a devastating impact on our environment. The average worker, who isn't a millionaire, can't do much to change human impact on the environment, knowing that it's multi-million dollar corporations and private entities that cause the most damage and have the biggest negative impact, and need to make the biggest changes. But small steps are still steps forward. People like you and me, who have less than a million dollars, can create a wave of positive impact by making small changes, together. A big part of that is removing the conventional lawn and replacing it with native species that support our local ecology.

If you're ready to make a change, here's your guide:
https://lawnchick.com/kill-your-lawn-editorial

Resources For Disabled Gardeners

Wheel Chair Info:

https://agrability.osu.edu/sites/agrability/files/imce/Wheelchairs%20OAP.pdf

Tool Suggestions

https://agrability.osu.edu/sites/agrability/files/imce/2022_garden_tools_handout_OhioAgrAbility.pdf

Garden/Work Station Design

ADA Workstation Guidelines/ help:
https://agrability.osu.edu/sites/agrability/files/imce/Ohio%20AgrAbility%20poster2014-ADA.pdf

https://extension.unh.edu/sites/default/files/migrated_unmanaged_files/Resource000470_Rep492.pdf

Back Health

http://www.agrability.org/wp-content/uploads/2015/11/Back_health_final.pdf

https://agrability.osu.edu/sites/agrability/files/imce/Farming%20and%2
0gardening%20with%20arthritis%20handout_2.pdf

https://agrability.osu.edu/sites/agrability/files/imce/Don%27t%20let%2
0the%20dirt%20hurt_stretches_0.pdf

Gardening With Visual Impairment

https://agrability.osu.edu/sites/agrability/files/imce/Gardening_with_vis
ual_impairment_handout_2021.pdf

Arthritis Specific

http://www.agrability.org/wp-
content/uploads/2015/11/Arthritis_and_Ag.pdf

https://agrability.osu.edu/sites/agrability/files/imce/GardeningArthritisP
J.pdf

https://www.youtube.com/watch?v=kpu9oeQB88k&feature=youtu.be

More Resources

https://www.loc.gov/nls/new-materials/book-lists/gardening-people-
disabilities/

https://digabc.org/

https://idyllarbor.com/product/accessible-gardening-for-people-with-
physical-disabilities/3967

Wildlands Restoration Volunteers

Wildlands Restoration Volunteers (WRV) is a Colorado nonprofit
501(c)(3) that organizes thousands of volunteers each year to complete
more than 150 conservation projects throughout Colorado. Volunteer
events range in length from a few hours to multi-day campouts and are
located in beautiful natural areas from the plains to the alpine. By
volunteering with WRV, you'll meet great people while helping to heal
the land and strengthen our communities. Sign up for a volunteer project
today!

<u>Keystone Species For Species Diversity</u>

Native plants are core to the wildlife garden. Intentional use of native plants, which have formed symbiotic relationships with native wildlife over millions of years, creates the most productive and sustainable wildlife habitat. While some plants play a singular role for one or limited types of wildlife, others are essential to the life cycle of many species.

The local species of these plants vary by ecoregion, that is, areas where ecosystems (and the type, quality, and quantity of environmental resources) are generally similar. Keystone plant genera are unique to local food webs within ecoregions. Remove keystone plants and the diversity and abundance of many essential insect species, which 96% of terrestrial birds rely on for food sources, will be diminished. The ecosystem collapses in a similar way that the removal of the "key" stone in ancient Roman arch will trigger its demise. Learn your ecoregion and get help choosing native plants at

https://www.nwf.org/Garden-for-Wildlife/About/Native-Plants/keystone-plants-by-ecoregion

- Olov Brändström, Star Spangled Banner In Minor Key, 2018

- Rising Appalachia, "I Believe In Being Ready", Leylines, 2019

- Wayne Silas Jr., "All or Nothing", Wild Rice - Songs From The Menominee Nation, Canyon Records 2006

- Marcus Miller, "Let America Be America Again", Marshall (Original Motion Picture Soundtrack), Warner Records 2107

- Nina Simone, "Sinnerman", Pastel Blues, Colpix Records 1962

- Phil Collins, "In the Air Tonight", Face Value, Atlantic Records 1981

- Stray Cats, "Cry Danger", 40, SurfDog Records 2019

- Kittie Harloe, "Fight The War", Kipo And The Age Of Wonderbeasts (Season 1 Mixtape) Back Lot Music 2020

- Bad Cop/Bad Cop, "Warriors", Warriors, Fat Wreck Chords 2017

- Bon Jovi, "We Don't Run", Burning Bridges, Mercury Records 2015

- The Gaslight Anthem, "Changing Of The Guard", The Songs Of Bob Dylan Honoring 50 Years Of Amnesty International, Mercury Records 2015

- Bon Jovi, "Brothers In Arms", 2020, Island Records 2020
- The Interrupters, "Be Gone", Fight The Good Fight, Rude Boy Sounds 2018
- Bon Jovi, "American Reckoning", 2020, Island Records 2020
- DJ Spooky, "Not In Our Name", Celestial Mechanix, Thirsty Ear Recordings 2004
- Playing For Change, "All Along the Watchtower", Playing For Change Foundation 2018

Quoted Chapter 22

- Gil Scott Heron, "The Revolution Will Not Be Televised", Pieces of a Man, Flying Dutchman/RCA Records 1971
- Bon Jovi, "Beautiful Drug", 2020, Island Records 2020
- Tom Petty And The Heartbreakers, "Let Me Up (I've Had Enough)", Let Me Up (I've Had Enough) Geffen Records 1987
- Neil Young, Rockin' In The Free World (Fahrenheit 9/11 Mix), Rockin' In The Free World, WMG 2012
- The Interrupters, "By My Side", Say It Out Loud, Hellcat Records 2016
- Deap Vally, "Turn It Off", Femejism, Cooking Vinyl Limited 2016
- Björk, "Army of Me," Post, One Little Indian Records 1995
- Royal Cinema, "Rebels", Rebels, Orchard Enterprises 2022
- Pennywise, "Revolution", All Or Nothing, Epitaph Records 2012
- Bon Jovi, "Never Say Goodbye", Slippery When Wet, The Island Def Jam Music Group 1986
- Tony K, "Don't Want It", Single 2018
- Emmanuel Jal, We Want Peace, www.wewantpeace.com 2010
- The Interrupters, "Outrage", Fight the Good Fight, Hellcat

Records 2020

- Archive, "Bullets", single 2009

- Bon Jovi, "I'll Sleep When I'm Dead", Keep The Faith, The Island Def Jam Music Group 1992

- The Gaslight Anthem, "Blue Dahlia," Handwritten, The Island Def Jam Music Group 2012

- The Interrupters, "Loyal", Say It Out Loud, Hellcat Records 2024

- Bon Jovi, "Knockout", This House Is Not For Sale, 2016 Island Records

- Five Finger Death Punch, "Wrong Side of Heaven", The Wrong Side Of Heaven And The Righteous Side Of Hell, Volume 1 (Deluxe), Prospect Park 2013

- Muse, "Uprising", The Resistance, Studio Bellini 2009

- Run The Jewels, "Lie, Cheat, Steal", Run the Jewels 2, Mass Appeal 2014

- Gary Numan, "My Name Is Ruin", Savage (Songs from a Broken World) BMG 2017

- Five Finger Death Punch, "Lift Me Up", The Wrong Side Of Heaven And The Righteous Side Of Hell, Volume 1 (Deluxe), Prospect Park 2013

- The Offspring, "You're Gonna Go Far, Kid", Rise And Fall, Rage And Grace, Columbia Records 2008

- Run The Jewels, "Close Your Eyes And Count To F*ck", Run the Jewels 2, Mass Appeal 2014

- Streetlight Manifesto, "Everything Went Numb", Everything Goes Numb, Victory Records 2003

- Unknown Mortal Orchestra, "American Guilt", Sex & Food, Jagjaguwar 2018

- The Brothers Bright, Blood on My Name (Acoustic),Blood on My Name, Whitestone Nocturne 2015

- The Heavy. "Short Change Hero", The House That Dirt Built, Counter Records 2008

- Gary Clark Jr., "This Land", This Land, Warner Bros. 2019

- Reina del Cid, "My Country 'Tis of Thee (Land of Inequity)", Candy Apple Red, Flickertail Drive 2022

- Rising Appalachia, "Closer to the Edge", Filthy Dirty South, Independent 2012

- Sturgill Simpson, "All Said and Done", Sound and Fury, Elektra Records 2019

- Marina, "Purge The Poison", Ancient Dreams in a Modern Land, Atlantic Records 2021

- Saul Williams, "List Of Demands (Reparations)", The Inevitable Rise And Liberation Of Niggy Tardust, Fader Label 2007

- The Freeze, "American Town", Land Of The Lost, Modern Method Records 1983

- Disturbed, "The Vengeful One", Immortalized (Deluxe Edition), Reprise 2015

- Vita Nova, "Halocene", Vita Nova, Independent 2020

- Green Day, "Working Class Hero", Working Class Hero, Instant Karma: The Amnesty International Campaign to Save Darfur, Amnesty International 2007

- Brother Ali, "Uncle Sam Goddamn", The Undisputed Truth, Rhymesayers Entertainment 2007

- Halocene, "Bring Me That Horizon," Throne (ft. Ai Mori) We've Got It Covered: Vol 8. Independent 2021

- Frou Frou, "Holding Out For A Hero", Shrek 2 (Original

Motion Picture Soundtrack), Dreamworks 2010

- Grouplove, "This Is The End", This Is This, Canvasback 2021
- Europe, "The Final Countdown", The Final Countdown (Expanded Edition), Epic 1986
- Titus Andronicus, "A More Perfect Union", The Monitor, XL Records 2010
- OMNIA, "Free Bird Fly", Earth Warrior, Paganscum Records 2014
- Kansas, "Dust in the Wind", Point Of Know Return, Epic Records 1977
- Phlotilla, "Going Down Fighting", The Old Guard Soundtrack, Netflix 2020
- Kara Nodrik, "Growing Light", 2mørVs 2023 https://www.youtube.com/watch?v=b-iqV6mfIlE&list=OLAK5uy_nE1wi_7Y7QK8IAhIus4IQ9aQ1vJdeY7p4&ab_channel=KaraNodrik-Topic
- The Weeknd, "Nothing Is Lost (You Give Me Strength)", Avatar: The Way of Water Original Motion Picture Soundtrack, Republic Records 2023
- The Greatest Showman Cast, "This Is Me", The Greatest Showman Soundtrack, Atlantic Records 2018
- Sinéad O'Connor, I Believe in You, A Very Special Christmas 2, A&M 1992
- Rising Appalachia, "Thank You Very Much", Thank You Very Much, Independent 2022
- Sara Thomsen. "Somewhere to Begin," Somewhere to Begin, Whitebark Music 2014
- Genevieve Chadwick, "Days Like This", Listen To The Music, Playing For Change By PFC123 2016
- Nahko And Medicine For The People, "The Wolves Have

Returned", HOKA, Side One Dummy Records 2016

- The Five Stairsteps, "O-o-h Child'', Riding In Cars With Boys - Music From The Motion Picture, Legacy Recordings 2016

- The Staple Singers, "I'll Take You There", Be Altitude: Respect Yourself [Stax Remasters], Stax Records 1972

- Nimo Patel & Daniel Nahmod, WE SHALL OVERCOME: LOVE WILL RISE AGAIN, Empty Hands Music 2018

- Tom Petty And The Heartbreakers, "Even The Losers," Damn The Torpedoes, UMG Recordings 1979

- Naethan Apollo, "Night Watch", Tales From Cazilor, UnderCurrent 2023

- Defiance Ohio, "You Are Loved", Defiance Ohio, Midwestern Minutes, No Idea Records 2010

- The Oh Hellos, "Soldier, Poet, King", Dear Wormwood, The Oh Hellos 2015

- Bon Jovi, "Reunion", This House Is Not For Sale, Island Records 2017

- Sinéad O'Connor, "The Emperor's New Clothes", I Do Not Want What I Haven't Got, Ensign 1990

- Bon Jovi, "New Years' Day", This House Is Not For Sale, Island Records 2017

- The Who, "Street Song", WHO, Polydor Records 2019

- Bon Jovi, "Born Again Tomorrow", This House Is Not For Sale, Island Records 2017

- Steve Perry, "Running Alone", Street Talk (Expanded Edition) 1984

- Sinéad O'Connor, "Jerusalem", Lion and the Cobra, Chrysalis Records Limited 1987

- Demi Lovato, "Confident", Confident, Island Records 2015

- Bon Jovi, "Because We Can," What About Now, Universal Music Group 2019
- Mike Shinoda, "Happy Endings (feat. iann dior and UPSAHL)", EP Single 2021
- Paradise Fears, "Battle Scars", Battle Scars, DigSin 2013
- American Authors, "Best Day Of My Life", Oh, What A Life, Island Records 2014
- Rachel Platten, "Fight Song." Columbia Records 2015
- Collective Soul, "Shine", Hints, Allegations & Things Left Unsaid, Rising Storm 1993
- Talking Heads, "Once in a Lifetime", Remain in Light, Sire Records Company 1980
- Bon Jovi, "Limitless", 2020, Captain Kidd Corp 2020
- Pat Benatar, "We Belong", Tropico, Chrysalis 1984
- Neil Diamond, "America", The Jazz Singer, Columbia Records 1980
- Dennis Timothy, "Star Spangled Banner (Rock Guitar)", 292 Records 2021

<u>The Aces High, Jokers Wild Series</u>

Aces High, Jokers Wild Book 1: The Hands We're Given

Aces High, Jokers Wild Book 1.5: The Boys of Summer Have Gone

Aces High, Jokers Wild Book 2: Call the Bluff

Aces High, Jokers Wild Book 2.5: After Hours Game (A Wildcards Christmas)

Aces High, Jokers Wild Book 3: Raise the Stakes

Aces High, Jokers Wild Book 3.5: Bad Hand (A Wildcards Halloween)

Aces High, Jokers Wild Book 4: Aces and Eights

Aces High, Jokers Wild Book 4.5: Follow The Lady

Aces High, Jokers Wild Book 5: Draw Dead

Aces High, Jokers Wild Book 5.5: Draw Out

Aces High, Jokers Wild Book 6: Deuces Are Wild

Aces High, Jokers Wild Book 6.5: Fill The Pot

Aces High, Jokers wild Book 7: Odds Against

Aces High, Jokers Wild Book 7.5: Call the Clock

Aces High, Jokers Wild Book 8: The Games We've Played

Anthologies

Neon Dreams and Nightmares: Mixed Punk Works of Dystopian Futures

Dark Horizons: A Collection of Near-Future, Dystopian, and Cyberpunk Sci-fi: Multi author 5 book box set

We Came To Dance: A Queer Anthology Benefitting Club Q

Playing With A Full Deck: Stories of Hope in Hard Times

About The Author

Bringing their own experiences as a marginalized author to the page with flawed but genuine characters, O.E. Tearmann's work has been described as "Firefly for the dystopian genre." Publisher's Weekly called it "a lovely paean to the healing power of respectful personal connections among comrades, friends, and lovers."

Tearmann lives in Colorado with two cats, their partner, and the belief that individuals can make humanity better through small actions. They are a member of the Science Fiction Writers of America, the Rocky Mountain Fiction Writers, and the Queer Scifi group. In their spare time, they teach workshops on writing GLTBQ characters, plant gardens that showcase sustainable agricultural practices, and play too many video games.

www.oetearmann.com